PRECIOUS JEWELS

Dale Martellino

ISBN: 1539031969
ISBN 13: 9781539031963
Library of Congress Control Number: 2016916029
CreateSpace Independent Publishing Platform
North Charleston, South Carolina

DELILAH IN TUSCANY, 1975

Delilah mulled over why the magnetic pull was stronger toward a country than to her handsome fiancé lounging in the room below her as she soaked in her tub. She closed her eyes tightly and sank into the bathwater surrounding her. Her damp hair floated in dark rivulets that danced atop the steamy surface. With her knees awkwardly jutting out like atolls in a warm sea, she rested her head on the hard metal shell of the elaborate tub.

A warm Tuscan breeze fluttered the sky-blue drapes as her thoughts hopscotched from this dilemma to that dilemma facing her as a soon-to-be bride getting married in this faded villa. She never even noticed the heavy brass key on the table put there for privacy.

Carmine, their self-proclaimed guide for the paid-in-advance Wedding Encounter in Tuscany, said it was "no problemo" to find a rabbi in his beloved city, although he never had bumped into any. To Carmine, any situation in life was either a "problemo" or "no problemo," which amused both her and her fiancé, Philip.

The package deal that they bought last year on the Internet promised to procure a priest for the wedding service, but that would never work for Delilah.

She remembered the stocky tourists carrying walking sticks and sporting pointy green-felt hats waiting outside a mundane structure that had an attached block of wood with Hebrew letters on its lintel. The cardboard sign, scribbled in Italian and tacked up as an afterthought, was what drew everyone's attention.

She attempted to read the Italian, but her Italian was not as good as her French, which was not really good either. The five sweaty tourists, listening to their private guide, would not budge from the blocked sign or its doorway.

A carved walking stick, connected to a pudgy fist, kept jamming against the doorbell until a demure, dark-haired woman adorned in black from the tip of her head to her midnight sandals arrived at the building's edifice. The group in front of her paid no attention to the tearstained face, the red eyes, or the cluster of tissues she tightly held in her hand.

A misshapen Tyrolean hat, which held Delilah's eyes, sat atop the roundest face in the group.

"Signorina, ve will enter the Juden Tempel now!" the boisterous woman proclaimed in English that more than hinted of German syntax. "Ve leave Siena at one o'clock for goodt."

"Ritorno," said the woman with the sad eyes.

"Nein," said the bouncing green beanie.

"Si," whispered the signorina.

"Nein, nein, nein," said the voice with the shaking stick.

The signorina, cringing from the exchange, sheepishly let them in while wiping off her dampened cheekbones.

"We have got to get out of here," whispered Philip, who knew that anywhere was better than where they were.

Philip began steering Delilah toward the campo. It was time for a "Phil-up," which was one of his favorite phrases and guaranteed to ease tensions.

After their gelato break, they returned to the Jewish temple, devoid of any signs. Delilah gently pushed on the doorbell and was greeted by the signorina again.

"Parlez Anglesey?" asked Delilah in a language composite that was tricky to decipher if one did not know French or Delilah-speak.

"Shalom. Our tour of synagogue just begins," was the answer in English, relaxing Philip from the panic that gripped him every time Delilah attempted to speak in a foreign tongue.

During the tour, Delilah spotted a well-dressed gentleman in the sanctuary, maneuvering a solitary bulb into a socket. He periodically paused from this simple task to listen. At the end of the tour, Philip asked how many people from Siena had perished in the Holocaust.

When the guide faltered, the voice from the ladder delivered the response. "Nineteen people were sent to Germany from this town and never were seen again." The man then confidently stepped down from his perch and asked if there were more questions.

"What is the Jewish community like at this time?" asked Philip while looking directly at the man, who obviously held a position besides maintenance.

"There are around ten families in town and a handful more than that if the students from the university here are included. We function somewhat like Hillel, a Jewish student organization at colleges." The man appeared more like a rabbi as he spoke.

Without really thinking, Delilah almost coughed out a request like a projectile that garnered more import as she uttered it. "Rabbi, marry Philip and me next Saturday night," she blurted out to the equally stunned rabbi.

The rabbi cleared his throat, glanced at the barren pews, and without even blinking replied, "Si," which drew sustained claps from the startled guide.

The promise to her dying father that a rabbi would sanctify her marriage flew in her head seconds before the words had taken form. She was more astonished than anyone when the rabbi replied yes.

The cooling water jarred her thoughts, as did the strange knocking noise, which she ignored.

"My fingers resemble prunes," she thought as she stared intently at the folds in her fingers.

She carefully stepped out of the tub, moving those wrinkly prunes, and grabbed the dense, bright-white towel being warmed on the stainless metal bar positioned behind her. She rapidly bundled the soft cotton around her damp body and tucked it in snugly by the narrow dip in her breastbone. She then turned around and squared off with a "problemo": Carmine, her preassigned guide for this special wedding weekend, was staring at her from the open doorway.

"*Aahhhh!*" Delilah screamed. "*Aahhhhh!*"

The staring Carmine took a large sharp breath but could not muster any words.

"Wha, wha, what is going on here?" Delilah stammered in total disbelief as to how in the world this driver could have let himself into her private bathing quarters.

"Sorry, sorry. No problemo, no problemo…I leave," he said abruptly as he slunk out of the door and away from the shocked Delilah, whose eyes trailed him as she stood, still wrapped in a skimpy towel.

Carmine furiously ran to his parked car as he absconded from the scene of the crime.

"Marone," he exhaled as he clapped his hands on the hot metal of his car.

"Why… why I so frozen at the image of the Madonna?" he thought. "Why I go in bathing room?"

But he knew why his muscles could not maneuver him away from the bathroom that he had stumbled upon.

She was naked in there.

She was naked…and…she was beautiful.

She was naked, she was beautiful, and she had no idea that he had been staring at her.

As she had stared at her fingers, he had stared at her curves, her dips, and her delights.

"Oh, marone! I am Pinocchio, and I am turning to wood."

He then drove away, completely forgetting why he was upstairs in her bathing area in the first place.

The oversize espresso machine, resplendent in chrome and copper, impressed the American tourists, which was what the owner, Sylvie, was hoping for when she stood at the checkout counter making her final decision on such an outlandish purchase. The pungent aroma of the coffee wafted around the ground floor of the villa, enticing its residents to partake in its bounty.

Anna, standing adjacent to the monstrous coffee machine, was waiting for Delilah with the rest of the wedding entourage. Delilah's childhood friend Kerrie was seated with her boyfriend of the moment, Mike, who was perched on the arm of her chair leaning toward her bulging cleavage. A policeman by trade, he was only with them because he was willing to travel to Europe at the last minute. Kerrie had images of him running up to a pickpocket and thrusting his badge in the cowering criminal's face, at which point the criminal would peer at his small physique and commence laughing. Kerrie tried not to think of such things during their lovemaking.

Anxious for the evening to begin, Philip looked toward the steps impatiently. "Get your act together," kept running through his mind as he tried to control his eyes from reverting to Kerrie's protruding chest.

When Delilah burst into the room with the poise of a queen and the sweet aroma of self-confidence, it broke his reverie. His negative inclinations disappeared as his catcall whistle exploded.

Kerrie had noticed Philip staring at her, and she liked it. She liked his blond hair that he kept long and curly around his ears. His eyes were a strong greenish color that reminded her of the eyes of cats ready to pounce. She watched him closely as he lifted up Delilah and saw his muscles flex under that crisp cotton shirt he always wore; it seemed to repel wrinkles no matter how twisted it became. Nothing about Philip ever seemed wrinkled. He knew what to say, and he knew how to act. At this moment, she knew that he wanted her friend, although a few seconds previously, she knew that Philip had desired her.

"Carmine described a sweet place for our dinner tonight. He told me he was going to mention it to you, Dee," said Philip.

"Hmm, I'm not sure," murmured Dee when she realized that was the impetus that caused him to barge into her bathing room.

Carmine was waiting outside for the wedding party in his luxurious black Mercedes wagon. He jumped out of the car as they waltzed toward the vehicle.

Delilah bore her eyes straight into his. "I will not retreat into some silly embarrassment from what obviously was a mistake in *his* judgment," she thought.

"Nice to see you again, Carmine," came out of her clenched teeth.

"Si, yes," mumbled Carmine into the cool night air.

Philip dictated his manifesto for the night's festivities. "My princess goes in the fancy car. Since Carmine also rented this miniscule one and I am the only one with an international license, I will steer this old Fiat to dinner tonight. I am offering a sequel to Mr. Toad's wild ride. Now, who is game?"

"I always liked the *Wind in the Willows,* so I reserve my seat," Kerrie quickly responded.

This took Mike aback. He did not relish the idea of bouncing from here to who knows where in a peanut of an automobile. He was not about to let Kerrie ride with Philip alone, though.

"I guess I'll be giving my ticket to Mr. Toad then," said Mike to the others.

Philip continued, "My princess will sit in the front throne, and Anna will have the entire backseat to lounge in her chauffeur-driven carriage. We peons will bounce along behind Her Majesty."

Nobody chose to argue with the boss.

"Enjoy the ride, my sweet Delilah, for in the future you will be seated next to Master Toad for the long haul."

"I think I should be in your car now, Phil," whined Dee.

"Sorry, Princess, the seats have been chosen. Now, gather round to hear the plan. We will wind through narrow roads and curvaceous bends to an establishment with a stone mill that ground the wheat of olden days into flour. Carmine tells me there is even a water source inside and a...wait...I do not want to ruin the surprise. The chef is a good friend of Carmine's and has told him that he will be preparing a prewedding feast fit for our court."

After his pompous speech, the group grudgingly piled into cars that went from the sublime to the ridiculous. In Philip's clunker, Kerrie sat in the front seat. It contained a small spring that dug into the tiny space between her two butt cheeks.

Mike slithered into the back and angled his body sideways so he was facing the side windows. He had his derriere on the driver's side and one foot in the seat well, which necessitated one foot to be angled up awkwardly. You could hear a distinct "eww" when he bent down to enter the car and an "oh, shit" when he eventually settled into his cramped position.

Meanwhile, Philip smiled contentedly in the driver's seat, anxious for their *aventura* to begin.

Carmine opened the passenger side for Delilah as a footman does for a queen. She had her Italian-knit white sweater draped over one arm; it had little rosettes delicately sewn on to add dollops of red color. It appeared as if she had just won the Run for the Roses, with the patterned rosettes forming a blanket over her arm. Her other hand reached up and just so slightly put pressure on Carmine's hand, which was extending toward her.

Anna shook her head in confusion because her brain had noticed something before her consciousness had; these actions of Delilah and Carmine appeared as foreplay to the casual observer.

Originally the two cars drove in tandem, with Philip cranking up the old Fiat with its faded allure to a speed where he had no idea how it compared to miles per hour except that it was middling to slow. Carmine tried to handle the discrepancy between the monster motor he was containing and the faint grinding of gears he heard behind him in the pitch-black night.

After an hour of this misery, Philip finally honked his silly-sounding horn and rolled down his antiquated window while creeping beside the Mercedes at a haltingly slow speed.

"Just go ahead of this contraption," yelled Philip to Carmine with a wave of a hand and a kiss blown in Dee's direction. "We'll meet you there."

"No problemo," resounded from Carmine's mouth as Dee clasped her cheek to receive the imaginary kiss thrown into the night's wind.

And with that, the two divergent machines inevitably parted.

Philip vanished. The Benz's sleek aerodynamics let them shoot out quickly after their final rendezvous with the clunker. Carmine smoothly took control of the road, seemingly alone on it.

"Why don't you show us what this powerful car can achieve?" cooed Anna, who just felt like shaking things up in the night that was not going how she had imagined.

"You like?" Carmine whispered to Dee.

She barely responded. "If it is what Anna wants."

That was all it took for Carmine to put his pedal foot down to the floor and roar like the lion he was presently pretending to be.

The few stars that twinkled between the darkening clouds illuminated the night. The road narrowed to one lane, resembling the Daytona International Speedway. Their increasing velocity made the girls hunker down in their seats and grab at the doors, where handholds were attached. Dee nervously realized that perhaps she had made a mistake in letting Carmine have free rein. This pit in her stomach was not what she should be feeling before her nuptials to someone who was not in the driver's seat.

"Slow down, cowboy," was what Anna meant to articulate from her gaping mouth, but nonsensical syllables were elicited in its stead.

The darkness outside was peppered with large, looming blocks of trees moving faster and faster as Delilah peered through the side windows. The thump of her heartbeat could be felt throughout her body, as if dominoes were falling from her arms to her trunk, to her legs, and bouncing to her head in bizarre patterns.

"Eh, you wanted some action, Anna? Now you have it!"

Dee glanced at Anna, who was grabbing onto the slippery side panel of the car.

Carmine leaned toward Delilah as she shook her head ever so slightly from right to left, which Dee was assuming, though incorrectly, was the universal action for no. Carmine unfortunately was not located in her American universe of international language. So instead of slowing down, he pushed his foot forcibly on the pedal and propelled them into spatial chaos.

The girls first swayed to the left, and then they swayed to the right as the car hugged the bends in the road. The olive trees lining the asphalt became a solid thorny wall that blinded them from all that lay behind.

It finally dawned on Dee that whatever Carmine was thinking, it had to be quickly diffused. Sign language could only get a gal so far, and it was time to literally put on the brakes. She instinctively started pumping her foot on the floorboards. She gasped in panic.

A mass was looming ahead of them. Her instinct kicked in, and loud screams streamed from her mouth. Her destiny in a split second became linked with the unknown before her. She barely saw the mix of flashlights and flags parading in front of the windshield. Bright words inconceivably jumped off a large banner in a mishmash of blood-colored letters. Those letters appeared to be dripping down as nonsensical words juxtaposing themselves in an atmospheric confusion that started swirling around her like a tornado. She was being transported to oblivion.

Carmine grabbed the steering wheel with an iron fist and slammed his foot on the brake pad, while veering to the right side of this massive black hole that suddenly appeared alive with a cacophony of noise and bodies disrupting the solace that he alone had felt from the speeding vehicle. This lifesaving maneuver put them barreling toward saplings that were scattered around the forest behind the ancient olive bushes.

Initially, the car flew slightly airborne with the grace of a leaping ballet master. It then descended into the low growth, feeling as if it were scraping the bottom of their feet as it continued through the tumble of metal and twigs. Carmine's persona was that of a ballplayer dodging imaginary opponents, which were actually large trees.

The car was petering to a halt when it hit an unknown target. The safety bags popped as Dee and Carmine started puffing on clouds of powder that made them appear as if they were those heavenly creatures in celestial paintings that were plastered on the ceilings of the local churches.

Anna's pasty visage was not caused from talc, for there was no bag that inflated in the backseat. It was only the paleness of her injured body that caused the hue. One burst of noise blended into another, sounding similar to a symphony tuning up before the conductor arrives.

"Delilah, hurt you?" yelled Carmine in his confused English.

It was not until Delilah tried to form words that she realized that the noise being picked up by her ears came from her mouth; she was the one who was screaming. She then discerned another octave of vocalization coming from the far reaches of the vehicle.

"I'm alive. I'm OK," said Delilah, barely audible as she finally pushed the words through the higher decibels of Anna's cries. "Anna, Anna, Anna," whispered Dee into the powdery interior.

Distinct moaning was then heard from Anna's smashed-in area of the car.

The driver's door jolted open as a crush of bodies descended upon the car. People started appearing everywhere from the dark void. They were all speaking at once in a language that Dee recognized as Italian, but now sounded more like jibber-jabber. The yelling never ceased as Dee and Anna sat shaking in the podlike cocoon that seemed to suffocate them.

"Anna," pleaded Delilah, "answer!"

But the whimpering only continued.

The clatter stopped suddenly when Carmine grabbed Dee's hand and held up his other hand as if directing traffic at a busy intersection.

"Important, Anna, must we see," whispered Carmine as he peered around the seat.

Delilah turned her focus to the world around her. Some of the staring faces were old, and some were young. All of their expressions freaked her out. Confusion reigned in her head, and she could not conceive how so many people could suddenly appear in the middle of nowhere in the black of night. A wave undulated through the crowd as one individual waded into the sea of bodies.

He opened the door to the backseat, saying only "Dottore" while intently staring at the motionless Anna as if she were a slide under a microscope.

Tiny beads of sweat began to appear in a light mustache above her lip and in gathering droplets that were forming on her forehead.

"More medico," said Carmine as he quickly started a conversation with another individual who also appeared to assess the situation.

Anna gently closed her eyes to calm the rough seas within her.

"I am doctor," said the pensively staring man in front of Anna. "Massive hurt where?" he continued in his lovely singsong voice.

"Hmmmm," said Anna. The sudden throbbing in her head pointed out clearly to her that she was not dead. The side of the car seemed to go in where her hip went out. Her right arm just kind of dangled, and she felt something crusty on her face with her left arm that slowly inched up to it.

"I'm scared," she now articulated.

"Don't be," echoed the kind voice in the distance as the world slowly moved out of focus and gently tumbled her into the void.

The young doctor with the singsong voice proceeded to command the debacle. "Patient in back needs to be in hospital, veloce veloce. Other doctor must take her in car we have and leave immediately. I will stay with two other passengers and take to sanctuary."

Carmine and the younger doctor then began a swirl of conversation that definitely was not in English. When the conversation wound down, the younger doctor carried Dee out of the car. She nestled in the arms of this strange man and put her head delicately on a jacket that smelled of night air and some kind of nutty essence. Carmine appeared next to her and began a conversation where only bits and pieces could be understood because of the enveloping fog that was clinging to her.

"Doctors will look and if OK, off to convent and wait for ride."

She could not figure out why she had to join a convent in the middle of the night, but she was too confused to worry about it. She was not aware that Jewish women who had been in accidents were sent off to convents.

She muttered, "I will get used to a life in this new denomination and will wait for salvation."

Carmine only heard the word "salvation," crossed himself, and quickly informed the mass of Italian marchers that they would wait in the convent for a car to pick them up and the crowd should continue with their business…whatever that was.

Carmine and the doctor carefully carried Delilah to a soft mound of auburn leaves next to a bushy group of trees that shielded her from the cool night wind. A large, faded cart previously laden with crops that had been dumped unceremoniously appeared near the snake of people who had wound around the forest area that they now occupied.

While still holding Dee, the doctor placed his body sideways against the old wood that comprised the bed of the cart. He then swung his legs around to form a mold, with Dee's body sunken in the middle. They stood out like two unlikely figures resembling an odd pietà. Carmine sat on the crooked front bench, while another man controlled an ancient horse that moved decidedly and did not get spooked by what seemed to spook the cart's occupants. Delilah felt almost comfortable as she melted into the repose, similar to another religious duo.

Carmine nervously began chattering in Italian to the other travelers, with Dee periodically picking up words and phrases.

"Muslim" kept being repeated over and over, as well as "mosque." She had heard previously that a big rally was supposed to happen near the site of a proposed mosque in the Siena area. Many nearby residents did not want to share their land with a large mosque that could accommodate more than the local population of Islam. The fear was that this religious structure would bring in more Muslims, who would never be considered Italians by the locals. As she glanced outside the window, she spied a severed head of a pig on a passing gate.

"Mosque, mosque" came across loud and clear from the front seat.

Staying awake proved too difficult, and she closed her eyes and let the darkness of the night engulf her.

The convent, La Certosa di Pontignano, appeared suddenly amid the olive groves. The doctor, Delilah, and Carmine entered through a small creaky door that was dwarfed by the large structure surrounding it. Once Delilah was ushered into the interior, a lush courtyard took shape through her sleepy eyes. They veered into an office framed with weathered wood crosses at each corner. After a brief visit with the Mother Superior, the doctor, who still held Delilah firmly to his chest, carried her to one of the cells deep in the darkened cloister. They passed mute nuns wrapped in black fabrics who silently shuffled by them, not bothering to peek through the starched white cardboard that framed their faces.

Mother Superior had explained that Sister Katarina's command of the English language would be more comforting to Delilah than the other nuns, who only spoke dialect Italian and were busy with a variety of duties like farming, making jellies, and other household chores. She told them that this tiny nun took care of all of their injured animals and was the gentlest presence in the cloister.

They nodded in agreement and then collectively said "grazie" to the Mother Superior by the assigned cell door.

"I will inform you when comes your ride," she said curtly as she shut the door that enclosed the unlikely roommates entombed in this ancient monastic cell.

They squinted at a minimountain of black positioned in the corner. They were caught by surprise when the dome sprouted arms, warmed a smile, and spoke in lilting English. Delilah felt her body relax the instant she heard the dulcet tones.

"Do we have an injured bird here for me to heal?" the tiny nun asked from her perching position.

"Si, yes. I am Dr. Rescondito, who accompanies her," said the humble doctor.

"Eh, bene. Welcome. Sister Katarina is how they refer to me, signori," replied the sister, with two kind eyes that sparkled as she spoke to the attending physician and the quizzical Carmine, who stood agape in the middle of the room.

Carmine focused his attention on the neatly made bed that was held up by an old wooden frame; it was where the doctor had gently laid Delilah. Dee's eyes appeared shut, which elicited a hush as the two men quietly sat in two rickety chairs that were positioned next to a desk filled with a surplus of papers in a deluge of piles.

"Tell me what brought you to this moment," Katarina softly said to them.

"I am driver, but was completely blindsided by those appearing camouflaged in the night," Carmine responded in Italian.

"And how did you happen upon this moment?" she asked, glancing at the doctor.

Dr. Rescondito paused, cocked his head to the right, and inhaled deeply before replying. "Mia madre, originally from the Mideast, has lived in Italia my whole life. My Italian father had been in the military and stationed in Persia, where he met my mother and actually married her in a local civil service. It was permissible for men to have multiple wives in my country, but my mother was convinced that she was his one and only. Her family initially was not happy with this wedding and told her it would be a tragedy to move apart from them, but she ultimately had their permission. My father originally hailed from Rome but brought his young bride to Siena. Unbeknownst to her, he had a wife and three children living in Roma. After two years in Siena and a one-year-old child, my father went back to Rome and his other family, leaving us with no income. My mother eventually obtained a job as a housecleaner in a small hotel to support us.

"My mother is a Muslim, but I do not adhere to her practices now. It was her faith and the Arab community around here that contributed to my solid upbringing. I owe my life to the Muslim community around Siena. I had great sadness when our own town did not accept the plans for a new mosque outside of Siena, even though there was plenty of land available. It is hard for me to understand how all of these neighbors who know of our pious lives could try to deny us a holy sanctuary.

"We decided to march this very day to the spot where the mosque was to be built. We had been told that a severed pig's head was placed where we were heading. This was a message from the people of the town. We marched in solidarity to remove the head and cleanse the area from the blood that had been spilled. When we heard a car whizzing down the dark road, we were concerned that there might be trouble coming. It was a problem, but different from what we had anticipated. The car careened out of control, but luckily nobody was in its path except some underbrush."

"I am so sorry," Carmine said. "I was hired to drive for wedding celebration, and now the bride does not look so good and your march has ended poorly."

Katarina's delicate hand pushed through yards of fabric and touched Delilah's cheek, instantly relaxing her tense muscles.

"She will be fine; she will be fine," whispered the nun while she gently stroked Delilah's cheek, "and so will you," she said as she looked at the young doctor.

From this light touch on the cheek, Dee's eyelids unfurled. She saw before her captivating dark eyes with slightly sagging lids. An oval face with perfectly formed lips devoid of lipstick completed the portrait "How can a good Jewish girl end up in a convent, Sister? Please tell me."

Dee choked up when she asked Sister Katarina this, but the nun, thinking that the question referred to her and not the girl, said, "I will tell you how a good Jewish girl ended up in a convent, my dear."

Dee closed her eyes while concentrating on the melodious tones of Katarina.

Katarina began her story. "Over one thousand years ago, there was an Arab-Jewish merchant with the name of Ibrahim Ibn Jacob. He wrote about Prague, mentioning that Russians, Slavs, Muslims, Jews, and Turks were arriving in Fraga (Prague), which was then the biggest trade town. In the years 995 to 997, Jews were allowed to settle in Prague, and there they founded their own township, a ghetto, as a reward for fighting pagans alongside the Christians. So it was not unusual for Jews to be in Prague since there was a very long history of them in the area. Therefore it was not unusual for my family to be living in such a magnificent city as practicing Jews many centuries later.

"The Jews had lived a very content life with the independent Czechoslovak Republic of 1918, but things changed. In 1941, there were approximately fifty thousand Jews living in Prague, and I was soon to be counted as one of them. The memory of my parents is so dim, it barely exists. It comes solely from an old photograph that I would like to show you."

The sister shuffled to the simple wooden desk situated by the heavy door. Her dark robe was quite long and swayed with her steady gait. Only the rounded toe of her shoe peeked out from under those oppressive folds.

"Might I help you, Sister?" asked Dr. Rescondito kindly while watching Katarina fishing for something.

"I almost have it," she replied while pushing her arm so far in her desk drawer that it almost disappeared.

Katarina twisted her body to the side and elongated her torso while whispering, "Aha," so softly that Dee barely heard her exhale.

Carmine was the first to see the faded image.

"Magnifico!" he proclaimed while looking at two obviously well-heeled people. Even though the image had become crinkled and faded, he still could see the remnants of a fur hat adorning a gentleman's head and a long wool coat with added animal trim that covered a slim body. The woman in the picture was delicate and held a bundle that resembled a fuzzy fur football, with a form barely recognizable. Upon closer inspection, he realized it was a little dog. The woman's face was a beautiful oval, with perfect lips that formed a delicate smile.

The camera had frozen a slice of life from another era stubbornly held on to by this nun. She passed the fading image to the doctor and then placed the photo in Delilah's hand, which rested atop her chest, which heaved up and down in anticipation of seeing the old portrait.

"Mio padre Rudolph e mia madre Naomi," were the slowly formed words that were barely audible to her curious guests.

Delilah, in her stupor, imagined the couple in the picture as her own parents. She saw her mother, young and pretty, with her father so obviously smitten. She imagined herself somehow transported as their little bundle, not the dog it actually was. Her thoughts jumbled while staring at the black folds next to her. She initially was not aware that the story she was about to hear was not hers.

AND NOW...TO A DIFFERENT TIME... AND A DIFFERENT PERSON... NOVEMBER 1941

K atarina Orbhan marched through the streets of Prague surrounded by a series of gray buildings blocking out the sun's warmth. The occupying Nazis had sporadically plastered cloth swastikas that flapped within the breezy corridors. She was tired of watching the machinations of their occupation unfold in front of her and was constantly worried about the endgame. She felt abject horror that the red and black insignias found everywhere were staining her fleeting youth.

She strove to climb out of her personal downward spiral. She fretted that blood and bones were now seeping their way into the surfaces where she walked and were wantonly easing into the bowels of the earth, where they would reflect on all Czechs who would tread there for years to come.

"Halt," commanded the young guard who jumped in front of her while she obsessed on her own state of the state.

His baggy uniform draped over his average frame, but Katarina concentrated on his searing blue eyes. Those same eyes viewed an extremely attractive girl around nineteen, with her own beautiful set of blues that melted his recently trained military vigilance.

"I am halted," responded Katarina. "I am a social worker, sir. Here are my papers, which are all in order, you will see. I need to work now, please."

He lingered near her hand as she held out the papers. He could feel the slight tremble as her scrunch of papers passed to his solid grip.

"Young women like you should not enter the dirty ghetto no matter what sort of documents you show me. A quarantine has been posted."

He could feel himself being drawn in by this assertive fräulein. She made him regret enlisting at nineteen. Opportunities to meet girls were infrequent while on sentry duty surrounded by barbed wire and guns.

"I will get fired from my job if I complete this report without the necessary interviews from this Jewish sector."

Katarina opened the folder that she had stuffed in her bag with page after page of scribbles.

"I was hired to evaluate the conditions in the ghetto. You see, I really am an official social worker, and my government office has been working side by side with the authorities. You recently arrived in my country, and I stand here welcoming you to my city. I would appreciate it if you would welcome me to this area where only documented personnel are allowed, considering I do have all of the proper documents. Thank you for your concern, but I will be fine. I am not afraid of a quarantine, whether real or imagined."

But she was afraid from top to bottom. Not of the Jews who were behind a barrier that kept them tucked away from the rest of Prague, but of this young German soldier, whom she felt forced to flirt with even though she was cognizant of the danger he posed.

This same young soldier, on the other hand, was seemingly alone in a hostile foreign land and surprisingly did not pose the danger that she feared. His father had insisted that he join Hitler's Youth Program to keep safe during the terrible economic and political times that he had convinced himself were totally caused by the Jewish dilemma.

The Jewish presence in Germany and the surrounding countries, which theoretically should have been considered German territory, was sucking the lifeblood out of his motherland. The area's economy was disastrous, and his family's was even worse. His dad was frozen in fear that his only son would sink in these troubled times, as well as deplete his own meager savings.

His father looked toward the Hitler Youth Program as a way out of this dilemma for both of them. Having fought in World War I, he knew the dangers of combat but ultimately knew Bertie was better there than in front of a firing squad, which would happen if he did not enlist like the other youth in their small town.

All of these dilemmas and solutions tangled up in him to form a complete hatred of the Jews. The son was aware of his father's beliefs and, as a dutiful child, felt similar thoughts about Jews coursing through his own veins.

"What are you called by your friends?" the suddenly flirtatious young man blurted out without giving it too much thought, which even surprised his newfound capricious self. He yearned to make conversation with this pretty girl. The lack of females crept into his solitary bunk every night in the darkened barracks and often reared its head when the sun shone. Not many people in Prague chose to speak to him civilly, let alone look into his eyes as this brave girl had ventured. He liked her.

Engaging in idle chatter would cause him embarrassment as inappropriate youthful actions if his superiors spotted him. Seeing this stunning girl in front of him was worth the risk of a transfer to the front. She might even be of German descent, which would please his parents. He had seen many girls in school who resembled her in appearance. There was a petite nose, her complexion was similar to his, and she spoke with a sweetness tinged with that sassiness that he ultimately found irresistible. He convinced himself that even his mother might approve of her.

He longed for contact so dreadfully much that his draw to her resembled an intense magnet unable to combat the cellular interaction of its makeup. It was true animal attraction, and all human safety features eventually vanished in its all-powerful draw.

"I am called Katarina, but I will soon be called mud if I do not complete my task."

She played the part and giggled while pursing her lips in an effect that resembled the initial moment before a new kiss was to happen. She had reeled him in, and she knew it.

At this boldness, he produced a hearty laugh and volunteered his Christian name, which by this time she must have realized was not standard operating procedure for guards standing sentry by the ghetto.

"My friends back home call me Bert, and my parents call me Bertie," he said with a wink and a smile aimed to please.

Katarina pondered the situation while she deeply inhaled the crisp morning air and slowly exhaled the warmer exhaust that had passed through her lungs. Miraculously, she felt calmer. She knew she had to move decisively; she might never get another chance like this one unfolding before her. This handsome young soldier could possibly be used to her advantage. But she remembered what her father had sternly informed her of last week:

"Young Czech girls should not fraternize with any German soldiers ever, and do not even consider talking or even looking at Jews. The war will eventually come to an end, and history tells us what happens to those who inadvertently or especially on purpose pick the wrong side in a conflict. There will be hangings, I promise you; there will be people shot, and there will be many put in prison. I have seen it before. Nobody knows for sure when the final spin in this game of chance will happen and who will be proclaimed the so-called winner in the final insane moments. In regard to being female, you, my daughter, make no mistake about what I am telling you. If you fraternize with a German soldier or a Jew, your final chapter will be so horrendous that I would rather die with you because I could not even bear to witness it."

"You are scaring her, Papa," her doting mother protested.

Margharite Orbhan knew that her husband was correct, but she also knew that Katarina was capable of defying her father if she believed strongly in a cause, such as the Jewish dilemma.

Madame Orbhan blamed herself for Katarina's innocence as well as kind spirit. Both women felt strongly that all people had buried goodness in them, even if some kept it well hidden. She hoped Katarina could flourish without her husband's harsh suppression.

She also knew that people were capable of very bad decisions and quite hurtful actions. She feared that it was the latter that possibly she had not stressed enough with her lovely Katarina.

"No, Mama. I am very mature, and I really do understand the ways of the world. We cannot live our lives in fear, though."

Hearing this made both parents exhibit those wrinkles that appear on the forehead when anger and surprise spring to the surface.

"You are a child!" roared Papa, "and this proves it. You are forbidden to put your life—and therefore that of your family—in harm's way. We live in serious times, and I must be confident that you will not fight me in this decision. We are not talking about being kind to pets; we are talking about a regime that is more violent than anything you have ever seen in your young life."

Katarina Orbhan pinpointed this exact moment as the second she knew she had to do whatever it took to make a difference. It was time for her to help the world and ignore her father.

⇥ ⇤

Working for Social Services was a job she acquired by luck. The Germans had established a "Zentralstelle fur Judische Auswadering" office, or basically a central office for the Jewish population in Bohemia and Moravia. They were hiring new people to help them in their Prague office. This was the job that Katarina sought. She knew people liked her. Her laugh drew attention. and not because she snorted, but because it was infectious and those around her wanted to join in with her merriment. She was especially beguiling when her face lit up, which was reflected by the smiles she elicited from the lucky ones who positioned themselves near her.

But it was what she said at her interview for the position and how she said it that turned the tide crashing into her, for better or worse.

"Young lady," said Mlle. Zelinsky, who conducted her interview, "I see you have no hidden star to set you apart. There is not even a shred of Jewishness in your file."

There is a way that a person can state something that makes the listener of that statement think there is more to the words than the words themselves. The young Katarina sensed a pause around the word "Jewishness." An adult, who is hardened in the world of double entendre and political statements, might have shrunk from giving a response of force, but not young Katarina. She was ready to save the world, and she wanted this job to be the vehicle that drove her ideals forward, especially to show her father. She threw back her shoulders and looked directly into the eyes of Mlle. Zelinsky, whose lips curled upward in anticipation for the outpouring that was obviously perched on this young woman's tongue.

"If it were up to me and there was even just one person in Prague forced to sew on a Jewish star, all of us would sew it on. Seeing this star gives permission to be derogatory and degrading to the wearer of such a previously innocuous six-pointed emblem. It is only because I strive to be dutiful to my father that I don't complete an action of civil disobedience."

"My dear," she instantly responded with authority, "I suggest you keep such opinions quiet, or you will find yourself in serious trouble. Because this position will place you in the middle of the Jewish sector, I must be crystal clear that it is not to assist those who reside there, but simply to take notes and then write a report on your actual findings. This office is permitted to do this by the city of Prague and the German military force that is occupying us at this time. If they were to think that anyone was assisting the Jewish population, our office would be abandoned, and our staff would probably be interned with conditions far worse than what you will see when you enter the Jewish area. As for what might happen to you...even a father to such a dutiful daughter would not be able to save you. I beg you not to verbalize such words again for your safety!"

Katarina did not know whether to say sorry or thank you, so she said both.

"I am sorry if I spoke out of turn. I have been told before to curb my tongue, and I am constantly working on that acrobatic feat. But just as I strive to be dutiful to my parents, I will be dutiful to this position, and you will like my astute reporting. Please let me formulate my utmost gratitude to you, since you mentioned I could possibly be in this position. I apologize for adding my unsolicited

opinions of present-day politics, which leave everyone confused, especially me. You are so right to remind me about
thinking before speaking, and I appreciate your concern
and know you are correct. I promise I will not be so de-
monstrative in the future. I do not know what happened
to me. I must be terribly nervous because this is such an
important interview. My school record will inform you
that this outburst was an oddity, and you can be confident
that it will not happen again."

Mlle. Zelinsky shook her head and looked at the naive
young girl sitting on the edge of her seat in front of her. She
had no idea what this impulsive girl was up to, but she realized that something was percolating, and that cinched her
own resolution to use her to help her favorite Jewish doctor.
She found a use for Katarina's obvious flaw in wanting to
help the oppressed.

Eva Zelinsky never would have chanced doing something
so outwardly foolish as assisting a Jew herself—before last
week. But this week was a different story concerning her un-
characteristic motive. She developed an explosive itch that
started on the back of her red right hand and then climbed
up her dry arm and extended to her itchy trunk. The rash
then took a turn toward her back, and now it looked like it
was crawling again toward her chest. The hue of her face
began to get red as welts formed, which added to the panic
that set in a few days ago. She tried to get an appointment
at her doctor's office, located on Maiselova Street in what
used to be a Jewish area of the city. A new physician had

taken over his office. The young doctor, arriving without prior notice, was rumored to be from Germany.

Dr. Rudolf Bonn, her favorite physician, was out of commission because he had a Jewish mother. Eva felt forced to see the newcomer, even though she was not fond of newcomers or invaders, depending on which word was more apropos.

She had seen her dear handsome Dr. Bonn last year, where he had been as thorough in his exam as he was kind in his spirit. He was sporting a yellow star on his white coat and joked that it was because he had been a star pupil at the Charles University Medical School he attended years ago in this, his hometown of Prague, where she knew his family had resided for generations.

She tended to get quite nervous when she experienced anything out of the ordinary from her usual aches and pains. She called his office frequently and saw him more than the average healthy person might see a doctor. This kindly gentleman in his late thirties always made time for her and never made her feel rushed when she would discuss at length her concerns. He was one of the smartest men she knew, and that helped to promote the little romantic crush that had formed.

He was tall and handsome, with strong arms and a delicate touch, which she felt was great for surgeries and even better for the personal contact that she longed for during her sleepless nights. Even though he was happily married, he never made her feel awkward when she gave him those lingering smiles and pats on the arm. She was aware that he was in a good marriage because he was always mentioning his wife and even insinuated that his wife was possibly with child. She was too flustered when he confided this to ask for clarification in this murky area. One way or the other, she was convinced that a baby's picture would soon be added to one of the multiple shots that he proudly displayed on the rear surface of his cluttered desk.

Eva Zelinsky became consumed with the other woman's probable pregnancy and obsessed with what it must be like to have a child in one's uterus. She pictured herself as the lovely Madame Bonn and started to pat her belly. She would look at her sparse wardrobe and pick out looser clothing. She put her soft rabbit's fur sweater back in the armoire and chose a loose chemise that gave her a blockier rather than sexier look. She also got in the habit of going to the library reference section and looking up articles on gestation, with illustrations of the wonderful things that occurred each month in the nine months awaiting the birth of a child.

She began to note such facts, like how stress was not good on a fetus and how important good nutrition was to the modern expectant mother. At least Rudolph Bonn was a doctor, and thank goodness he was aware of all of the amazing facts that she had become acutely familiar with through her recent extensive reading. He would know how to take care of his wife, or her, or whomever he was married to in her mind at that moment.

It was a terrible blow to her when she learned that Jews were no longer allowed to work at their professions and were concentrated within the Holesovice quarter, which was an older section in Prague that made gray days seem even grayer because of the lack of paint and the poor upkeep on the facades.

There was talk that the Jews were going to be moved to Terezin, which was around thirty-eight kilometers from Prague center and took around forty minutes or so to get to. She was fearful of that news, not because of the many Jews in the city who would be affected by this decree, but that her own precious doctor would be included in that unfortunate lot. How could she know what was going on at Terezin, being that it was so far away from the city?

German soldiers occupied every corner of the state, speaking a language that sounded similar yet undeniably foreign. German beer was tasty, but everyone in Prague knew that Moravian beer was superior because of its delicate flavor.

She had no desire to frequent anything German, from their beer to their politics, to their even more viral hatred of the Jews, that was stronger than the walls of the Prague Castle. The people of Prague did not seem to hate the Jewish population as much as the German invaders did. It was with apprehension of anything German that she feared for the safety of her dear doctor and his soon-to-be-born child.

Eva also knew that she was not meant for intrigue. A month ago, she ventured close to the Holesovice district out of curiosity. There were actually very few streets that were a corridor into that section, which also housed a small square that had a church with a blackened stone carving of an oversize vulture looking ominously at those within its gaze.

The church had what looked like an odd stick hanging from one of the interior rafters that was rumored to be the arm of a beggar that had been chopped off in punishment and placed there to remind the sinners that they would have to pay on this earth as well as in heaven if they broke commandments, such as by stealing. The area housed at least two old synagogues, no longer used by the local Jews since they were forbidden to practice Judaism.

Eva was taken aback when she encountered a German sentry posted by the main venue into the district. She knew when she was approaching the Jewish quarter because the city around her changed its personae and became older and oddly more innately decorative in its architectural detail minus the coat of much-needed paint. She was aware that at one time these buildings held color and shone vivacity to their beholders, but now they were in need of a good washing. She carefully changed her projected direction from the Jewish quarter and veered to another street, which basically put her into a horseshoe pattern of traffic without ever going into the originally desired location with the feared sentry.

She produced a sigh of relief when she realized her nature was more timid than adventurous. She was painfully aware that she held a certain level of fantasy in her thoughts that never broke through to reality as she marched back to the safety of her familiar busy streets. They were devoid of the scattering of yellow stars that had previously appeared in her precarious city, which seemed to teeter on a precipice of new ideas and iron-fist controls.

It was in this climate of uncertainty that a German officer had ventured into her building and demanded that she hire a new worker, who had to be young, attractive, and female. This intern would be responsible for collecting numerical data in regard to the Jewish population of the city. Her initial distaste of this officer gave way to the possibility that she could hire someone else to go into the ghetto to find the exact whereabouts of her Jewish doctor.

She pushed down the bile that was rising into her throat from having to converse with this coarse individual and agreed to post a temporary position for such an unsuspecting frivolous youth, who would not be aware of the imminent dangers of such a simple-sounding assignment.

Within a week of the order to procure a young girl, there stood before her the perfect specimen: Katarina Orbhan.

And now before Katarina stood a young man named Bert, whose thoughts were exploding in his head as he looked at the absolutely striking girl with curly blond hair in front of him. He blocked his hostile environment; he blocked the steadfast ruthlessness of his immediate superiors; and he blocked his common sense, as his gaze kept bouncing back between the document in his hand and the potential receptacle for his youthful lust.

As is usually the case with young men, lust won over, and he blurted out the only thing he could think of: "See me."

"Pardon me?" smirked Katarina because now she was certain that she had hooked him, although she was not certain if she would reel in a barracuda, an eel, or a minnow. She added a quick, "I see you too!"

Her large smile formed tiny grooves on her rosy cheeks, and her perfectly formed ears seemed to wriggle in excitement. And that sealed the deal for him.

"I am aware that it is very forward of me, but I would so enjoy just having a coffee with you. Permit me to ask your parents, for my intentions are honorable and I am simply a lonely Bertie in a foreign land."

Without hesitation, she then sealed her end of the deal, even though she knew a young German soldier could never be brought to meet her parents. She had easily fallen into her first great acting role of a career that might turn out to be extensive. Her paramount desire to help Jews was overtaking her common sense.

"Coffee sounds delightful, but I am unable to do it today. I really do have to observe and collect data in the ghetto. I cannot write a report on what I think is happening down those streets unless I see it for myself," she proclaimed in a breathy way.

Bert began nervously bouncing his foot on the stone surface as he tried frantically to appear calm.

"I get a day off on Thursday of this week, which gives you plenty of time to make up an excuse before then for not meeting me," Bert said with a tinge of sarcasm.

Katarina began to feel sorry for this soldier boy, who could not possibly be as offensive as the Nazi uniform he wore. His dingy insignias drew the focus of her waning attention. Her scheme, which was slowly evolving, could only benefit from knowing a German soldier with obvious Nazi credentials who guarded the Jewish quarter.

In her head she really did run through ten excuses for not meeting Bert, but blurted out instead, "Thursday would work during my lunchtime if you would like to add a sandwich or pastry to that coffee."

With his pathetic offer affirmed, he willingly gave his affection instantly to a perfect stranger. He then quickly rolled back on his heels, slapped his feet on the pavement, and rolled forward without giving the damsel even a second to change her mind.

"When would you like me to ask your parents' permission?" he asked with a twinkle in his eyes.

Katarina quickly responded, "There is no need for that. I am a modern woman, and my parents trust me to make the correct decision. I understand that a coffee is just a coffee. Why not meet at the Church of Our Lady Before Tyn on Celetna Street? I'll be at the front of the church by the steps at noon."

Bert acknowledged knowing where that famous church rested in the square and replied, "I'll be early, and I would wait forever for you."

Katarina blushed at his genuine demonstration of emotion and felt embarrassed that she was even planning to follow through with this capricious folly that had been tacked on to an even greater folly that had the potential of getting even more convoluted as her nonplan enfolded her.

She swung her purse over her head to hang delicately between her breasts and cleared her throat while she prepared to saunter away with her briefcase in hand.

She took a step forward as she whispered, "Bye," to this Nazi guard, who then clicked his heels and winked.

Her steps got quicker as her gait morphed into a jog. She commanded her eyes to look at the Jewish enclave before her and not the attentive young man behind her.

The neighborhood was not as she remembered it. Crowds traversed the packed streets as well as the adjacent sidewalks. A sea of dark caps wavered in front of her as pedestrians quickly glanced downward to avoid eye contact. Terror began to grip her as her familiarity receded.

This whole year she had tended not to travel outside the parameter of her neighborhood. She visited her local friends in a two-block configuration, where she could run to pick up a cut of meat at Pejskars or buy bread from the local street vendor.

A gnawing feeling started rumbling in her tummy as her thoughts jumbled into an explosion of fireworks that started taking off in her head and producing a headache. Did she really need the assistance of a Nazi soldier? Well, it could not hurt her, she figured. Was she in any danger? That answer was quite obvious.

She needed to attend to business first and blot out these anxiety-producing thoughts of saving Jews. Her job was to report to Mlle. Zelinsky what was occurring on the ghetto streets of Prague now occupied by only those of Jewish descent. She was given a contact that could assist her in her quest for a more realistic accounting. She remembered Mlle. Zelinsky's hand was shaking imperceptibly when she handed her the small pink square of paper with the name "Dr. Rudolf Bonn" printed on it in block letters.

"This gentleman might help you with your appraisal of the vicinity and interpret the local dialect for you. I am assuming Yiddish is spoken frequently there. He can assist getting a more accurate count than the soldiers can because the Jews consistently hide from strangers in uniform," she said hoarsely. Her voice took on the quality of an elderly woman, even though she was actually not that much older than Katarina.

Katarina was still confused about exactly what she was supposed to accomplish. She was not even sure what was to come of this report. If it were presented to the German invaders, they could possibly use it to promote more of their aggressive actions that were being inflicted on the Slavic people for the supposed good of that people, a disjointed concept in and of itself. If the city of Prague were to actually understand what was going on within the city limits, there was the possibility of change, but it was hard for her to decide if more damage could result with said report.

She was torn because she knew that whatever this report entailed, wherever it ended up, whether in a drawer or on the führer's own desk, it was not going to be the only task that she intended to do. She was determined to pursue her own covert agenda on this mission and accomplish things unofficially. She would not bury that burning need to do at least one thing that could help at least one person, no matter how small. She liked to think she could accomplish Herculean tasks that would secure a more copacetic relationship with the Jews in her community, but she knew this might not happen. She wished it were possible to exist in a world without barriers, but she knew this was not to be either. She had enough sense to start small, and she had enough sense to start soon or her window would be closed to such possibilities.

What better way to begin her mission than to be on Josefska Street, surrounded by Jews and armed with a notebook and pen that neatly resided in her tightly gripped, very professional-looking briefcase. She could do this, and she would do this. Her fears started to melt around her. She looked up and saw a hint of blue sky, then let her gaze drop down in a slide that ended with the gray cobblestones of a street she saw paved with hope. It was time to get to work.

Katarina opened to a blank page in her blue notebook while leaning against the damp surface of the uneven stone building. She had to set down her briefcase momentarily and was amazed at just how many people there were around her. The street was teeming with bodies, and they all had yellow stars on them. Some of the stars looked askew, as if they doubted whether this was a proper location for a star. Some of their yellow tones shone more brightly, while others were dulled from never being shed. If one only looked at the stars, and not the people, they took on the dimensions of a constellation, with groups of them darting around in front and behind her. She observed some tints that looked like an older group of stars because they had a trampled appearance. Some yellows seemed almost opulently oversize because the bodies connected to them were so undersize.

Her briefcase precariously leaned against her leg while her hair flew up in silly acrobatics and then nosedived every time someone streamed by her and affected the air currents that were trapped between the buildings. Her heart began racing again, and her eyes started darting around the unfamiliar landscape. She was coming to the realization that she really was petrified even though she tried to block it. She was more scared than she had been when talking to an enemy Nazi soldier, and this worried her quite a lot. She quickly grabbed her briefcase, as if she were a hostage who was not going to get released unless she unlocked her secrets contained in the blank sheets poised in the briefcase.

"Stop this silliness," came out of her mouth while her hair flew even higher in the wind.

"OK," said a voice that was coming from the five-foot-ten-inch frame that was suddenly blocking her view of those scurrying around her. "I will stop my silliness if you start walking a bit, or I am afraid that you will be the catastrophe on the sidewalk that will make these other people stop and gawk at you for causing quite the traffic jam on this pedestrian roadway."

This was all said with a smile that had two dimples on either side of a very friendly face.

"Follow me, the Pied Piper, or David as I am often called. I can see you need assistance, dear princess. You are in luck because I am a king, well, at least a kingfisher by birth. David Kingfisher at your service."

"Do I really look like I am in need of saving?" Katarina said incredulously, even though she felt an instant relief to be around someone who appeared quite entertaining and native to the area. "I am here on official business."

"Then I will officially introduce myself and will help you with your endeavors before you succumb to the madness of the crowds. David Kingfisher is my name, and assistance is my game, dear damsel in distress," he proclaimed with a flourishing bow that ended in a hand grab and flowed through a walk, which ended in a doorway that had evidently been close by even though she had not noticed it previously.

"I really did not want to frighten you, but you did seem out of sorts. You are now away from the path of the masses, and you will not be squished if you decide to again take out that bright blue notebook of yours."

"Hmm," she harrumphed as she freed her notebook from its confines. "You can leave now," she replied as curtly as possible.

She had no intention of having another conversation with another stranger. Seeing so many strangers was all quite shocking to her. Her friends had always been her friends for as long as she remembered, and those were the individuals whom she talked to—and usually it was only they. Occasionally some moved away and others arrived, but the majority of people who surrounded her in her insular life had been raised within the few blocks of where she lived with her parents and brother. She knew no one who did not know her parents. She was completely out of her element with this first job, and she was confused in these new environs with all of these strange poor people who looked so tattered. She was talking to odd characters on this first day of her job, and she found this very disconcerting.

David, meanwhile, had spotted this young woman immediately as being someone who did not belong in the ghetto. She was devoid of the yellow mark that kept Jews apart from the general society, and this drew him in like a beacon of light seen over a dark ocean night. He never had a problem meeting girls of any persuasion, and they never seemed to have a problem being around him either. He was attracted to brunettes, blondes, redheads, Jews, and even goyim, or shiksas, the name that most people around him called those females who were not Jewish. He was having a slight hitch with his usual intake of females as of late, though. His boyish charm and his striking good looks had always played into his getting at least a swipe of what he wanted, but everyone now showed fear in their actions and reactions.

His favorite uncle, Ike, with his bald head and his lengthy prayer shawl always wrapped around him, used to call him "spoiled," with a little "pith, pith" that came afterward almost spitting from his wide lips. He ignored his uncle's proclamation because Uncle Ike also had a favorite nephew, and that was he, the devilishly handsome David. Uncle Ike's wife, Sadie, often called him a "pretty boy," which he liked much less coming from her even though he was aware that both of their statements rang true.

His life had taken a turn into turmoil, with constant somersaults that made everything topsy-turvy. He was not at all pleased with what had been happening in his love life—or his life in general. He remembered when the air of change wafted into his parents' home.   Objets d'art began disappearing mysteriously, with no family member coming up with explanations as to where the valuable items were. First, it was the beautiful Ming vase, and then the silver candlesticks, and even the very large velvet couch! He thought it was a silver lining when he was told he could not attend the city day school anymore. He had to control his joy when he realized he no longer had to wake up and trot off to lessons that often put him to sleep. Schoolwork with his older brother soon became tedious, and oftentimes he missed the companionship of his playful school-yard friends.

When the yellow star was reluctantly sewn on his clothes, it felt like severed skin against him. Many edicts had chipped away at their existence, but this one took the largest toll. The star shape seared into his outfits like a bad tattoo that was indelibly there for all to see. He never knew when he would be the brunt of jokes or the receptacle for punks throwing garbage aimed at his face. He was afraid that he was starting to be consumed with the fear that overtook him on the teeming streets.

No longer in their home, they squeezed into a minute apartment with Uncle Ike, Aunt Sadie, and two stinky cats. He slept on the couch with one cat, which always inched toward his face and loved to rest under his nose feeling the steamy air blowing on its fur. A dark, fat cat slept by his long bony feet that peeked out of the covers; it attacked him if he even moved an inch. This was neither where he wanted to be nor how he wanted to be living. His instinct now drove him toward this girl. She was able to enter this ghetto, so she was able to leave it. He recently had been concentrating his energy on a way out of Prague. He wanted to be wherever he could rip off the yellow star.

"Tell me what you are doing here, Princess. I know the streets, I know the people, I know you do not belong here, and I know I have some time before I am due home for the banquet that graces my table nightly—not really that part, you know."

Katarina realized she could use a little assistance. This whole day had discombobulated her so much that she was beginning to get a pain behind her eyes, which was not a good sign for anyone who was prone to headaches.

"I am from the official Office of Social Services of Prague, and I am sure that my office would approve of you assisting me, even slightly, while I begin the process of writing a report on this area of town," she proclaimed as she mustered her most official-sounding voice, which was meant to intimidate this much too good-looking young man.

"I can definitely help you. I have reams and reams of information for you about this area. I am familiar with the streets, the obvious condition of the buildings, and the not so obvious problems. I am an expert on what it is like to live within these confines. You are officially quite lucky to bump into me, Princess. At your service, and no need to cut me into your salary."

"Offering you money never occurred to me. It sounds like we think quite differently. I suggest you move on," she added while thinking about the definition of a con man. "I spoke too hastily and will be fine without your help."

She was talking too much and too suddenly to this stranger. Just because he wore a yellow star did not mean he was harmless.

"Whoa, not so fast with the brush-off. I do regret my choice of words, for it looks like you misunderstood me. I do not need extra money living here in the ghetto. I was only attempting to be cute, which I guess failed. Seriously, I do want to help you figure out this crazy labyrinth filled with people bumping into one another and stepping on one another's toes. It is a gauntlet of confusion here. I would want someone to help me if by some miracle I was just thrown into this chaos and told to describe it. Forgive me for the comments that affronted you. Can you be so kind as to give me another opportunity, Princess, to prove myself useful? Remember, David did take down Goliath, and there are a lot of giants out there who might not listen to such a lovely, refined young woman as yourself. Besides, I am...David."

Katarina thought about his words of reconciliation. He was actually charming, and he did have a familiarity with these streets that she did not have, so she replied, "We must get on better footing. You are living here, which is a plus, but your 'cuteness,' as you referred to your banter, irritates me. I could use someone who knows his way around to help me with the ins and outs of this area, so maybe we could sit at some point and have a real conversation on the trials and tribulations of life here."

She knew she sounded all over the map, but her head hurt, and this day was just becoming too much for her to handle. She did not even know if there were any cafés nearby, which confirmed her suspicions that she might possibly lead a sheltered life and was not quite as savvy as she had previously thought. She was not ready to give up on this endeavor though. She still held on to her personal mission of wanting to help Jews. Obviously this guy she was talking to was Jewish, because his star prominently showed on the front and the back of his jacket. At least this was a start.

Today was especially overwhelming, from interactions with the Nazi guard to this David character. She could hardly believe she was just in her first hours of this daunting task, which was now appearing to be more monumental than she had initially assumed. She needed her comfort zone. She wanted to see her stern papa wagging his finger at her, and she needed her loving mama's consoling arms embracing her. She even yearned for her brother to tease her a bit, pointing out to her that she was still a child. Being demure and mature was not the draw she initially considered it to be.

She said, "I think we should have a conversation tomorrow and not today. Let us meet at 9:00 a.m. in a café of your choice, if there is a café around here."

"There is a café at 13 Bilkova called Trini's. It is behind the Spanish synagogue, so it will be easy for you to find.

You see, it is right around the corner from here if you look to your right. You will only have to walk straight into the ghetto and turn right at this first corner. They will not mind if we spend hours there nursing just one cup of the colored hot water that they call tea or coffee."

What he was not saying was that it was the only café left in the Jewish town, so there was not much of a choice and there really was not much of a menu. Trini, the kind owner's wife, kept the establishment open just so people could socialize and pretend it was operating normally. The Germans permitted the café to exist, although he'd heard that soon the doors would be locked forever. He still needed her to think that he was essential and cafés were in business as usual.

Anyone sitting at Trini's would have been more than happy to offer his or her opinion to this pretty girl, who did not look threatening to anyone. The prerequisite hushed tones and notably no strangers present would have to occur for conversation though.

The day's delay of their next meeting would give him time to figure out how he could use her to get out of this hellhole. All anyone wanted to do these days was complain ad infinitum about what was occurring to them, around them, and the injustice of it all. He was more impulsive and wanted action, not so much kvetching.

The odd chance that this sweet face could pass on pertinent information to anyone of importance was astounding. But now was not the time to question anything in regard to the lovely girl who was plopped into his path. Few people showed interest in his people's plight. The entire population of Prague seemed worried for their own survival. After all, the country had been invaded, which distressed everyone. Personal survival was on everybody's mind, not altruistic thoughts for the chosen people. Someone out there had bestowed Katarina a task that was obviously too large for her, which meant they must have considered the possibility that she might fail in her endeavor. That made more sense as to why she was there. It could be just for show. Nobody was really interested in what was happening in the ghetto. But he hung on to his conviction that she must hold some vital key for his escape even though she addled his brain.

So, he smiled his warmest smile and twinkled those beautiful eyes of his and waved to her with the words, "See you at 9:00 a.m. tomorrow morning at Trini's on Bilkova Street."

Katarina smiled ever so slightly with her fake smile that she had previously mastered in front of a mirror weeks ago, quickened her steps toward the openness of the free square, and anxiously ran to the safety of her waiting home.

Katarina walked into her somewhat ordinary house, with the narrow three floors now appearing opulent. Even though her ghetto visit was short, her anxiety there had been great. She grabbed the first trolley that came along, and it eventually delivered her close to her destination. The tree-lined street of her neighborhood shaded her from the sun, which was just starting to trickle out after a day of clouds and gloom. These moderately sized homes were lavish mansions compared to the ones she had just seen. Each home here held different generations of the same family, sharing the combined space as well as the gene pool.

Once she saw her front door looming in the distance, she had the desire to do her little skip exercise that she got a kick out of doing when she was a spry eleven-year-old. The walk up to her front door had a variety of lines made from embedded stone that crossed at odd angles. This challenged the hopscotcher to reach new heights while navigating its intricate course. Even though she was getting much too old for such frivolity, her thoughts returned to the game today, but now she wanted her actions to be more in tune to the adult she was trying to be. The door was graced with a beautiful knocker in brass, which was of a capped young man who had his arm up and his back bent slightly. When you grabbed his hind end, the arm rapped on the door, which tended to delight the person knocking. When the occupant opened the door, a smile was the first thing he or she confronted. This delighted everyone.

Katrina started yelling, "I'm home," even before the door completely shut.

"Who cares?" yelled her brother, rollicking down the formal staircase.

"I do," invoked her gentle mother, who was just walking into the floral-carpeted hallway from the chandeliered dining room.

Katarina almost mowed her mother down when she gave her a bear hug that was worthy of a big grizzly.

"That is the kind of greeting I should get every time one of my darlings walks through that door!" her mother said while kissing the air instead of her daughter's skin because she had put Katarina's head in a vise.

"We are so lucky, Mama."

"Of course we are, my little cupcake. Was your first day that upsetting that you should come home more delighted to see us than usual? You really do not need this job, Katarina. Please think about quitting."

Katarina could not tell her mother about the Nazi guard or the Jewish boy who showered attention on her today. She did not even have all of it straight in her own mind, so she was only able to say, "First days are always a challenge, Mama. You know that, because you try so hard to understand me, and I really appreciate it."

"I do try, but I am not always successful. I hope you might talk to me about what happened today, because you are acting a bit unusual."

"You are so smart, Mama. Going into the Jewish area did shock me somewhat. I guess I really had no idea how very crowded they are in those narrow streets and how sad everything appears," Katarina responded.

"Katarina, Katarina, you know you do not really need to have this job. Please call LouLou and ask her to take over for you. Papa would love to have you putter around his office and put away some of those large file folders that he always has lying around cluttering his office. Just say the word."

"I will say more than one word, Mama, and that is I started a job and I will finish it. Just because I appreciate my home does not mean I have to instantly quit my very first job. You used to tell me not to give up on things, but to give them a chance. There is always a chance that all of the kinks will disappear. The job is a definitive report for a short-term stint, and when it is complete, my contract will be finished, and then I will file for Papa if I am unable to get more work. Please, try to support me in this because I know that Papa is not too excited that I am working outside of the family, and I need you to be in my corner."

"After that impassioned speech, not only will I defend your job to Papa, but I will even offer my services to assist you when you go into that section of town to do your research. I am not sure it is as safe for a lovely young lady as we initially thought."

"Mama, *no*! I mean, thank you for this offer, but I was just being my usual silly self. The job is so good for me. I finally feel somewhat independent. Knowing that you are here and I can come home if needed gives me such security."

She now realized that she had been a little too dramatic with her entrance. It had previously been pointed out to her that the melodramatics she oftentimes exhibited over minor things were taken more seriously than she intended. She was not going to even whisper the names of her two new male acquaintances, but they kept clanging in her head. "Bert, Bert, David, David, no, no, no. You are both making me act crazy," she thought, but the words that came out were different.

"No, Mama. Thank you again for your offer. I am happy to know that I can count on you if I need to, but I am going to try to be adult, even though I obviously have a little way to go. Even I can see that."

Her childish appeal made Margharite Orbhan enfold her daughter in another big mama hug that caused Katarina to rest her head on her mother's shoulder and whisper, "I love you, Mama," which wiped the pained expression off Margharite's face.

⟻ ⟼

The following morning positioned itself with a potential array of problems that had a whole slew of possible answers that confused even Katarina. She definitely could not confide in her mama even though she did end up supportive the previous night during a somewhat tense meal that Katarina was now remembering.

"Papa, you would not believe the drama that Katarina brought into the house when she came home from her first day of work today," her brother, Georgie, blurted out right when the sliced warm potatoes covered with chunky salt were being passed under Katarina's alert nose.

But her mother saved the day and proclaimed that a little fluster was normal for a first day and Papa had nothing to worry about with his little girl. This deleted the tense lines that were beginning to form around his terse expression.

"She is a little girl, Papa, and she does not belong running around Prague as if she could really report anything other than what flavor of ice cream she preferred."

Georgie had gone too far with that statement, but Katarina was not going to bite that bait. Thank goodness Mama was perfectly able to present her case to Papa and terminate the discussion. This gave her a slight reprise from her tenuous situation, which she felt was slipping away from her control.

Today was a new day, though, and she felt somewhat up to a new challenge...especially when it presented itself as she was walking out the door.

She already had her hand on the smooth wooden door-knob when she heard the phone ringing in the distance. Petra, who was their housekeeper and nanny, answered it as Katarina started to turn the doorknob to the right. She noticed a pause in the conversation, and then something was muttered by Petra as she put the phone down. Katarina almost made it out the door before Petra caught up with her. Just when she thought she was free from the pull of her family, she got reeled in again.

"You must come to the phone, Mlle. Katarina, because there is a Mlle. Zelinsky who wants to talk to you."

This was not good news. She had to meet David at 9:00 a.m., which was one hour away. She knew that if she refused to come to the phone, her job might be terminated, which would solve the issue for her parents.

"Good morning, Mademoiselle. How can I help you?" Katarina presented her most authoritative voice, which was lower than Petra had ever heard her command.

"I wanted to discuss your first day on the job and make sure that you are equipped with all of the correct tools for success." She really just wanted to see if Katarina had con-tacted her doctor. She knew she should not press her in this matter of seeing him on the very first day, but she was hop-ing she had at least located him. "I would like to see you in the office today so we can discuss this matter."

Katarina haltingly responded, "I cannot...no, I mean I am meeting an acquired source to help me find the true source, which is the one from your recommendation. That part of town has changed immensely, so I enlisted a navigator to point me to the correct address at which to begin my research with the good doctor. Is it possible to confer with you after my visit to the district today? I look forward to our conversations because I am afraid I will need a little guidance before I can begin actually reporting."

Eva Zelinsky was sure that Katarina would need more than a little guidance and wanted to make sure that she was there for the culling of information that might overwhelm her while trying to report all of the delicate facts. She was sure of Katarina's naïveté and was not comfortable with her complete independence in this matter, even though she was the one who had hired her.

"Come at three o'clock in the afternoon, and we will discuss your findings from today's activities," Mlle. Zelinsky said curtly.

"Thank you, Mademoiselle. I look forward to this meeting and will see you at three o'clock promptly."

Katarina felt that she had just dodged a bullet as she crashed the receiver on its receptacle and ran out of the house. The door slammed behind her as she sprinted to the clanging streetcar that would deliver her to her new career, which was starting to eat away at her confidence at an alarmingly fast rate.

The checkpoint where she had first met Bert was manned by another soldier, who had a few more age lines on his face than young Bert did. This time, she was not at all hesitant as she whipped out her credentials and assignment sheet printed with the combined letterhead of the Nazi party and the Prague Office of Social Services. No words were exchanged, and he simply motioned her to move in her intended direction. Her thoughts of Bert would have to wait until her thoughts of David were not so intrusive. The bustle from the scurrying people did not jangle her nerves as much as it had previously as she walked toward the well-known establishment of Trini's.

All of the buildings on the street seemed to connect to one another, with just a minute amount of space separating the different styles. The building that Trini's was housed in had four floors, with a series of four long windows in each section. There were ornate details of curlicues and leaves above each window that could not be drowned out by the dismal situation that its inhabitants found themselves in at this time. The upper floor of the building looked like a roof, pointing to the sky, but a mansard roof actually sat on top of that floor, with two windows resplendent with curlicues peering down to the street below. The street level was canopied, with three rolled-out and tattered canvas coverings stating the names of three establishments located in the building printed in block letters. Trini's name sat boldly in the middle of the three signs, with a large water-stained glass window positioned so all could see out as they eyed the street to sense if danger was approaching. As she peered inside through the dingy window, she saw a single large room, with dark wooden tables and small wooden chairs crammed full of people who seemed to be bouncing up and down in motion. She soon realized that it was her head that was bobbing as she tried to see anyone who resembled what she only half remembered David to look like.

A gentle tap on her shoulder made her whip around quickly, and she found herself locking onto David's dark-brown eyes boring into hers.

"Sorry to scare you, Princess. You are right on time, and I am ready to be your tour guide and assistant extraordinaire."

"Before we enter, David, I would like you to explain again why in the world you would possibly want to help me. You realize I cannot pay you, even though I do appreciate your assistance."

"We went through this, Princess. Just a guy with a lot of time on his hands who sees a princess who could use a prince, not to mention me, as a helper in this crazy part of town that has been sectioned off from the rest of civilization. I also want you to immerse yourself in this neighborhood so you can accurately write your report. You do realize that the majority of people living on these streets were not previously housed here, and it is more than awkward for everyone involved. But let us sit down. I am anxious for you to get a sense of what is going on around here."

"David," said Katarina, "I do not want to give you the impression that I have any importance in this city or that my simple report is going to effect any kind of change around here. I would like to think it would, but I realize that it is impossible in these times to have one report or one person impact the outcome of an entire community. I might have somewhat inflated my importance, and for that, I apologize."

"Not to worry, Princess. You seem perfect for the task, so let's enter Trini's and get this show on the road!"

"Sounds good," muttered Katarina as she followed David to a very small, battered table in the back corner that had two narrow chairs squeezed in an area that should only have accommodated a simple table devoid of accoutrements or chairs.

Once inside, the two young people huddled together closely in a surprisingly intimate way. It might have been the overwhelming crowd or just their need to be close to another one of their age that drew them in toward each other. As they talked more, the space between them kept shrinking.

"I need to see various housing facilities, as well as see what sanitation and recreation are available to the constituents of this district," whispered Katrina while inching in a little closer yet. "I also have the name of a certain doctor, Bonn, who is living here with an expectant wife. I definitely need to speak to this individual, so please prioritize meeting him at this beginning of our collaboration." Now her breath was puffing toward his face and made him slightly blush.

David thought intently about her somewhat easy requests. One could see immediately if one was truly looking carefully at the surroundings that sanitation was minimal. The stench was hardly tolerable on a warm day, and recreation comprised only solo occupants staring into the beyond with diminishing hope. As for this doctor, he was immensely popular and quite well-known. Any stranger could lead her to his doorstep, but this did not fit into David's plans. He needed to spend time with this girl to set up his escape route. It helped that she was pert and pleasant and had sweet breath. She had long thin fingers that he found very attractive, as well as a lean build. It was an oddity that fingers were where he focused when initially meeting a female, but his gaze was drawn there quite often. His Aunt Sadie had stubby fingers that were mottled in color and rough like sandpaper. His mother's hands used to be soft. He noticed this when she touched his forehead while testing for a fever or grabbed his arm if she needed to balance herself quickly. She now had fingers that had evolved into something less than the elegant long tapers he remembered from his recent youth.

He had seen this girl as his ticket out of this dreadful situation, which looked worse not better as time progressed. He needed to proceed cautiously if he were to have any success at all with her.

"Why don't we walk around a little bit today, and after you leave, I will procure an appointment for you with your doctor at a specific time, which will eliminate the need to wait alongside sick patients who might be communicable and inadvertently give you a gift that you would not want."

"It sounds good not to get a disease, David, while visiting a man that is supposed to heal, not infect," Katarina said with a nod of her head and a smile on her pretty face that brought a wink from her growing admirer.

Katarina's notebook quickly filled with dramatic scribbles as she timidly walked next to David in the dank, dark Jewish quarter. She wrote of the tremendous crowds of people of all ages who walked in massive groups. Occasionally you could see a pattern when parts of the herd shot into a passageway or opened a door quickly along the way. She was reassured by the presence of David, who quickly got in step with the throngs who moved through the foreign sidewalks. She stumbled along, crushed beside his assertive figure. He walked her by magnificent structures, such as one he called the Jerusalem Synagogue, which was dedicated in 1906. A steel gate had been erected around it, and big chains encompassed the metal parts that made those passing by it painfully aware that there was no religious attendance in that forgotten house of worship, no matter how grand it looked.

David explained how Jews could no longer practice the religion openly, but he insinuated that some still continued to keep at least the outward manifestations of the religion alive within their own family units. "This particular information is not for your report, Katarina, because lives could possibly be lost if it became flaunted, even though it is common knowledge that something or another is occurring in regard to religion and the people confined."

"I respect you asking for privacy, and nothing will be added about religious practices to anything I write," she said as she quickly wrote down that private conversations were not to be added to any report. She even starred the sentence beginning with the word "religious" and starred again the word "private."

Before she knew it, they were back at Trini's, exhausted and ready to take their places by the ragtag table again. David ushered her to their spot, and they plopped into their somewhat beat-up seats.

"I think this constitutes the end of our first day, Princess, and I hope you found our walk educational. Same time, same place tomorrow?"

Katarina's date with Bert was the following day, which she did not want to advertise, so she steered her date with David to Friday morning.

"That will give me a little time to write some things down that I have witnessed today," Katarina explained as she abruptly stood up in close proximity to David's chair.

"Rushing off so soon?" he said while gazing into her eyes above his. "May I give you a peck on both cheeks as if we lived in Paris?" he asked with pleading eyes.

"We are not in gay Paris, monsieur, so adieu the Prague way, where one gives a hardy slap on the shoulder," she said while slapping his shoulder area as hard as she could.

"See you on Friday, champ," he said to her back, because she was already out the door.

Katarina quickly shot off to her impending meeting with her superior. She arrived at the office with twenty minutes to spare and knocked timidly on the door of the Office of Social Services. Mlle. Zelinsky opened the door herself to a room that was devoid of a secretary but filled with files and stacks of papers precariously placed over the flat, large desk, with only a few cleared spots peeking out from the amassed clutter. She seemed a bit flustered as she watched Katarina glance around the messy space, with her eyes resting on the two small Nazi flags that adorned the disarray.

Ignoring her stares, Mademoiselle ushered Katarina into the attached office, which was less cluttered and had a very large red and black Nazi flag attached to the otherwise blank wall behind where she sat. This cube was somewhat larger than the first and was very neat and structured in appearance. The blotter sat smack-dab in the center of the flat plane of her desk, with three pencils, one black pen, one red pen, one blue pen, and two rectangular tan erasers. She glided into her large wooden chair while motioning for Katarina to sit in the rickety one opposite from the chair she regally occupied.

"I see you have redecorated your office with a new flag, Mademoiselle," Katarina said before thinking her statement out completely.

"I am sure that you approve of the new decor, Katarina, because if you voice otherwise, you know your jobs will be limited in the entire city of Prague, not just in this office."

Eva Zelinsky was always taken by surprise with the brashness of this youthful figure before her. She just hoped that this outspokenness would not be her own demise, as well as this child's. She would be a lot more comfortable once this ridiculous errand she had this naive girl on was finished and she could lock the door behind her so no one could reenter with potential trouble.

"I need your notes each time you enter the restricted area, and you will write up your report at the desk in the front room that you just walked through on your way to your present seat here in my office. The report will be added to the report from the Jewish Council of Elders, who are accounting for all of the occupants of Prague's Jewish community, as well as a report from the military attaché's office. Each report will complement the others, and a full picture will be realized when the dossier is complete. You have exactly one week from today before you place the file on my desk with the contents that you have been conscribed to perform, and then your job will be over. Are there any questions?"

With her mouth agape, Katarina was able to partially get out the word, "What?" before Mlle. Zelinsky continued.

"As you might be aware, we are an occupied city. Do not fool yourself that there is any autonomy left for our occupants. I could possibly have given you a different view of your temporary position, but this is how it has to be played. Herr Captain August will be coming to this office unannounced this week. He will ensure a smooth transition of the report to his office."

And with that statement, practically on cue from an off-stage prompter, a Nazi captain came sliding through the anteroom and into the interior office.

"Herr Captain, this is quite humorous because I just mentioned your name to my new intern, Katarina, and lo and behold, you appear!" Mademoiselle said this with a laugh that was hard to be interpreted, whether one of nervousness or girlishness or both.

"Ladies, I am here to check on your progress. The Nazi party is fully aware of all that goes on in the vermin-filled quarter, but is always open to seeing things from various viewpoints. Your work will be shared with the Red Cross as long as it is completed by a week from yesterday's date. Now, let me see what has happened as of today."

Katarina did not want anyone to see her notes, which she had promised David would not be in any report. She could not believe how stupid she was to write down what he explicitly told her was private. She had never previously spoken to a Nazi officer, but after meeting Bert, she was hoping that all had a certain humanity that she could expose with her wily charms.

"I need to write a more formal report, Herr Captain, and only have my schoolgirl notes that will be hard to decipher by anyone other than me. Everything will be ready next week," said Katarina while she exposed her beautiful white teeth and a grin from ear to ear that was meant to entertain.

The Nazi Captain August calmly walked up to her, positioning his somewhat bulky body next to her as he clutched her shoulder in a hug that was too harsh to ever be considered friendly. Then he twirled her to face him, eliminating the space between them. His hot, smelly breath made her nose twinge in this unwanted encounter that hunched her back and bulged her eyes.

"You are a child, with a woman's physique, that is doing the job of a common worker for the glorious army that occupies your weak city while sealing your weak fate. You will give me your notes now, and as I read them, you will take my worn jacket that is quite dusty and go outside and make sure all the street particles are removed. Then I will give you back your silly notes, and you will write it up not as a schoolgirl, but as a worker for the Nazi party, my little blond, blue-eyed dolly."

A shocked Katarina gingerly exchanged the notes for the offered jacket and left through the first office door. She heard the Nazi yell, "Close the door," which she quickly did, and ran outside, stifling her tears.

Meanwhile, the captain quickly locked the same door as he pushed a shocked Eva against the wall, lifting up her oversize skirt while covering her open mouth with his damp, sweaty palm. The wide-eyed Eva was incapable of making a sound while the captain unzipped his already unbelted pants and pulled them down around his hairy ankles. He then coarsely ripped off her undergarment that was demurely covering her private parts, while her eyes transformed to saucers above his clamped hand that was still blocking her mouth. He then kicked her legs from under her as he jumped on top of her, covering her with his full weight. He lunged into her and aggressively penetrated her, breaking her intact membrane. The newly broken membrane was being saved for Dr. Bonn in her twisted thinking, which kept repeating over and over in her jangled head. She was having trouble focusing on anything that came close to the reality around her and now simply squeezed her eyes shut in horror. After no more than three minutes, which felt like a stretch of three years, the captain stood up, zipped up his wrinkled pants, told her quietly to stop acting like a fool, and looked triumphant at the spoils of war allotted to him in his split-second decision.

"Mademoiselle, I had no idea that it was a virgin that I would be blessed with today. I was being such a gentleman by not ravaging that sweet young thing earlier that it never dawned on me that you had not partaken in the joys of adult lovemaking. She will be saved for a later date, but we will be fornicating again very soon, my dear. You will learn the intricacies of satisfying me and be grateful that I will give you the opportunity. Now, my obedient pet, do not even hint about any of this to your young intern, or I will stop calling you my pet and will simply call you a casualty of war. You did a good job today, Eva. I will now assign you the task of looking over these notes that the little bird made. Store them safely and only give them to her when she begins to write the silly report that will probably sit on my desk until the end of the war unseen, or until we need it for purposes other than information."

With that said, he saluted her, blew her a kiss, and walked out the door, leaving her choking back the emotion that was lying in wait and ready to pour out as soon as the monster left.

Every muscle in Eva's body was reacting so fast that she could not determine whether she was standing, sitting, or lying down. She quickly grabbed some tissues from the top drawer of her desk and wiped the blood that was trickling down her frozen legs. She realized the back of her dress was soiled and immediately sat down in her chair. She did not want to chance Katarina bursting into this horrid crime scene.

As she stared at the neat array of pencils, pens, and notes on her desktop, she slowly began to collect herself. Her mind scrambled to put what had just occurred into neat columns.

This foreign monster, bedecked in a military uniform, had violated her, which placed him in the first column. She decided anything in the first column gave her the police option...but then the police really were no longer, and the army was definitely in control of the city, so it would never work.

She then moved to the opposite realm of reality, where another column was placed. This column would be titled the secret column. No one would know the secret hidden in this column except the evil monster. She leaned toward choosing that column.

She then concluded that she'd better pick up her ripped undergarment that had been thrown unceremoniously on the floor or there would be no secret.

She stuffed the soiled garment in her bottom drawer and moved her thoughts onward to yet another column. This was the column that she was going to fill with innuendos and lies that would enable her to keep the little bit of sanity that she had remaining intact. She added a bizarre possibility to the new column: the horrible Nazi had never been inside her, and it would never happen again. She quickly realized the improbability of that since the captain had made it very clear that this was just the first encounter of many. She worried she could not survive this brutality.

This necessitated a final column, designed to help her in a life with this distasteful man doing abhorrent crimes to her whenever it suited his whim. She titled this her *death column*. This made her muscles go to taffy, and she dropped her tired head onto her very neat desk and cried her eyes out with oceans of tears.

Meanwhile, Katarina was banging on the captain's jacket with such force that dust was being emitted nonstop. She gave explosive whacks instead of occasional thwacks because she was so agitated.

This simple task instilled great fear in her because she was so petrified of the scary officer. She worried that even this extensive beating of his jacket would not be sufficient for his Nazi attitude. She continued her cleaning of the garment by putting the cloth between her hands and even trying to press out some of the imbedded wrinkles, as if her hand could possibly mimic an iron. The smell of his stale body odor had been infused into his military-issued jacket and wafted to her open nostrils. This caused her to experience a slight nausea and made her pallor turn to olive green. When finally done with this task of servitude, she sat on the curb to catch her breath before attempting to go back into the office.

Abruptly, she felt the pressure of a fat leg on either side of her slumped body. Two dirty black military-issued shoes peeked out from the two sides of her delicate thighs.

"I see the fräulein has time to sit on her pretty ass," whispered the captain as he bent down toward her ear. To the bystanders, this display of a Nazi captain straddling a young girl appeared distasteful and inappropriate, but not so much that anyone wanted to stop and diffuse the unfolding situation. Everyone just kept hurrying by, but now eyes were averted instead of staring.

"Herr Captain, I have just finished with your jacket," said Katarina quickly, while wiggling out of the compromising position that he had clamped upon her.

"Give me my jacket. Then, hurry upstairs, little bird, and complete your writing like you were told," he barked. The thought of her finding Eva in a state of disarray would help his cause and give her an inkling of what was in store for her without even bothering to verbalize the inevitable.

"Yes, sir, Herr Captain," she said while looking down at the ground, which was beginning to be blurred by the tears that had just started to creep from her young, clouded eyes.

Katarina lumbered up the stairs while roughly rubbing her eyes with her own dress, which was now filled with some of the polluted dust particles that had escaped from the jacket. She did not want to appear as immature as she felt in front of her supervisor, so she quickly pressed her hands against her dress, as if this would remedy the situation. The door did not budge as she turned the handle to enter the office. She listened with her ear to the wood and heard some muffled sounds coming from the interior, so she knew that Mlle. Zelinsky was there. She slowly tapped on the door and waited for it to open.

Eva Zelinsky had not realized that she locked the door earlier, but it was clear to her that this young girl should not see the bloody stain that burned through her dress and announced her late loss of maidenhood. She quickly went to her middle drawer, where she found an old woolen patterned shawl that she sometimes put over her shoulders when chilled. This time she wrapped it around her hips like a young gypsy might while begging in front of the church. Seeing Gypsies was a frequent sight before the Nazis had arrived in Prague and dispersed them to the ends of the earth or possibly heaven.

Eva was not really surprised when the young Katarina entered with her downcast, swollen eyes and did not even seem to notice her attire.

"Take your notes and do not disturb me until you have transferred them onto the office stationery to complete the first draft from your first day. Then put the two documents in two separate file folders located in the front desk, and leave for the night."

Eva Zelinsky then marched into her office and quietly closed the door. She had not checked Katarina's notes for errors as that monster had demanded, but she knew that she would be able to do it once the documents were safely in the files and Katarina was gone. It was essential to act official and to get Katarina out of the office before she realized that she was a possible witness in a travesty of justice.

Katarina had meekly taken the notes from her obviously distressed supervisor and then collapsed at the front secretary's desk. She had no idea if anyone had bothered to look at her scribbling, which unfortunately contained off-the-record statements about ghetto occupants still practicing their outlawed religion.

She remembered that the dangerous part of her notes was delineated with asterisks, so she got out her eraser and attempted to remove the identified phrases that might be construed as subversive. She looked at the smudged paper with the blank spaces on it and knew that even for notes, this would look suspicious to someone who probably saw deceit wherever he glanced, whether real or imagined. She decided to write in "religion is no longer practiced," thinking that this feeble attempt to doctor the notes was adequate for their safety.

She then quickly typed up the paper, put both documents in their respective file folders, and walked out, letting the door slam enough to make a clap that Mlle. Zelinsky could hear even if she were sleeping, which she was not even close to doing.

Katarina would not utter even an iota of the day's events. She knew she'd better act like she loved her job, or her parents would instantly make her quit. If that happened she would have accomplished absolutely nothing other than deceiving them and flirting with two pushy boys located on opposite spectrums of life.

She mustered her courage, put on her smiley face, and ventured toward home. If tomorrow were not better, she feared she would lose her resolve to continue. This espionage business was a little more difficult than she had realized.

⇒ ⇐

The next day, Katarina managed to get out of the house without friction. She wore casual clothes in anticipation of her imminent encounter with the young soldier, Bert. This outfit seemed friendly to her and not adversarial, which was how she felt. Her white collared blouse had two buttons undone in the front, which she felt signified casual, not formal attire. She wore her loafers with her clean white socks, which made her look even more youthful than her nineteen years. The sun was shining as she walked briskly to the trolley stop, which would eventually get her on the crowded bus that would take her to the front of the old church where Bert would be.

Meanwhile, Bert was already standing in front of the church, anxious for his rendezvous with this foreign beauty, who he worried would not muster approval from his elderly parents because of her nationality. At least she looked somewhat blond and definitely had blue eyes. Most importantly, she was not a Jew or a Gypsy. He was confident of his ability to spot subversives within the general population. He assumed this was one of the reasons why he was placed on guard duty by the high command at the entrance to the ghetto. His eagle eyes were his asset.

He scoured his immediate surroundings, anxious to see the sweet, young girl he so quickly had taken to his heart. He yearned to hold her. He wanted to delicately surround his arms around her, not brutishly like a soldier, but gently, like a lover. He needed the world to disappear for just a moment in time, and she suddenly held the key to that.

He was tired of this soldiering business and wanted to be simply a young man again, without a gun. He was tired of using his acute eagle eyes to penetrate strangers' souls to see whether they were the evil devils whom his superiors had trained him to spot.

Bert saw Katarina as she turned around the distant corner and began walking doggedly toward him, adeptly avoiding the occasional person in her path. His demeanor softened when he caught sight of her bouncing toward him with her hair flouncing up with each wave of movement. She was even more radiant than he had remembered, and she looked so innocent and untouched by the war that had engulfed him. He now felt an urge to protect her and keep her from any danger that could be lurking in unseen places. Observing Katarina, with the sun shining on her like a spotlight, made Bert fall deeply in love for the first and, unfortunately, the last time.

"Here I am!" said Bert as he began running in ecstasy to Katarina, overwhelmed with the sight of her.

The only real crowds on Celetna Street at noon were the parishioners who were exiting the church. Katarina peered into the group to try and discern from which mouth the anxious words of arrival had been spoken. She quickly rested her gaze upon a young man that looked so different than the soldier she had previously met two days ago that she was not sure it was the same individual.

"Bert?" asked Katarina tentatively.

"It is I, and I am so very pleased to see you!"

"Such a nice greeting," proclaimed Katarina with a laughter-filled smile.

"Walk with me," he said. "I passed a charming-looking restaurant that I thought we could try."

"The only one in this area is Kopak's, and that is quite pricey for us locals."

"I have korunas in my pocket, and I would love to spend them on you. This is my treat today because I am so happy to be with you," he said unabashedly.

And spend time and money they did. After a light lunch with fare that was more accessible before the war than during the war, they continued their time together by strolling around what had always been known as a charming city.

"May I hold your arm?" Bert asked while offering his length from shoulder to digit for her inspection.

"That sounds lovely," she cooed as she took him up on his offer while winding through the city streets.

"Might I accompany you home?" continued Bert, relishing the touch of her resting hand through the crook of his elbow.

"I have had such a truly lovely afternoon, Bert, but I would prefer if I went to my house without an escort this time. I would like to prepare my family for meeting you and not surprise them, for they have no idea that I actually had lunch with you today. You have been a gentleman, and I know my parents will like you, but please, I must prepare them for you."

Bert's frown shocked Katarina a bit, but she did not sway in her conviction to go home alone. "Let's meet on your next day off," she proclaimed to appease him for the unintended slur that had stung him.

The new date erased the hint of displeasure and put a smile in its place. "What about the day after tomorrow when I get off sentry duty, before I am required to be in the mess hall? That usually gives me around two hours, which I would love to spend with you. We could continue our walk through the city of Prague, and maybe you could mention me to your parents before then, so I could actually meet them."

"Bert, I would prefer that my parents not be involved with us at this time. Please understand that I just do not want to answer the countless questions that they would grill me with about a gentleman caller. I think it would be better to just wait a bit, if you would."

"As you wish," he said while kissing her hand gallantly.

A blush came over Katarina as she said, "Time to go now, Bert. What time and place for Saturday?"

"Same place," he said, "but four o'clock instead of noon. I will be thinking of you every moment until then."

Katarina gave a big grin about this forward proclamation, then turned to leave.

"See you soon, Katarina."

"Ciao," said Katarina, who could not figure out why she offered the Italian good-bye instead of a simple "sbohem" in Czech.

All of the way home, her thoughts kept going round and round in her head. She could not help herself; she really

liked Bert. He was strong, which she knew was partially because he was so well fed. The German soldiers had it somewhat easy in Prague compared to what she heard about in
other cities that they had invaded. These soldiers were in a
large cosmopolitan city, and they were the kingpins, not the
pawns. This German liked her, as well as being very solici-
tous to her and kind-natured.

During their lunch he never took his eyes off her. He
was concerned that her soup was too hot when put in front
of her because of the emitting steam, which dampened
her brow. He looked playfully at her when she spoke of
her brother and his crazy antics that drove her up a wall.
He kept asking questions about her mother and learned
that she was always kind to Katarina and took her side
during sibling rivalries. He looked more serious when he
asked questions about her father—what he did, and if he
had a good reputation within the community. He agreed
with her father about Katarina being too carefree and
was not at all alarmed that he was as strict as Katarina
claimed.

Bert also seemed to question why she was out working
and not staying at home and helping with the household
duties. That part she was not crazy about, but after all, this
was just their first date. She then proceeded to be shocked
because she thought of this encounter as a date. She initially felt that it was good insurance to be friendly with a
German guard, but now she looked at him not only as a
Nazi guard of the ghetto who could help her if she needed
it, but as a suitor.

He had attained the status of a gentleman caller who
was not quite a caller, because she continually refused to

have him come to her door to call on her. That notion of her potential romance she wanted to avoid.

She knew her parents would be offended and shocked if they were aware that there was a Bert in her life, although he did not seem bothered by them.

Dating a Nazi was an absurd proposition that was going to stay in her secretive world for the time being. Meeting Captain August pointed out the other side of a Nazi soldier, which made her frightened. She did not associate Bert at all with those mean characteristics. She refused to dwell on any scary aspects. She sensed she was toying with danger but refused to address it.

She pushed away her illogical logic and concentrated on her immediate issues. Bert was extremely likable and he made her feel desired, so maybe she was not as immature as she was thinking. His being a Nazi soldier should be irrelevant to her dating and only important when thinking of how to use him to make a difference for the Jewish people, who were in an extremely uncomfortable spot with their own bleak future. She felt more comfortable placing the two German men on opposite sides of the spectrum.

The soldier who stormed into her new office was the true Nazi. He was terribly scary, large-boned, and rude mannered; he did not have any redeeming qualities that came to mind. She was petrified to be around him, yet knew it was inevitable that she would see him again quite soon. She would ask Mlle. Zelinsky if she could keep him away from her, though she suspected that it was not possible. She was happy that she only had to work three days a week for this small contract, not the intended five days.

"A Mlle. Zelinsky called," was the message that was sitting on the counter waiting for her when she arrived home. Her home felt eerily dark when she unlocked the door because of the early sunset in mid-November. The note, written in crisp block letters, was left on the very clean counter in the kitchen with one of her favorite biscuits and an empty glass that Mama knew would be filled with milk when she consumed the biscuit. "We are at Cousin Mary's. Left without you, assuming you were working today. Please explain later. Love, Mama."

Katarina quickly dialed her office number before pouring her milk in the waiting glass. The line barely rang before she heard Eva Zelinsky's breathy voice almost whispering on the other end.

"Katarina, you must come to the office after getting data every day after you leave the Holesovice District. You are to work each day, with no days off until your report is complete. Your three-day-per-week schedule has been changed. You must arrive at the office at 4:30 p.m., not a minute earlier and not a minute later. Am I clear?"

Katarina knew not to respond with anything other than a, "Yes, Mademoiselle." And then she tried diligently to put the receiver properly on its receptacle even though her hand was finding the task difficult. She did not understand why there was such a sudden change, and she worried it was because of her erasing some of her notes and switching their intent.

The person on the other end of the line was also having difficulties putting the receiver down. Captain August's hand encompassed Eva's and was squeezing it so hard that the pain was numbing. Once the receiver was in its receptacle, he whipped her around and lifted up her dress while ripping off another pair of her diminishing underwear.

"This cheap cloth is worthless, so don't look so surprised that it will no longer be of use. I will supply panties that will be more appropriate. You should not even bother wearing this silly cloth around my reconnaissance base."

His breathing was hot, and she felt a poisonous cloud descending upon her. It was not the loss of underwear that she was lamenting, but the loss of her life as she previously lived it. She was drifting down a stream with a gushing waterfall swirling toward an abyss, and that made her worry that she too would swirl into oblivion and drown in her own future. She acted like a helpless invalid who was no longer able to make decisions on her own and vowed as he clutched her to him that this was going to change somehow.

"Why did your supervisor call the house if you were with her, my dear?" asked Margharite Orbhan with an incriminating look.

Katarina knew that the "my dear" was synonymous with "you naughty girl," and it instantly took the flush out of her cheeks.

"Mama, I had to go into the Holesovice District to gather the information for my report. You were correct thinking I was not in the office. You and Papa will want to celebrate because my job will be winding down sooner than I expected, although it might be ramping up a little bit before it terminates. I must now report to the office every day at four thirty after visiting the district until I've finished, which should be sooner than later with all of those accrued hours. The commanding officer involved needs the report earlier than previously stated."

Margharite Orbhan pushed her arm down slowly with an extended hand, as if she were stopping an onslaught of gorillas.

"What kind of officer is involved with you? I thought you only had to report to a female superior. Is this an SS Nazi officer?" she said with terror in her eyes, making the wrinkles around them look like a Chinese fan Katarina once owned.

"Mama, you know there are Nazi officers all over Prague, and contact with them cannot be avoided, even though I agree with you and would rather not be around them at all. I believe they are evil," she said, which brought the color back to her pale cheeks.

"Katarina, men in uniform are capable of scary things… I insist you quit tomorrow morning. You are too young to be around SS soldiers. Your father was right, and I am ashamed I intervened. Before we take this matter to him, I need to know you are safe from harm's way, under our roof and behind our locked door."

This time the fear was in Katarina's face because she knew that quitting was impossible right now.

"This officer is not receptive to anything other than getting this report done immediately, and I do not feel it would be wise to cross him, Mama. I will work every day diligently until it is done, including the weekends, and then I promise you, I will never go back to that office again. Whether it was right or wrong of me to begin this job, I have a commitment. Nazi officers are more than capable of horrific things if people go against them. We have all seen the men, women, and children gathered into trucks for who knows what reason. I am OK, Mama. I just need to finish this job—quickly…I promise I will quit when it is over. Most of my dealings will be with Mlle. Zelinsky, and hopefully I will not have much to do with Nazis."

Her impassioned speech struck a chord with her mother, who backed down quite quickly, which surprised Katarina even more.

Margharite replied, "Listen to me carefully, my precious daughter, worth more than any paycheck you might bring home. You are now in a place you should not be. I must give your father a general outline of what we discussed today, but will eliminate the officer part. You are to finish this report in three days. I know this is a lot of work for you, from what you have previously explained, but finishing the document will enable you never to return to that sinkhole again. You must divert your gaze to the ground whenever you see a Nazi coming. Katarina, this small mannerism is important. Never look them in the eyes, always show submission, and get away from them as quickly as possible. There are good men everywhere, but right now I am going to accept your definition of evil and say you must have as little contact as possible with the men you encounter. Three days is what you have. I will confess the complete story to your papa after that."

She floated to where Katarina stood looking so downcast after hearing her mother's ultimatum. She gently raised her delicate hands to her daughter's face and stroked each side. "Do you understand?" she said with a heavy heart and a tear in her eye.

"You present a daunting task, but I will do it," responded Katarina, whose submission was seen in her body language.

"You must do what I say...not just try. Wake up early tomorrow refreshed. It will be the second to last day of your job," asserted her mother, appearing more like her father than the often-soft parent.

The next morning, when Katarina entered the blockaded district, she noted a different guard on duty and gave him her papers without bothering to look up, as her mother had suggested. Her lowered glance wandered around the dusty ground, filled with the uneven cobblestones, intermingling the gray and blue hues. She noted the guard's pant leg was too short for his stocky frame, as bare ankle skin appeared above filthy-looking socks while he perused her entrance papers from above.

"Bert says 'hi,'" came out of a mouth that was missing a front tooth that would have normally blocked the spit that unfortunately was now being sprayed from this void. His feeble attempt to get out the word "says" minus soaking the listener was not succeeding.

"Ya...he told me a beauty might be walking into the Jewish cesspool and to be particularly nice to you. So, willkommen, dear girl, and"—he sneered—"you'd better treat our Bertie nicely, or the whole SS troop will come after you!" This he declared with a laugh that scared more than humored Katarina.

"Of course," she replied meekly, while only slightly looking up as she grabbed her papers from his hand, which was streaked with so much dirt that it appeared striated deep into its core.

She hightailed it so quickly to Trini's that she was a tad early for her planned meeting with David. They had not actually set a firm time, but she assumed morning meant 9:00 a.m., not 8:00 a.m.

Katarina almost felt comfortable seeing the tarnished café. She walked into Trini's, the sole working café in the district, and went up to a small, square frame that looked like it should house a window to the back wall. She strained her vocal chords as she called into the kitchen, where a lone man was bustling around with cooking utensils battered from many turns in a pot. "By any chance do you know where I could find a Dr. Bonn?" she called into the food space, remembering her other contact. A gaunt man, who was approximately fifty years old in her estimation, kept working with his clanging pans and only gave her a sideways glance as he whispered that he could be found around the corner, on the second floor of the brown faded building that had no windows on the first floor.

She heard just enough to know where to go and thanked him as she turned around and walked out of the odd café. To her amazement, the faded building was found quite easily. She came across a large wooden door with a minute triangular window on top and a gnarled knob to turn. The door looked like it might have been painted green at one time, but only a slight residue of color remained. She opened it to find a multilevel stairway extending to a darkened area above.

She began climbing the creaking stairs, which she confidently assumed would announce her arrival, but it failed to bring any curiosity seekers. The landing on the second floor was so dimly lit that she could barely decipher the dingy card pinned on the door that listed Dr. Bonn as one of the occupants.

She rapped on the closed door and began bouncing her foot nervously. She faintly heard voices mingling in unison behind the closed barrier. It was essential to find this doctor and ask him a few questions, because it would fulfill her obligation to Mlle. Zelinski, who had been so adamant that contact be made with only him.

Katarina's impatience got the better of her, and she slowly turned the knob and cast her eyes on a circus of people. Mothers were clutching crying toddlers, whose muffled cries sounded like animals lost in a forest. There were elderly men and pockmarked teenagers, as well as a series of sniffers that were lined up against a wall that badly needed another coat of plaster.

"Excuse me," she said as she cleared her throat, trying to get attention.

The sniffling paused, the crying diminished, and all faces turned toward the sound that had come from her delicately shaped mouth, well-coifed hair, and immaculate clothes that were devoid of a yellow frayed star.

"Could I see Dr. Bonn, please?" was what she queried to the pale, emaciated inhabitants of what appeared to be some sort of medical waiting room. Almost magically, a space formed that led directly to another door at the opposite side of the room. She carefully placed one well-heeled foot in front of another and walked to the entrance as if a book were on top of her head and she was partaking in a Saturday morning deportment class. She gently tapped the door, and a very pretty pregnant woman answered it with shock drawn on her face.

"Katarina Orbhan here. I am from the office of Prague Records and was told to contact Dr. Bonn by Mlle. Eva Zelinsky." This she proclaimed in the only official-sounding words she could muster.

A kindly looking gentleman in a suit that had been sewn together many times to keep it from falling apart peered around another's outstretched arm that he was cradling and observing. There was oozing yellow pus that was dripping into a rusty pan positioned below the outstretched appendage.

"Enter, Mademoiselle. You are feasting your eyes on Dr. Bonn," said the voice of authority with a hint of humor as he gently put the damaged arm down that he had been holding.

"The most important thing is cleanliness, Jacob. Wash the arm with this black soap three times a day and come back if it does not clear up within two weeks."

He finished with his patient, then turned to the woman heavy with child, motioning her to usher the young man out of the room. Everyone seemed to need assistance from the sole physician before her, and all craned their necks to try to peek into the slight space that was made when the door creaked open.

Katarina noticed that the woman he constantly eyed was quite puffy from pregnancy but had beautiful high cheekbones and long dark hair that was braided and pinned up in a handsome manner. She bent down upon returning from the waiting area to pick up some papers that must have momentarily eluded her and emitted a minute squeak that was barely audible. As she stood up, Katarina noticed her eyes had started to squint and her shoulders hunched in an awkward curl. There was a puddle forming around her feet that looked as if she were attempting a surprise trick that had promised a puddle to magically appear. Her dark eyes moved down to the puddle and then strained over to her observing husband.

Dr. Bonn had never really taken his eyes off this woman, who obviously was strongly connected to him; he quickly moved to her side and urged her to sit down in the seat he previously occupied.

"Mlle. Orbhan, you must excuse us at this time," the doctor said calmly. "My wife and I are going to have a baby," he continued as he gazed into his wife's eyes with a reassuring nod. "I am more than happy to speak to you tomorrow, if that could be arranged, because I must deliver a precious baby right now! To life! L'chaim!"

At this announcement, a young boy who had snuck in the room without being noticed stamped his feet as if they were hands clapping and ran into the connecting waiting room, yelling that a new baby was coming into the ghetto, ready or not.

A flustered Katarina blushed as she clamped her hand on her mouth and murmured, "I will come back at a more convenient time." She made an attempt to emit the words "Good luck," but they sounded like a bunch of consonants with no meaning because the vowels that belonged to them were not in the configuration.

She then hurried through the crowd, almost tripped down the steps, and gushed into the street, which was filled with more people in tatters and yellow stars sewn on their clothing than earlier. She ran to Trini's and felt calmer when she spotted David waiting for her right in front of the large window where they had initially found each other.

"Slow down, Princess, and tell me why you look like you just ran a marathon," said David as he put his strong arms on either side of her shoulders in a reassuring way.

Katarina pushed him away and asked him to follow her through the now familiar door.

━◁ ▷━

Around the corner and up two flights of steps, a crowded room was emptying as Dr. Bonn ushered his wife to the other side of the apartment, where a bed awaited her.

As primarily a dermatologist, Rudolph Bonn had only been near a delivery room while he was attending medical school. Moving his wife into their bed and not a hospital gurney was not what he had in mind when he thought of the birth of his much-anticipated first child.

His pursed lips were upturned on either side as he helped his wife, Naomi, get neatly situated under the thin covers that were stretched from many years of usage. She slipped on her yellowed, threadbare nightgown and began a short wait for the onslaught of pain that would render her helpless. Within an hour she started to writhe in discomfort, which he knew was typical of the long birthing process for a first delivery. It was when he decided to reexamine her that an inkling of fear invaded his calm, and he knew this was not going to be the typical birth that he had witnessed in his short training segment in women's health.

Their apartment was shared with Naomi's parents and her mother's sister's family of two more generations. Space was at a premium, but everyone was more than happy to give them the only real bedroom in the apartment to act as a birthing room. Rudolph instantly asked for Naomi's mother and aunt to assist him. They were more than happy to assist and noted from the look on the dermatologist's face that this delivery of their new grandchild might not be as smooth as he had anticipated. He asked her aunt to stay with her as he whispered to his mother-in-law that the baby was breech. Lena, his mother-in-law, gasped uncontrollably, which set Naomi crying into her aunt's hand.

"We will do this together, Naomi. Dry your tears and let's get to work on this baby," said her husband, with such unfamiliar panic in his voice that even though Naomi normally felt so safe with her physician husband, she let out a scream that could be heard echoing below.

⟞⟝ ⟞⟝

Meanwhile, Katarina confronted David at Trini's. "You did not bother to tell me that Dr. Bonn is only around the corner and obviously I did not need your assistance to find him!" Katarina scolded David as she glared at him across the table.

"Now, Princess...I am of more assistance than simply finding a doctor in this confusing ghetto," responded David, while giving her his camera-ready smile that seemed to melt most of the ladies who came in contact with this Romeo.

Katarina was uncomfortably aware that she had only three days to complete her task, and one of them was disappearing faster than she wanted. She actually needed David to help her sort through all of these mean streets and masses of people who were stuffed in them. She also knew that Dr. Bonn was having quite the time in his own life and was not going to be much help to her, so she decided to change her tone and stop berating her informant.

"I am on a tight schedule now and must be in my superior's office by four thirty each afternoon until the report is done, which my mother demands is three days, with this as day one. I need to go up and down as many streets as I can and calculate some sort of average of inhabitants per street." Her eyes welled up with tears as she confessed, "And there is a Nazi commandant who is watching the office as well as me, who makes me so very nervous I cannot even think straight."

Katarina was surprised at how much information she let out in so little time, while choking back the tears that were ready to come flowing out again. This whole expedition had proved to be a lot more difficult than she had ever expected. She had no understanding why she could talk with David but was unable to be half as forthcoming with her father.

This news about the speed of her impending report seemed to affect David more than she was expecting. He looked panicked and blurted out without much time to ponder the consequences, "Katarina! You must help me before your work is done here. I need to get out of here. It is so much worse than you can imagine because you are looking only on the grimy surface of this imprisoned bit of land and not really getting a feel for what it is like to be here day in and day out. I am so sorry to involve you, but you must hear my plea. Guards walk around the district every day and simply grab people who are never heard from again. Parents cry every night for their children, and children cry every night for their parents. Many are herded into trucks, and others who will not go willingly are shot on the spot. They are told to kneel on the ground, and then a bullet is fired into their heads as they fall over like a wooden puppet that has lost its strings. They end up in the same waiting truck with those who are still alive but managed to crawl in the truck of their own volition. It is amazing that you have not seen any of these incidents since you have come here. This probably just means that there is another awful thing that will befall us soon, because they have not done their usual random pickups of innocent people.

"I will do absolutely anything to get out of this sinkhole. I know I can be listed as your assistant on that official paper that you are always waving around here. Let me copy that entrance paper that gives you carte blanche access to come and go, and add only one name. On the remaining days, I will give you all of the accurate numbers that only you will have and that you desperately need so quickly. On the third day, I beg of you, I beseech you, take me with you, and I will owe you my life. I know we can accomplish this safely. You come in and out of here with absolutely no problems, and you know it. You have got to help me, please, I am begging.

"There is an artist who resides here who will make a copy of your entrance papers and simply add my name after yours. The authorities will never know the difference, I promise you. Right now, let us drop off the paper, and I will show you how this can be done with no harm to anyone. I would never jeopardize your safety, Katarina. Remember, I will give you all the pertinent facts that you could need, and it will be more accurate than anyone else could possibly get from here. I beseech you. Do not ponder too long on what I have said…just help me…please. It is a mitzvah that you will be blessed with for the rest of your life if you can save at least one person from this district that reeks of death and impending doom."

Katarina had trouble wrapping her head around the patter of pleas that she had just witnessed being shot off in quick succession. She paused to think about what he had requested. David was enlisting her help to get out of a despicable life that he was being forced to live.

Her initial reaction during his long request was to change her original resolve and absolutely never help anyone ever, due to the frightening consequences that could result from it. But now, her second reaction was the complete opposite. She found herself reverting back to her initial resolve as to why she took this job in the first place. She really did want to make a difference in the world. She needed to be part of the solution, not part of the problems that were plaguing her beautiful city.

She was working for Germans who were occupying Prague. She was living with the shadow of a Nazi officer who loomed menacingly in the distance. So far she had done nothing but compromise her ideals, so she instantly made another rash decision that feebly justified her job, which had only cost her problems so far. This young man standing before her solidified her original thoughts concerning why she ventured into a poverty-stricken area filled with desperate people. She should not have been surprised that someone would ask for her assistance. She began to see herself as his only hope. In a split second, Katarina chose to help the boy that stood before her.

Katarina slowly removed her stamped visa from her bag and passed it covertly to David's lap as they sat huddled in Trini's. He grabbed the paper with one hand and with the other hand touched her face as if she were the most delicate china doll in the world, then fluttered his lips near hers in what may be construed as a kiss in some cultures. The deal was sealed.

The screams were muffled coming out of that second-floor apartment around the corner and up the stairs. Rudolph Bonn had his entire arm practically immersed in Naomi's uterus while attempting to right the baby. Each time the baby made a slight turn, it inched its way back as soon as his retreating hand reached the stagnant air of the worried room. The cord was tangled around the baby, and somehow a cesarean operation was going to have to be performed in these not so antiseptic conditions that were minus a real hospital, a real gynecologist, or any semblance of a real nurse. The birth of the Bonns' firstborn was moving from bad to worse as those around Naomi watched her painful expression and her deathly pallor multiply as the moments ticked by in the tense atmosphere.

Katarina shadowed David's brisk pace through a series of small crowded streets, which led them into another dingy apartment building that looked similar to all of its adjacent structures. They walked up five flights of steps to the top floor, where a large door was located in front of them. Instead of knocking on the door, David reached up and rapped six times in succession on a piece of ceiling that probably opened up to the above crawl space. He then called out the words "Dick Tracy," which really confused Katarina. The comic strip character had fame with her brother, and she had teased him many times about the silliness of the detective's ways. The rectangle opened like it would have if it had been in her brother's comic book. They proceeded to climb a rope ladder that danced down when thrown from the void above. She felt relief after climbing the rope and silently thanked her gym instructor for insisting that all girls master rope climbing.

Upon entering, she saw four men who sat precariously on four scratched and rickety chairs. These chairs adjoined some old schoolroom desks that were scattered around the attic space in disarray. Nobody looked like the suave Dick Tracy. The men in front of her all sported long beards of light brown, dark brown, reddish brown, and gray curls. All wore the tallit that signified their conformity to the most religious in the community. A language was spoken that she did not comprehend and assumed to be Hebrew or Yiddish, not that of the famous detective.

David did a lot of pointing, some fast mumbling, and then some heartfelt hugs to one particular gentleman. He then introduced her to the various men but did not offer any of their names in return. He placed Katarina's document on the front desk. With no need for prolonged conversation, he quickly ushered her down the ladder, through the hall-way, down the stairs, and into the bustling street.

"We will pick up your original document at two o'clock today, so you will not have any concerns about leaving safely today. Tomorrow, the two of us will discuss the specifics of our plan, which will give us a full day to remove the kinks before its execution," said David. "I will see you first thing in the morning at Trini's?"

"Execution," whispered Katarina. "Why would you chose that word?" she said incredulously.

"That poor word choice is the only mistake that I will make, dearest Katarina," he vowed as he squeezed her hands in solidarity.

They continued their day, with David speed talking as well as speed walking, while Katarina quickly scribbled bits and pieces of the information he delivered whenever they slowed down enough for her to write.

"There were around ninety-two thousand Jews on Prague's doorstep before the war. There are many less here now. As you can easily see, there are crowded conditions, terrible sewage, unbelievable health problems, and many families sharing crowded quarters meant for one quarter of who lives here. Everyone you see has had their prior home confiscated if they had previously lived outside the district. Very few Jewish businesses outside the ghetto have been al-lowed to continue, and only a few Jews assisting the new owners with the transition have been allowed to travel to their own companies. There is a scattering of people who have permission to leave this section as long as they return on the same day or have definitely secured permission to do otherwise."

He spoke on and on...until 2:00 p.m. arrived, and they went back to the attic location to pick up her original document and confirm the altered document could be picked up early the following day.

Dr. Bonn's insulated world had changed in the hours since his wife gushed the opaque puddle from underneath her dark, dank clothes. He no longer had any thoughts of patients or the political debacle that encompassed his world before his wife was forced into this horrible abyss, unable to climb out of it. He was aware that he had failed his trusting companion, and his conscience felt crushed with this weight of failure. Now, his only concerns were for the minute-old infant and the safety of his wife, whose life was jetting alarmingly out of control. The amount of blood soaking the sheets was not anything close to normal. No one should ever lose that amount of blood and not receive a transfusion of new blood. Extra sheets and towels deposited from neighbors, as well as freshly boiled water, were positioned near the simple wooden bed frame. The space was shaded from the light of day by sheets that hung from the sole window, with barely a breath of fresh air that could squeeze into the room heavy with the uncomfortable smell of oxidized blood. A faint muffled cry was heard from the recesses of the room.

Naomi glanced weakly at her husband, saw her parents huddled in the corner, and then closed her heavy eyes.

She lightly patted the lumpy mattress that supported her anguished body and moved her practically lifeless hand to search for her aunt's hand, which she knew was nearby. She whispered, "It is for the best. I could never stand the pain that this world is now producing. Do not blame Rudy. I just cannot proceed to the future."

Rudolph was unabashedly crying as he pleaded, "Hold on; we are a family now. We have a beautiful little girl. I cannot live without you," but she had already slipped into the unconscious prelude to death, and no one knew whether she even heard his protestations or not.

Katarina trudged from the ghetto to the impending doom of her office, knowing that no matter what had happened in her day, she needed to be standing in that stifling space by 4:30 p.m. She actually made it with time to spare since she was so acutely aware of the hour and so deathly afraid of arriving after her requisite time. She tried to rap more assertively than timidly on the protruding door of her destination. She then walked into the office, making a racket intended to wake even the dead.

She heard the familiar, "Katarina?"

"Place your notes facedown on my desk," ordered Mlle. Zelinsky, peeking out from the door frame. "This time I must see them before you change anything."

When Eva Zelinsky perused the young girl's scribbles, she froze when she came across what looked like an offhand remark on the top right of the first page. It mentioned the name of her beloved, Dr. Bonn, and had a question mark with the word "baby" before it.

"Did you see Dr. Bonn?" gushed Eva, just like a schoolgirl asking about her first crush.

Katarina quietly laid out to the agitated Mlle. Zelinksy that Dr. Bonn's office was quite filled when she arrived there to see him, but unexpectedly emptied when his wife surprisingly began labor right in front of her.

Eva gasped loudly and grabbed her lower abdomen in an involuntary fashion. All of this registered surprise for Katarina, but she attempted to mask her emotions and simply said, "I will meet with him tomorrow and be able to report back to you then. I am sure there will be a healthy baby at that time. But on a more important note, I want to inform you that my report will be completed the day after tomorrow. I realize it is with greater speed than I originally thought, but since the captain is pushing for a fast completion of this project, it might work to both of our satisfaction. I worry that my safety is not at the level I presumed it would be when hired, and I prefer to end at least our professional contact after this, although we can keep our social contact, of course," she added superciliously. "Thank you for this opportunity for my first real job. I will be forever grateful to you for giving me a chance."

Eva responded, "I hope for your sake that the report will completely finish your dealings with this office, but you are not finished with this assignment yet, young lady. The power I hold from this office is minimal during this occupation time," she added as a weak afterthought.

Katarina knew that she was referring to the captain and became concerned that Mlle. Zelinsky was confessing the truth.

"I want you to type up the information from today, and use the 'white paint' that is located in the front desk to clear your note about Dr. Bonn. You are to see him tomorrow and then report directly to me, not the captain, about this particular matter that I am having you do privately. I picked you for this position because I had faith that you would do the right thing when asked. You must have realized that you otherwise would never have been allotted this assignment since your complete lack of experience and your youthfulness were not great credentials. You must do what I ask with total discretion. I cannot ensure your safety otherwise."

Katarina now realized that her brother, Georgie, had assessed her ability to procure a job better than she had. As the light became clearer, it finally dawned on her that everyone she had become involved with recently was using her for his or her own purposes. An onslaught of head pain made her eyes squint.

She thought of her previous decision to help David escape from the ghetto. This deception would save his life. She could not waste time concerning herself about deceiving this ragtag Social Services group that had hired her under false pretenses. Helping David had to be paramount in her mind. This job enabled her to do good things inadvertently from the tasks at hand.

Katarina's head pain began to ease as she moved to the front desk and started to make a professional document out of a series of incomplete sentences. She carefully erased any mention of the curious Dr. Bonn, whom Mlle. Zelinsky constantly mentioned. She located the white paint in the top drawer, twisted the lid open, and carefully removed any smudges.

Eva returned to her recently cleaned desk and mulled over the news Katarina had told her of the kindly Dr. Bonn. She desperately wanted to get him removed from the gears of the Nazi machinery engulfing him. She started to concoct her own plan to use that official machinery for her own selfish purposes. The young girl in the front office and the mass underground that all citizens heard rumors of on a daily basis could be players in the scheme that she was conniving. She wished there was a way to tap into the unhappy populace of Prague to play a part in this plan, whatever the plan actually was.

The portly Captain August anxiously climbed the steps to his imagined harem, or as the tiny sign stated, "Office of Social Services." His growing anticipation was not for the uptight Eva Zelinsky this time, who had already begun to bore him with her initial complacency, but for the younger, more supple worker, who he knew would be waiting there for his own personal uses at the designated time of 4:00 p.m.

"Mademoiselles," the captain barked as he entered the dimly lit office where Katarina was working with her head down, "I would like a bucket of beer to enjoy while I begin reading what this silly intern prepared for me." He brushed by Katarina and barged into Eva Zelinsky's office.

"Here are some korunas," he said, throwing them in Eva's direction.

Even though Eva did not want his sexual advances, she knew that she would have to endure them until he lost interest. She hoped their awful encounters would cease shortly because of her obviously lackluster performance.

A flash of maternal instinct for her young charge overcame her as she realized that Katarina was probably next on his list and would be in first place soon. She feared that this young ninny was safer in the teeming ghetto than she was alone with this gross monster.

"Would it be better for Katarina to run this beer errand, Herr Captain?" said Eva as the captain walked up to her, stomping painfully on her toes, which were only lightly covered with worn leather.

After the captain's pointed silence, Eva said, "I see that is not an option"; she realized that it did not make any sense to question anything that the monster demanded.

As Eva Zelinsky bowed her head and scurried out of the office, she became pretty certain that Katarina and she would soon be sharing the same fate at this Nazi's dirty hands. She trod lightly to the closest tavern while planning ways to ensure his demise before he ever stepped foot on a battlefield. The man had to be eliminated, and not just for her and Katarina, but also for all women in Prague, Germany, or any country where he might be posted. She had extra time to consider her budding idea because the tavern was located a hefty four blocks away and another four blocks back.

Meanwhile, the staring captain, hot with sexual tension, waltzed up to the petrified Katarina, who was quaking at the front desk and listening to everything that had been said. Captain August simply stated in his deep voice that only he considered sexy, "Strip, or I will shoot you," with such a slow deliberation that Katarina knew that this was a fact he was delivering, not an idle threat.

Katarina's hands shook so hard that her body began to almost convulse, which had the opposite effect on her experienced rapist. He started to smile as he unzipped his pants in glorious anticipation of a new virgin to deflower.

Things had never been this easy in his small hometown of Suhl, Germany. He was overjoyed when he was asked to join the SS unit of the military, where his uniform alone, without even the assistance of a weapon, could command obedience. He was proud though of the magnitude of the gun located in his loosened belt that made his native town famous. Suhl was a gun-manufacturing town. There were times in battle where weapons were useful, but he knew that in this confrontation that he was joyously having now, his strength lay in other deep, dank areas. He put his locked famous weapon on the floor with the safety secured to ensure that it would not ejaculate bullets without his command. He then went over to this young girl and moved his hands up and down over her now naked, strong body. He was overwhelmed that in this imagined Garden of Eden she did not even voice objections to his flagrant request. He knocked her off-balance with his foot, caught her with his arms, and snaked her to the floor. He swelled with power over this helpless young female, whose tears ran down her face, and entered her, with her stifled cry coming through her projecting sobs.

Eva's muscles ached from her long trek that took her from the scene of the latest crime to a tavern for unwanted beer, which was not what the disgusting captain even desired. She needed her plan to be quickly put in place. She could not continue another day without feasting her eyes on her dear doctor, who in a split second had also become her gallant savior. This saintly man had given her solace in the past from physical pains as well as mental somersaults, and she desperately needed his help now. She felt only her doctor was capable of confronting this horrible captain about the indignities that he was showering upon her and now the helpless Katarina.

On her quest for beer, she also quested for ways to the captain's imminent demise that she was planning. She had disjointed thoughts that kept darting around her head. Doctors gave shots to cure sick people, so was there a shot that could cure her sick tormenter as well? She remembered asking Dr. Bonn why he always snapped his thumb against his second finger that clicked on the glass of a soon to be given medicinal shot. He explained in his comforting tones, as patiently as he always did, that air in the tube could be dangerous in large quantities if it were shot into a vein. He carefully ensured that even a little bubble could not be an issue in any shot he gave because he preventively tapped the glass as he pushed the injector up just a tad. A little liquid would dribble out as well as any air that was contained therein, and he explained it would not be a concern for her.

She envisioned Dr. Bonn giving the monster an inoculation full of air while she held an overstuffed pillow over his ugly face to make his well-deserved death occur faster. Loss of life was an unavoidable consequence of a monster's actions, and she knew that death was so commonplace in war that one more body racked up in the evil column would not keep her out of heaven, away from her forgiving God. She had no idea whether Jews believed in heaven or not, but she assumed they did not, so Rudolph Bonn should have no problem helping her. Eva also knew that the answer to German bureaucracy was miles and miles of useless paperwork. The Germans documented every little incident with statistics, annotations, and revised copy after copy, which was why her office was still in existence and why she'd hired this girl originally to do her dirty work of paperwork.

When Eva arrived on the scene, she quickly became cognizant that the monster already had eaten his prey. The captain had slithered away, but Katarina still wept, with her head collapsed down on the messy desk now damp with moisture. Eva slowly crept toward her and attempted to comfort her by resting her own hand lightly on the damaged child. Katarina appeared fully clothed, but was bare with emotion from the recent crime.

Knowing that the captain would just continue his demented escapades whenever he chose brought Eva to tears also. She realized that 4:00 p.m. would be Katarina's time of assault for at least the duration of her assignment, but she feared hers would not be so predictable. Eva became engulfed in her own sorrows as she practically fell on top of the poor girl.

She yearned for the larger-than-life Dr. Bonn to come to her much needed rescue, but she knew that in this topsy-turvy world, she would be obliged to save him first, which was the thought that stopped her tears.

She remembered the reason she had hired Katarina initially, and she needed to get back to that task and not be swayed by the distraught girl lying disheveled in front of her, even though she intimately knew how Katarina felt.

"Wash up in the sink, wipe your tears as I will wipe mine, and start writing the report that will get you out of here sooner. Just putting one step in front of the other will make you feel like you can go on in this world. I am sure you will agree with me on what the next step must be," she added to the overwhelmed girl, who really was not thinking of any possible steps.

"You will bring Dr. Bonn to this office from the ghetto," she said to the shell-shocked heap in front of her. "I know that he is the answer to both of our troubles. We must stand together in this, or we will both fall apart. We need the strongest, most helpful man in the world to stop the horrid Captain August, or he will be violating more unsuspecting females on a whim. You met Dr. Bonn, and it must have been obvious to you that he has immense skills. He will know how to help us."

Katarina froze in fear as it dawned on her that Mlle. Zelinsky was now telling her to somehow bring Dr. Bonn out of the district to actually kill Captain August. Assuredly, the thought of him dead did entice her, but she did not want to terminate her own life in the process of trying to save it. David was counting on her to take him out of the district with forged papers, and now she was simply to add Dr. Bonn to the mix that Mlle. Zelinsky had no clue was even in the works?

She howled in frustration as Mlle. Zelinsky tried to quiet her by saying, "We will figure this out, Katarina. By tomorrow, we will be rid of this useless man. I must concentrate now and figure out the details of such a plan."

Katarina instantly let silence be her mode of communication and just waited for Mlle. Zelinsky to proceed with the details of her insane plot. Her maturity had multiplied by large increments today, but she got no pleasure from her new status as a desecrated woman or from her newfound patience. She pictured her family waiting for her at home with the loyal Petra. Fighting with her brother and tolerating her overprotective parents now seemed like a luxury that was quite opposite what she was dealing with in the real world.

Her rape had miraculously taken a backseat to her worries about this crazy new scheme of Mlle. Zelinsky; she worried it would get her killed, even though a part of her had already died earlier in the office.

As Katarina plodded through the writing of her report, Mlle. Zelinsky devised a plan to bring Dr. Bonn to the office. She typed up a formal request on an official paper similar to the one that Katarina had to show the guard, to get Dr. Bonn out of the district and to the office at 3:00 p.m. tomorrow so they could wait together for Captain August to arrive at 4:00 p.m. Once August arrived, the doctor would pretend to be Katarina's father and would threaten August with exposure to his superiors if his behavior did not stop. If that did not scare him, and she knew it would not, then she and Katarina would distract him while Dr. Bonn injected him with a fatal blast of air.

Katarina looked at Mlle. Zelinsky with the odd expression of one who looks at a deranged person. She knew not whether this plan would succeed or not, but she did know that she did not want any part of it. David had already made plans to leave tomorrow, and if Bert were on duty, he had to be convinced to let her pass out of the ghetto with this stranger and into freedom without a hitch. Even if she had a burning desire to have some fictitious savior swoop down and save her, she was certain that it was not this Dr. Bonn, who seemed quite preoccupied at the moment.

"If you are not at the office by three o'clock, Katarina, with Dr. Bonn, I must inform you that I will tell Captain August where to find you," her superior shockingly added. "I demand your assistance, dear, and do not worry about the little details that must be planned. They will become clearer as we proceed with our mission. Good will triumph; it always does."

Eva added this last phrase with such animosity that Katarina could not decide whom she was actually more afraid of, the abusive captain or the deranged Mlle. Zelinsky.

The Orbhan housekeeper, Petra, was making dinner in the kitchen when Katarina sulked in through the front door. She had raised a daughter of her own and had been with the Orbhans for twenty years now, so she was quite familiar with the disjointed moods of burgeoning young women. Her radar picked up the signal immediately that something was amiss with Katarina.

Katarina's clothes were just that much askew, and her wrist was blotched with red welts when Petra overtly stared at them. Her hair was not neatly tucked in beneath her hat, and her breathing sounded almost like sobs.

The atmosphere of oppression and war was thick in the world outside of the Orbhans' cocooned existence. Petra was familiar with what atrocities lurked in the paths beyond their well-manicured walkway. She accurately guessed that someone, quite possibly a soldier, had used force on this poor innocent girl, now wandering back to her home dazed and confused.

Even childhood spankings were a rarity in this nonviolent household, which used words more than force. Petra knew any type of assault would weigh in strongly on her delicate Katarina. The placid Orbhans, who offered Petra space to live and paid her occasional expenses as well as a small salary, had no history of aggressiveness within their doors. She frowned, thinking that outside problems were slithering into inside problems.

She padded over to the young girl and gingerly led her to the bathroom without the need for idle chatter or explanations of what might have occurred during Katarina's toying with her nonsensical employment. Petra was silent and unable to verbalize what she accurately sensed.

Many years previously, a scrawny, dirty soldier had come like a rat to steal food from the kitchen and had raped her daughter, who was living with her at the time. She asked at the butcher's, at the baker's, and finally at the bread man's establishment who to contact to right this wrong, which in reality could never really be righted. She sought biblical justice, an eye for an eye, or close to it for her sanity. She procured a rough individual, who later became a member of the underground, to do the deed. The vermin who had violated her daughter was found lifeless in a ditch two weeks after her contact with this savior, and Petra was forever indebted to those honorable men in the underground who were willing to fight back when she could not muster the courage or the strength to do so herself. She pondered contacting them again while looking at the tearful girl in front of her unable to control her emotions.

Petra kept her connection through the years with the underground by donating anything she could muster that would not be noticed from the Orbhans' well-stocked home. The Orbhans never really missed the food, small knives, or cracked dishes that disappeared from their kitchen, and they never asked what happened to the old clothes that did not return from the hamper after the wash was long folded and put away.

Petra had no need to press the poor, disheveled Katarina as to what exactly had made her depleted and scared, but she felt obliged to tell Katarina that there was assistance out there if she wanted vengeance. She also knew that the ravaged girl would be too scared to mention any of this to her parents. She had every intention of keeping this dear girl's secret.

Katarina's naivety was immense, and Petra could only imagine what trouble she had gotten into while cavorting on her own, oblivious to the dangers around her. She was shocked when the Orbhans practically gave their blessings for her to accept a government position, of all things! This just pointed out that the parents were almost as naïve as the child.

She could not tell Mr. or Mrs. Orbhan how to raise their children because she did not feel that successful when raising her own sad daughter. She was the hired help, no matter how many times they assured her she was a member of their family. Many times she felt immersed in their caring atmosphere, but there were other times, especially as she cleaned up messes that could have been cleaned by the makers, that she realized she was not a part of their family unit.

She was always convinced that if a girl were traveling in Prague away from the imagined security of her locked home, it was only a matter of time before said girl, Katarina in this case, would arrive back at that door in this despondent condition.

"Now listen, mine munchkin," she soothingly said while helping Katarina bathe the dirt and bloodstains from her soiled body, "I have very secretive names that I cannot even say aloud, but I can contact them if you need someone to help you out of what appears to be a situation that you will hide from your parents. There are people living in Prague helping their compatriots survive with their miseries these days, and they might be able to assist you. You do not have to answer now, but please remember that this option exists. I am here for you, my sweet angel, if you need me. Thank goodness there are fighting people who will try to save us from even ourselves. This conversation is only for your munchkin ears, little Katarina. You are my sweet child, and it saddens me to see you like this. Now, let me help you sponge off some of this grime, and then you can decide how much of your story you want to impart."

Katarina then wept in Petra's maternal arms as the servant held her limp body, which now was convulsed with sobs. She was so thankful for this barely noticed woman who up until now had rarely made a memorable statement in anyone's direction.

Petra was always there to watch her cavort amid the eccentricities that her privileged existence had afforded her. She was amazed at the care and attention that Petra bestowed on her in her moment of need. Her guilt dripped right through the large tears that were dampening this servant's worn apron, but Katarina did have enough presence of mind to stay mum on the events that had upset her.

It was hard for Katarina to register how virulently her peaceful life had suddenly vanished. She now questioned why she had left her little insulated world of middle-class Prague when she foolishly acquired her first job. She was acutely aware when she was placed in the warm tub that turned dingy with dried blood and salty tears that she had stepped way out of her league, which had been comprised of uniformed schoolgirls and knickered, silly boys. She refused to tell Petra about the sudden cracks in her life caused by dry lightning that burst through the rainless sky of her existence.

Knowing that there was an underground out there that could be contacted was information she needed, which did imprint through the heaves of sorrow that she could not control. She remained numb with fear, however, as she wailed in her tub of tears.

"Shhh, dear girl. I will get you into bed before anyone comes home. You will feel better once you are resting in your clean bed, with the crisp sheets I put on just this morning. You are alive and in your own home, which is more than many poor souls can say at this time. Now let me get you dried, powdered, and into your sweetest nightgown, with the pink, embroidered flowers."

As soon as Katarina's washed and shiny hair hit the fluffy down pillow, she was in a deep slumber that would not be broken until daybreak.

≔ ≕

Katarina woke up when the first shadows cast by the sun peeked through her opaque shades. Petra must have presented a good excuse to her mother to allow such a long, undisturbed sleep to occur. She tried to push away the horrors of the previous day. She had to concentrate on what she knew was paramount for survival in this chess game, where uncertainty was the only given other than the king. She knew the king was the boss, Captain August, and he could move in any direction he wanted. Initially, she assumed it was her parents that carried the crown, but she now knew that was false. She was a pawn in a game where she had insufficient power to overcome a king.

She had to get to David to tell him of the new twist and see if he would agree to let Dr. Bonn temporarily take his spot and leave the ghetto.

She dressed in her somber brown skirt and old beige blouse. She had to fold over the skirt waistband because it was too loose around her middle, and the heavy cloth dropped to her protruding hipbones, which made the length fall awkwardly. The fit was made for happier times, when cookies, cakes, and tarts were consumed with no thoughts of limits or supply. The oversize skirt was too big for her and not at all in style, which appealed to her. She decided to wrap a large babushka around her shoulders that would keep off the morning chill that galloped into Prague this time of the year.

Katarina slowly peered out from her slightly open door and tiptoed downstairs, not disturbing even the little mouse that she saw scurrying into the kitchen. She then quietly opened the front door with just a tiny creak that could barely be discerned by her mother or Petra, who were both restlessly turning in their beds, which happened to drown out the oddly ominous sound coming from the foyer door.

Arriving at the ghetto, Katarina was taken aback when she realized that the guard on duty was her friend Bert. Unfairly, she had barely given him a thought because of the deluge of horrors that had tumbled down upon her recently.

Bert's face lit up when he heard delicate footfalls and looked up to find it actually was the girl that had occupied his every waking thought since he had last laid eyes on her. His brow began to seriously furl when he noticed that she looked quite ashen in the morning light; he knew that something was amiss.

"I am surprised to see you here so early, lovely lady. I have been counting the minutes until my shift is finally over and we can see each other in a completely unofficial way," he said cheerily, though he knew that he was not cracking her serious demeanor. He worried that her parents had convinced her to stop contact with him and she had intentions of making excuses for their intended date. He would do anything he could to make sure that avoidance of him was not in her actions today or any day in the future.

"I have to be at my office by four o'clock every day except Sunday until my report is complete because of Captain August, the military liaison assigned to our department. I will not be able to meet today because of this," Katarina weakly explained to him.

Bert knew of this Captain August by his reputation as a harsh, mean man unable to compromise. His undesirable characteristics were dangerous to those the feared officer came in contact with, whether civilian or military. Bert's facial muscles actually twitched when he heard the infamous man's name mentioned, and he feared for Katarina to have any dealings with him, no matter how slight.

"Why don't we meet after you are done at the office? That could still work with my schedule, and at least we would be able to see each other for a short amount of time. I can pick you up at your place of employment—if you could confirm its location, of course," he added a little sarcastically.

"Bert showing up at the office would absolutely not work at any time of any day," Katarina thought. Mlle. Zelinsky was a loose cannon, and the monster August was totally out of control. Mademoiselle's plan for getting rid of the captain was still in the insane stage. She wished that she had met Bert at a different time in her life, where unwanted distractions would not derail a possible relationship. She was savvy enough to realize that Bert was an asset to her at the present time even if he were not a suitor. She needed to stay connected to him, whether easy or not, because she might need him in her back pocket if things did not go well with all of this craziness that was happening so quickly.

She insisted, "Let me just meet you tomorrow, in front of our church, at noon again. It is Sunday, and I will be able to maneuver this. Meeting you by the church worked the other day, and we had a very good time together. My timing is too fluid to know exactly when I will finish today. It will be better on Sunday. I hope you understand my dilemma, Bert."

Staring into those pleading, dark eyes of hers mesmerized him into acquiescence. Bert could not refuse his Prague beauty in person, but he decided to secretly check up on her by 5:00 p.m. at her office anyway. Her nervousness today reminded him of soldiers anxiously awaiting a call to battle. This was not what he expected from this sweet girl. It was obvious she was not about to tell him what was really bothering her.

"Of course; I will abide by your wishes, dear Katarina. Tomorrow it is. I want you to be careful today in the district though. There were some trucks here earlier to pick up some workers for the new Terezin fortress that is being retrofitted. If you see any trucks, please avoid them and go inside whatever structure you can to stay absolutely clear of them. They are here for young, strong-looking Jewish males only, but you should always err on the safe side. It saddens me that you have to be exposed to this. In fact, you really should not be exposed to anything that is going on in here," he continued in a growing agitation. "When will you complete your assignment here again? I think your father might not be as strict as you think and might have been correct that you should not be here."

Katarina had no idea what he was talking about with trucks to Terezin or why he would even mention her father. She'd heard mention that Terezin was a small town thirty-seven miles from Prague where there was a small fortress. She remembered this from her class field trip.

"Why would young men be taken on a field trip?" she asked quizzically.

Bert realized that he should not have been talking at all about the plans of the German Army to his striking female friend, who was clearly over her head with this assignment or even understanding the seriousness of the Jewish dilemma. He'd heard rumors of a move encompassing all of the residents from the district being relocated to Terezin, plus an addition of more Jews and dissidents who were being rounded up in the surrounding areas to be added to the town. Terezin was to be a temporary holding spot for Jews being sent to other camps that were being established in Germany to supposedly house them. Rails would be the transport to the other spots in Germany.

"We will talk tomorrow, Katarina. Please, please just keep your visit here brief today. I am garnering curiosity about exactly what your job entails. We should talk about that tomorrow as well."

"I hear what you are saying, Bert. My family really wants everything completed shortly. That is why I am here so early today. My parents are good parents, no matter how much I might chatter about them otherwise," she responded.

"I am glad to hear that you will be done soon, and I did not mean to imply anything negative about your parents. Obviously they have raised a wonderful daughter, so they must excel at parenting," he said, quite visibly relieved that she would soon stop entering this hotspot of impending doom.

"I will meet you Sunday," he continued. "I know we will get along famously when we are no longer having chance encounters by this sentry post and are not donning our respective roles, which are cumbersome and hard to discard. Take care of yourself, sweet lady...Until we meet later," he said with a gentlemanly bow of his head, hoping that no one was looking at him like the foolish boy that he was, talking unabashedly to a pretty girl.

Katarina then gave such a coy smile accompanied by such a delicate curtsy that Bert was forced to present his toothy smile of joy.

Katarina proceeded to Trini's. A large truck with wooden seats around the interior perimeter and an open space in the center loomed into view as soon as the café did. She quickly whipped around the sharp corner of the cross street and peered cautiously from her hiding spot. She blanched in horror when she saw gun-toting Nazi soldiers grabbing mere boys, as well as any young-looking male, and tossing them in the idling truck with only a bark of orders and no explanation otherwise. The petrified boys had contorted faces as they were thrown belly first into the waiting truck, which never turned off its blaring engine. The vehicle slowly moved on, and the soldiers continued grabbing more prey as it inched forward.

She cowered flat against the building, then tried to peek out again. She squinted, clearing her vision as she watched the poor souls helpless in the truck. She inadvertently gasped when she saw her friend David was the third guy in the truck, slumped to the left, with blood streaming from his shoulder, clotting the fabric she remembered him wearing just the other day. The area around his eye had already begun to darken from a blow that had been previously delivered. It obscured his appearance, making him look more like an old gnome that graced many antique shops rather than a strapping young man.

Her legs remained planted by the side of the building, unable to move to the inside, as Bert had suggested. Her eyes followed the truck; with its hunger for strong youth almost satiated, it roared away toward the next tight street filled with unsuspecting males who wore dingy yellow stars. David stared straight at her as he left for hell and never even blinked. She knew she was looking at a cart that might as well have been going to the guillotine during the French Revolution, except that it was Prague, he was Jewish, and Bastille Day would be a long time coming.

She remained adhered to the cement until her scrambled thoughts cleared along with the street chaos. She had a flash about Mlle. Zelinsky and her tremendous faith in her Dr. Bonn, who was actually a major part of Katarina's planned events for the day.

Katarina ran past Trini's, around the corner, and up the stairs, only to be greeted by cries of keening and wailing. She walked in the entrance, which was ajar, to find two hunched-over women lost in tears and emotion. The doctor sat in the corner with his head bent, looking like a man who had crumbled like a useless paper that was thrown carelessly on the floor. A faint, high-pitched baby's cry could be heard through the sounds of sorrow.

Katarina quietly moved through the huddles of darkly wrapped people, who looked like they were bobbing for fish but were probably praying, as a mumble of words accompanied the movements. She walked up to Rudolph Bonn without anyone asking her why she was entering what appeared to be a house of mourning. She lightly tapped his slumped shoulder and obviously disturbed him; he slowly raised his tearstained face to greet her petrified glance.

"I cannot converse with you at this time," he said with polite brevity as he slumped down even more.

"Doctor, I can see this is a time of sorrow, but Mlle. Zelinsky deemed it of the upmost importance for me to speak with you. Not for what you might presume, but for assistance with something critical to her that she is unable to do alone, without your help specifically. Her faith in you is her strength in these hard times." Katarina's sincerity matched her insensitivity and brought a flicker of interest to the distraught man.

His prayer-filled thoughts were concentrated on his wife, but the young girl in front of him looked so well fed, healthy, and sincere that it instilled a vision of his lovely Naomi when he first set eyes on her. The girl before him also had that freshness of youth that fades in time, especially in the times that try one's soul.

Naomi would never turn anyone away from their doorstep, whether at dinner or bedtime or during their rare leisure times. She was the one who locked the doors when the day was over, and he knew that it was only the most rare of situations when she would actually turn someone away from their assistance even once the door had been barred and their personal time had begun.

This was neither the time nor the place for him to be speaking to this girl, but as he looked up again, he knew he wanted to take a chance and hear what this child, who was barely a woman, needed so desperately to say. He wanted to do this for Naomi. This simple act ultimately sealed his fate in the book of life as if it were Yom Kippur and fates were being sealed for yet another year.

"Let us move to the side that you were in yesterday. My sorrow overflows my very existence right now, and I cannot talk here amid the air thick from crying. My most wonderful wife was not able to stand the strains of childbirth in this time of stress, and my infant girl is without a mother's comfort in this disintegrating town of doom. Forgive me, young lady, but what appears before you is a broken man who could not be much help to anyone. I will listen to what you have to say, though, because I know my Naomi, may she rest in peace, would want it that way."

Katarina was rendered speechless and quietly crossed into the barren room that just yesterday was filled with bodies straining to see this well-known healer, who was welling up with tears right in front of her and did not look very strong at all. At least there was a little elbow room compared to the other space, which was the designated room for mourning and crowded with more than the usual body count squeezed into the limited area.

"From yesterday's potential joy to today's sadness must have been a bleak road for you and your family to travel. The birth of a new life should never bring the death of another to the forefront, and I am truly sorry for what has occurred here. Mlle. Zelinsky, as you might remember, was a patient of yours. She blindly trusts you, even for situations outside of these confining walls, in ways that I cannot completely comprehend but am coerced to do so. She has never lost this complete allegiance to you. Because of this, I too now hold you in the highest esteem. Her office, the same one that employs me, is a puppet theater for Captain August of the Nazi regime here in Prague. I am embarrassed to confess that he is terrorizing me; I only confess so under duress, with the hope that it will be our secret. He is doing the same filthy thing to Eva."

Katarina's voice started to quiver as she continued, "I understand her helplessness in this terrible position because I also do not feel like I am in a position to change things on my own. There is no one outside these walls that Mademoiselle feels has the stature, as well as the medical training, to provide the solution that she thinks might work to end this grave situation. I have no idea who to turn to either, because these last few days have practically paralyzed me. Mlle. Zelinsky has devised a plan though, and we are thinking it might be our only option. She wants you to confront Captain August. She is under the impression that without a star on your clothing, your presence will cow him into behaving possibly more like a gentleman than the monster that he is. Because you have had medical training, she was also hinting that there might be some sort of concoction that you could administer to him that would render him helpless and enable her to smother him with her own strength. She feels that one added dead soldier would not seem like an oddity to this devastated country of corpses. I realize this is a lot to ask of you, but when I explain the complete idea, you will see that it is very possible to accomplish this overpowering feat. Can I count on you at all?"

The doctor was dumfounded as to how unplanned this scheme seemed and how impossible it would be to enact. He was a virtual prisoner in his own city, with no rights and very little medication to administer if any, and treated subhumanly by most people outside the ghetto, especially anyone in a uniform. This young girl and that silly patient of his were bound to get everyone involved in their foolishness killed in the process.

"I am sorry, Mademoiselle, but you speak the unspeakable to me. There surely is another person who is not living in the district who can help you out of your predicament." He tried to say it more gently than he felt, but his expression deceived him. "The Nazis are terrorizing many people in Prague, especially the Jews located in this very district. My concern right now is for my infant child. I cannot help you in this far-fetched scheme that the two of you have quickly concocted."

Katarina noticed the look of abject shock that immersed the broken man in front of her. She knew she must appear so silly in this grieving man's eyes, and she felt she needed to redeem herself. This scheme of Mlle. Zelinsky initially appeared harebrained to her as well, and maybe she unintentionally communicated this while unfolding the plot in this darkly lit ghetto apartment. She realized that if she were to be successful in incorporating him in any endeavor they had, she'd better add more of what she was previously planning, which was definitely more organized than Mlle. Zelinsky's idea for the doctor.

David had spent time figuring out various escape routes and elicited the help of men who seemed to know what they were doing with documents and guards. Her original plans with David unfortunately vaporized moments previously, when she saw him zooming away with the enemy. She now impulsively decided to resurrect at least a fraction of David's plan.

She had never hinted to Eva what she was secretly planning with David. David had enlisted other helpers to ensure his success in leaving the district. His planning began to entice her more than Mlle. Zelinsky's. She hoped that Dr. Bonn would reconsider his initial response when he heard of this even better escape route. She decided to add even newer angles that were popping up in her head as she quickly thought of the latest add-on to her sketchy scheme.

"Today I watched Nazi guards roar up this very avenue in high-capacity trucks, grab young Jewish men and boys who did not appear like they were even in their teen years, and throw them violently into the waiting transports. I previously heard from a reliable source that Terezin was going to be used as some kind of camp for Jews and assumed that these boys were going to have something to do with its construction. My contact was a Jewish man, my age, called David, who was helping me navigate around the district to garner information for my report. I must confess again to you: David was forging papers that resemble the ones I carry to enable him to simply walk out with me as my documented assistant. David took me to a hidden attic in a building close to here, which produced the forgeries. We were to pick up the copies today. Your escape would be plausible if you left the district holding papers similar to the forged ones with David's name on them. David is obviously unable to escape because who knows when he will be returned to this horrid spot. I fear that the plan of the Nazis might be to have all of the Jews sent to Terezin. This seems like a crazy idea, but these men are capable of doing things that are unimaginable.

"Would you consider taking David's place with a new document that would actually have your name on it in a very official manner and not just inked on at the last minute?

The men who helped David could help you, and that would make at least leaving the district a little easier. You could be the one who walks out of the ghetto with official papers. You could then go to my office and help us contain this monster. After that, you would have your freedom, and you could head into the surrounding forest or even come back here if that is what you really want to do."

The young girl babbling in front of Dr. Bonn sounded like a schoolgirl skipping class, just walking out the door with no sense of consequences for her actions. He remembered that sometimes a skip could lead to truancy, but sometimes it could lead to a wonderful day romping on the beach. Some of the possibilities she outlined had potential, but the majority of them were not suitable to him for his present situation. His foremost concern was for his newborn little girl. His only willingness was to take a stab at getting her out of this poisonous environment.

Hearing about this new camp, Terezin, was not new information to him either. There were rumors about this dedicated space on the gossipy streets. Everyone feared his or her present living conditions were temporary, with the unknown being far worse than the known. There were always a few optimists weaving through the crowd who felt change benefited the masses, but his optimism died with his child-birthing wife. He feared it would never be resurrected. With Naomi dead, his future was no longer a concern. His immediate focus was only the projected life ahead for his daughter, which he hoped would be longer than her mother's shortened one had been.

Katarina's Terezin comments were upsetting because he had heard bits of it previously but was not aware that it was coming to fruition so immediately on the horizon. There initially had been a call by the council of Jews in the district to put together a volunteer work group that would go to Terezin and help build the added structures needed when the time came. Many men he knew had volunteered for this so they could ensure that it was being built properly and would not freeze its inhabitants in the winter with frigid winds or fall apart on its dwellers. He gleaned that not enough manpower had been sent voluntarily and now they were grabbing unsuspecting youthful males off the streets, who had no building experience but looked like there was more work in them than the older members of the community. He had also deduced that the reason for this facility could only be more bad news. He was not looking at this as an improvement over the present conditions.

He was aware that various train lines converged in this town. That fact brought more rumors to the local chatter that somehow it would all tie in together and the rails would be used to transport Jews to the feared Germany.

Either way, everyone knew their time was measured in the district, and this girl evoked enticing thoughts of a way out for not just him, who had little to live for, but his baby, who could have an entire future ahead of her if she were no longer associated with the Jews here. He felt his own hold on life was diminishing, and it was only the safety of his child that kept him breathing, as well as conniving for a chance of tomorrows.

He kept trying to think of what his precious Naomi would say, and he knew it would be, "Do whatever you can to save our child. She is our future, and we have no present."

With these integral thoughts, he proceeded to add to his conversation with Katarina alternative ideas that could possibly suit both of their needs and even that flighty Eva Zelinsky, whom he had always tried to humor.

"Can you lead me to the documenters you mentioned, since your friend David can no longer use those papers, at least right now? David was right to seek someone who is familiar with documentation and forgery. I am thinking this is the key to leaving this area. I will tell you honestly that my every thought is with my newborn now in this transitional period for me. Her new life is the most precious thing for our futures. The path out has to be clean for the innocents of youth, not just to appease the corrupted, who have already been tainted. I have decided to do whatever is necessary to ensure that my daughter can leave this subjugation. I will work with you to devise a plan that has more chance of success than the bits and pieces you offered.

"If you need someone to confront this Nazi captain, I will do this, but only if my daughter is guaranteed safety by you and Eva Zelinsky. If you need someone to administer a lethal injection, I will do this also, again if that helps little Naomi.

"I actually remember explaining why air must not be in a syringe to Eva. This must have made a bigger impression on her than I realized at the time. I have a feeling that she was considering this type of injection when her thoughts turned to bringing me on board with her scheme. My true plan is to save little Naomi at any cost. I will help both of you with your revenge on this Nazi if that will guarantee Naomi's freedom.

"We will get the papers, I will bring my daughter, and we will all go to your office outside this barbed wire, where she will stay with you until she has been placed in a position of safety. As for the captain specifically, you mentioned that if I confronted this monster, the problem would be solved. I do not think there is any chance of that happening at all. Even a forceful request to eliminate bad behavior will only incite a man like this. It is essential that he be given an injection immediately when he enters the office. I presume he always enters by himself, especially if he has divisive plans for either you or Eva.

"Once he has been successfully injected with air, things will move along faster because he will be rendered helpless, at least for a short time. If I give him a large shot of pure air minus any trace of liquid in the syringe, this will most assuredly stop him for an extended period of time. If luck is in our corner, this will immediately give him an embolism or at least the normally dreaded stroke or cardiac distress so he will no longer be a problem to you or anyone. If the injection alone does not kill him, a simple push down the office building stairs will simulate either fatal injuries from a fall caused by a heart attack, or a slippage because of imbalance of alcohol, which we could pour on him in the odd case that he did not arrive having a flask in his own pocket.

"This accidental-looking death should not cause you any problems if you proceed carefully and do not raise any red flags with your own erratic behavior. His death most definitely will appear happenchance if you do not hide it but contact his unit to report the tragic fall down the dangerous interior steps of an old building.

"I would then return to the district so there will be no repercussions for you or Mlle. Zelinsky while you keep Naomi safe in her new status as a Christian child. For the time being, her life as a Jew is over. Whether you place her with a willing farm family, keep her yourself, or take her to Switzerland, her ultimate safety will be up to you, as long as there is an option that can guarantee her safety. If there is a different avenue for her to escape persecution, I leave it up to you to provide it. You see, in this area, I trust you, just as you trusted me earlier with your intimate secrets.

"Your office works as a social services agency, and I know you will have various options that I am not even aware of at this time. I must be confident that you will save my innocent child in any way you or Eva can.

"I guess we must ultimately trust one another if we are to be working together juggling human lives.

"The district will need a man with medical instruction like me in the days ahead, especially if the local population is to be moved to a new, possibly hostile environment. I feel that I will be needed more there than with my daughter. She will be safer with you or the placement that you will provide.

"As for the immediate scenario at your office, two beautiful women will not raise alarm with the local military if you appear in control of the situation. Your only fear should be that you witnessed a deadly accident. The natural demise of a military officer in a war-torn country will not rise to importance because of their other imminent concerns at this time."

It was now clearer to Katarina why Mlle. Zelinsky had so much blind faith in this man adorned in a ragged suit who now sat presidentially before her. His ideas were more calculating than anything previously planned, and they appeared to even have the possibility of being somewhat successful. She was awed at the speed that he came up with such brilliant possibilities. She did manage to question some of the specifics though.

"I understand the documentation through my office, but what about your baby's papers? How are we going to walk out of this area with an infant?" asked Katarina. "How are we to render such a large man who has a loaded weapon helpless?" she added with newfound concern that showed intelligence enough to understand that it was in the details that the trouble always began.

"Let us start our journey by finding these men whom you previously used to alter your documents. The specifics will become clearer to both of us as this unfolds and we continually discuss as we walk. We must address all aspects of what we are going to do. We will methodically complete one task at a time and pray that everything will fall into place before we are through.

"First we go to the counterfeiters you mentioned. Now, tell me whatever little details you can remember about where this place was and who the people were."

Katarina explained how she assumed the men were religious because of their foreign garb and their speaking of what she thought might be Hebrew in an attic workshop that was only entered through a door on a peeling painted ceiling.

Dr. Bonn's eyes squinted with a glimmer of knowledge when she mentioned the look of the men, but he was unaware of their whereabouts in such a building with hidden attics.

"Take me on the route that you think you traveled yesterday. Your muscle memory might be better at zeroing in on the location rather than your brain," he said at the beginning of their roundabout, circuitous route through the district, where nothing at all looked familiar to Katarina. They began at Trini's and took a right, then went down a darkened alley and kept making concentric circles that brought them to a spot that looked vaguely familiar only because it looked like every other street they'd traversed.

Then they meandered back to Trini's, took a left, then another quick left, and then circled a crowded area teeming with gaunt-looking people and dark, looming buildings that provoked no flicker of recognition in Katarina's darting eyes.

After one and a quarter hours of searching in vain, Rudolph requested that Katarina wait in the office across from his in-laws near where they had begun their quest. His living space was still packed tightly with mourners dressed in the dark clothes that most Jews wore anyways, worn shoes, and draping, darkly patterned babushkas.

He deposited her in his barren office and told her that her wait would not be as boring as she might think because he was bringing his little daughter, Naomi, over to introduce her to Katarina as well as keep her company in case he was delayed.

Word had spread that his beloved Naomi had perished during a difficult childbirth. Sad-eyed women silently arrived. Many had just lost their youthful sons to the hostile soldiers who drove large trucks and grabbed the young earlier without warning. The stifling air was wrought with sadness and tears for Naomi and the boys who were now missing. There was a chance that the boys would be seen again, but everyone knew that there was no chance of the mother Naomi setting foot on this earth again. The only Naomi was now an infant, appropriately named after her dead mother, who was only allowed a fleeting glimpse of her child before death grabbed her.

Rudolph's concern was for the baby to survive this horrendous time, no matter what herculean effort it took from him or the hopeful Katarina. It would be nice to have days to plan an escape, but he knew that speed was of the essence and there was no better time than the present to try this daring adventure that could play out in a dozen different ways. The trucks coming so suddenly made him realize that he was not privy to information about what was to be and had to seize the moment only with what he knew was happening now.

Leaving Katarina in the small one-room space, he then went across the narrow hall to get the bundled Naomi, who was sleeping in a decrepit bureau drawer tucked in the far corner. He took the little bundle, tightly wrapped in a clean but dingy cloth, and told his anxious family that he had concocted a crazy plan with the girl across the hall to get Naomi to safety. The family just stared at him without a word uttered as he walked across the hall to show the baby to this basically unknown individual. The day had held too many surprises to jangle Naomi's parents out of their shock or to get a reaction from her elderly grandmother, who was keening nonstop next to her collapsed daughter.

⇥⊹ ⊹⇤

Katarina looked around the dark room, devoid of excess furniture. The few faded pieces seemed so ancient, it surprised her they remained upright resting on the scratched wooden floors. The dim sparkle that the waxed surface once held was long gone, and only the footprints of age remained. There were no rays of sunshine cheering up this sad room.

She paced back and forth until she saw the possibly once handsome doctor appear with a tightly wrapped bundle that she knew was a baby. It looked more like a basket of laundry that Petra might carry on washday than an infant. She was shocked when the small breathing bundle was placed in her previously dangling arms. Dr. Bonn's heavy steps slowed as he shuffled backward to eye his love transferred.

When Katarina held the wrapped little waif in her young arms, she incurred a strange sensation. She could not identify the emotion that had popped into her tired body, but it left a strong conviction to do whatever was needed to keep this love out of harm's way.

She previously was unable to verbalize to her parents why she was driven to work in the Office of Social Services. She now realized that helping at least one person achieve some level of safety in his or her life during this time of war was what she was meant to do. She wanted to be a part of humanity that helped people, not destroyed them.

Katarina peered into the wrapped package of life that was tucked into her arms, and she smiled with a warmth that the baby seemed to sense, because she slowly opened her eyes, then gently went back to sleep with a contented sigh.

"One of my female patients is next door and has been nursing Naomi, as well as her own son, who is almost a year now. When Naomi begins to whimper, just walk across the hall, and they will know what to do. They will be packing some containers of milk that you can take with you when we travel. The women in this apartment, who are related to me in various ways, are very appreciative of your assistance with our precious girl." Rudolph's words trailed off as he left to consult one of the many rabbis in the district. He had to deduce where holy men might congregate, especially if their mission was not praying but making the Nazis' job more difficult.

Katarina felt rejuvenated now that she held the precious cargo and had renewed purpose in her bizarre actions that were so different from anything she had ever done before.

Rudolph Bonn went quickly to Rabbi Schlectman, who could always be found in the building next to the Maisel or Maislova Synagogue on Maislova, the street named after Mordecai Maisel, who acquired a plot of land for the synagogue in 1590.

The building was now completely boarded up, with worn wood placed in a calico pattern haphazardly, but everyone knew its innards were filled with furniture from grand Jewish homes that no longer existed for their owners. It was basically a cemetery of furniture and belongings, with a neo-Gothic facade. The hope was that eventually the occupiers would return the things to their rightful owners, which as time went on became more dubious.

The synagogue and other warehouses outside the district had just become holding areas for Germans to store new acquisitions while the Jews in the district were being contained and stripped. The lavish jewelry, magnificent homes, viable businesses, famous art masterpieces, and miscellaneous items were slowly being distributed through the military and wealthy merchants to other wealthy people or those who would become wealthy after the war because of these acquisitions.

Before the doctor regally stood an elderly rabbi, slightly bent from the weight of the long coat that buttoned him up from the cold. A large brimmed hat, which was fur trimmed and blended with the dark brown fur trailing off his bearded face, obscured his sight.

As Rabbi Schlectman motioned to greet the esteemed doctor, he noted his ripped black ribbon that signified mourning, which he had been told was for his young wife. He shook the doctor's hand and offered him a seat in the drafty room. After the customary consoling was dutifully completed between the holy man and the mourner, Rudolph Bonn quickly got to the burning reason for searching out this particular rabbi, with whom he normally had little contact.

"A young Christian lady has come to me, and I think it is G-d's will," began Rudolph.

He explained to the rabbi that a young man named David had planned an escape by walking out of the ghetto with the accompanying papers of a certain Katarina Orbhan from the Office of Social Services of Prague, which was under the Nazis' thumb, of course.

Dr. Bonn chose not to include the questionable activities of a certain Captain August, but concentrated instead on getting the documents from the religious men who were assisting the young David.

He ended with, "And my ultimate concern is to get my infant daughter out of here. I do not want to cause any more trouble for my fellow Jews detained within these walls, and therefore plan on returning to the district after I have safely left Naomi. Is there any little tidbit of information that you can give me that will help me in this quest?" finished the doctor.

Rabbi Schlectman felt he understood the crowded streets and the souls and the motives of those who resided in the dejected ghetto around him. He was informed when the Nazis had asked for volunteers to build Terezin. He was aware Terezin would only be a harbinger of things to come. He feared for the lives of his local flock, as well as for the universal flock that was in danger from the present temperament of the rulers. He kept waiting for G-d to ease the suffering of his chosen people and feared for the future, just as any sane man around him would. He was well aware of the young David's activities when the reigning police had grabbed him while he innocently was putting one foot in front of another to not draw attention to any of his activities.

The rabbi was given a lengthy list just an hour earlier of those who had been taken by force, as well as those who had volunteered to go to the fortress. He was surprised how many loving family men had chosen a work camp with a dubious future rather than staying put with their loved ones even if told it was just a temporary measure. He knew that many opted for that dim path only to ensure quality work would be done in camp construction. They hoped that their sacrifice would help the structures be more viable, not just some wood slapped together that accepted cold and sickness in winter, with added heat and exhaustion in summer, to the many incarcerates who he knew would soon be arriving.

He looked at the man in front of him, who oozed charisma as well as tears, and said, "Here we need your healing gifts, Rudolph. Just like Terezin needs the stronger, younger men to build it, we need men like you to be a positive force here in this maelstrom of sorrows. You must give me your word that you will return to these distressed streets after you inhale a breath of freedom and your mission is accomplished."

Rudolph Bonn grasped the bearded rabbi and held him close as the holy man whispered the street, the house, and the names that Rudolph so desperately needed.

Rudolph quickly backtracked to his quarters and scooped up Katarina. They pursued their quarry with more purpose than their previous meanderings, where they were just wasting precious time they did not have.

He and Katarina had actually walked right by the drab, nondescript building earlier in the day, when nothing within eyesight even looked at all familiar to her. It was understandable, because the streets were all in disrepair. The people resembled one another, with similar looks of hunger and apparent sadness, and those expressions exploded on their faces when they occasionally looked up from their downward gazes. The common denominator was being lost in thoughts of locales other than their gloomy surroundings and frustrating circumstances.

They finally zeroed in on the forgotten building. They turned the old metal handle on the sluggish door and bounded up the stairway to what looked like the last floor on a dead-end hall. The stairwell was devoid of artificial light, but a shimmer of brightness flickered through the occasionally placed windows that appeared sporadically at the end of each floor.

Their hopeful eyes rose upward in unison and scanned the peeling ceiling for the innocent markings of a portal. They barely made out the slight, thin line that formed a rectangle in the ceiling.

They rapped within those parameters and called out, "Rabbi Schlectman's friends here." They waited for a tell-tale squeak from above, but nothing seemed to stir in the lofty space above them. They each stared somewhere past their heads on opposite sides of the hall while pondering their abject situation.

Rudolph knew that if he was the one positioned above deciding whether to reveal his lair, he would not even wiggle a finger in their direction with the simple phrase that had been uttered by strangers. Unfortunately, the rabbi had not shared any sort of "open sesame" wording that would magically unfold a treasure in a cave like Ali Baba had whispered in his story about the forty thieves.

Katarina decided to very formally start explaining how she knew of them as she strained upward toward the block of plaster above her. "I am Katarina, who was here with David previously. I am now with Dr. Bonn and need your help."

The creaking from the trapdoor brought forth a success-ful glance by the two hopefuls. Their task had been more difficult than they'd initially presumed. The rickety fold-away stairs quickly descended, and they gingerly climbed up, approaching a barrier of determined faces with no smile among them.

They stayed huddled around the ladder precariously as Rudolph assertively began to plead his case to the juried men. He spoke of how he happened upon them through Katarina via the rabbi. He mentioned his dead wife and his infant child as they stood passively listening without any visible wrinkles of concern or nods of understanding.

But when he began to speak of Katarina's friend David and how young David's fate had pivoted around in a flash by being in the wrong place at the wrong time, he got the attention of at least one of the stoic men. Dr. Bonn added, "Compared to those elderly who were milling around him, David looked like an Adonis and was quickly grabbed by the soldiers, who were not really looking that closely anyway."

A bent-over man with a long reddish beard and lids barely peeking from under his bushy eyebrows ran over to him and imploringly beseeched, "I pray that you are mistaken. Could there be an error in your identification of David being grabbed?"

This holy man feverishly looked from Rudolph to Katarina in the hopes that they would deny their aforementioned words. Word of David had brought passion to this previously impassive man.

Katarina's sadness over David's fate began to drip from her voice as she detailed what she had covertly viewed previously. The attentive holy man inadvertently gulped for air as she described the roundup details, ending with the truck rambling off, bound for other streets to grab more bodies.

All the holy men stayed quiet when Dr. Bonn reconstructed his association to Katarina through a past patient who now worked at the Social Services Office.

Katarina then explained how David's original plan had changed shape when it was adapted to Dr. Bonn's unique situation since David could no longer use her connections. She also decided not to mention the twist of Capt. August but did choose to mention that the doctor would be returning to the district so the papers would not be in question, as they would have been had David used them. David was not planning on returning to the streets of pestilence but had planned on pursuing a different path.

The wall of men's faces softened when Rudolph explained that his new motherless daughter had a chance of a future outside the ghetto, minus a star sewn on her nappy. Rudolph realized that when he mentioned his little Naomi, it always seemed to get better results for his ulterior plan.

Thankfully, their appeal succeeded. The red-bearded holy man did not give up on the phantom David so quickly though, insisting he should be an integral player in this scheme.

"What other information do you know about this round-up? Why are you both moving so quickly to remove David from the equation? What happens when David returns here and this young girl from the Office of Social Services is nowhere to be seen to help him? What gives you priority over David for these documents of survival? Is it just because you are a doctor and he is just a young boy without a chance yet to present his case again?"

These were all good questions that were volleyed at Dr. Bonn in quick succession. He did not waver when he responded, "If or when David returns, there is no reason for him not to proceed with his original plans."

And with that point clarified, even though it was a remote possibility that they were all aware would probably not happen, the holy men proceeded to attain the specifics needed for Dr. Bonn's document, while the red-bearded man uttered not another word.

Rudolph and Katarina sat quietly in the attic hideaway while the documents were being prepared. He wondered if this space would stay untouched if the building's residents were forced into eviction. He pondered whether any other buildings in the area had these crawl spaces and if the Nazis could possibly search all of them and rout out people's secret holdouts for survival. His thoughts went to his extended family, huddled in his cramped living quarters, trying to give solace and comfort to him and his in-laws while he was out gallivanting with this pretty young Christian girl. He began to feel guilty that he was even in this tucked-away attic far from those he loved.

David's advocate furtively peered in his direction while Rudolph scrunched up on the dirty floor next to this young woman he barely knew. Rudolph quietly parlayed his familiar worries about this imminent plan that appeared so convoluted back and forth in his own mind. It scared him that he was an architect to something that was doomed to failure, yet he was paralyzed from stopping its momentum. He reviewed the facts again: Katarina had to be at her office no later than 4:00 p.m., and actually a bit earlier if the plan were to succeed. He pondered the possibilities. Without a hitch, which he knew was highly unlikely, he would go to the Office of Social Services and ask Eva to hide little Naomi and try to get her out of the country. Because she held a managerial position in a Social Services office, the chances of placing the child in safety were increased, and therefore odds were increased for Naomi to survive the war.

But there really was no way of knowing the reliability of people in these drastic days of occupation. The people of Prague had traditionally been very accepting of their Jewish neighbors, but this was a different climate, with the winds of war blowing through the community from all angles. Eva had always presented herself as an honorable person, and he would just have to put his trust in her now, even if he had lingering doubts that he could not erase. He had no choice if this was the path that he was choosing.

He was hyperaware that his return to the district was going to be a solo adventure, with no added assistance from Katarina, whose youthful presence seemed to make people more amenable to whatever was at hand. He would not have the luxury of sticking around the Office of Social Services until Naomi's placement was secured. He had to administer the injection and then take off before trouble came racing after him.

He knew this whole series of maneuvers was only partially ensuring Naomi's safety, which caused his hand to slightly tremble. He had to leave her alone to face her fate, and this was unbearable. He closed his eyes and tried to picture Naomi safe.

The image of his child drove him, but it also petrified him. He had taken a Hippocratic oath to heal, not to kill. Did it matter that this Nazi had few redeeming qualities? There probably was a stocky Germanic wife back in his motherland pacing the floor while waiting for him to return, or a baby similar to his precious one who would now have only a mother and never a father. But having a birth mother around for sustenance and love was no longer something that Naomi would have either, and therefore he forced himself to behave differently than he'd ever imagined. This whole scheme was concocted with wild attempts to just get her in a place where she could simply have the chance of survival. He could not afford to dwell on the scary parts, such as a serious altercation with this Nazi captain. That part was the insane wild card.

His faith got stronger as he witnessed the men manipulate the documents. He watched the men slowly concentrating on their craft, bent over as if praying for a better time, and it gave him a glimmer of hope. They would soon achieve their desired result.

The red-bearded man inquisitively looked at Rudolph Bonn periodically, trying to pinpoint the reason why this doctor was allowed to obtain his child's freedom while David was off to toil in a distant camp that he too would probably be occupying soon. Rumors were rampant on every street corner in town about a dismal future. Staying optimistic about the present was becoming a challenge that he was not sure he sought adequately.

Within the hour, the men collectively looked toward Dr. Bonn as if on cue from a conductor. Then each nodded in assent that their work was finally finished.

Rudolph rose from his uncomfortable position on the floor and walked over to the huddled group, with every foot bone in his cramped feet faintly cracking. He and Katarina stood frozen as the bearded men explained the document that they had meticulously designed.

The red-bearded man began. "This gives your name right in this spot," he explained as he pointed to the top of the official-looking paper that had a straightly drawn line with his name printed above.

"It states that Doctor Rudolph Bonn is needed at the Prague Office of Social Services no later than four o'clock on this very day, and your expected return will be by seven o'clock on this exact same date. The Office of Social Services has been assigned the filing of this document, so a temporary pass will be issued. Issuing such a pass is standard for the guards to do, and we expect no problem with this. You do not want the guards to keep the document under any circumstances. This is important and has rarely been an issue in the past. There are still men and women here who are working in factories around the city and traverse the boundaries each day, which makes the guards used to letting out individual Jews at various times. It also helps that you are a doctor and are needed at an office that traditionally helps needy people. I sometimes wonder who could be in more need than the Jews right now, but imagine there are people outside the district who feel they are. Jewish doctors always have had the reputation of being more learned and better equipped in their trade than their Christian counterparts, so this level of thinking will also assist in your having access to the outside.

"Before your return to the district, you are to rip up the document and enter simply on the day pass. The paperwork will not be an issue until a future time because of the present upheaval in the district now. The right hand will assume that the left hand is in possession of the document and vise versa. Two and two will not equal four, but chances are nobody will even notice until the war is over.

"We are not addressing the infant that the two of you will be concealing. It is up to you as to the actual logistics of that task. Having a person from the Office of Social Services, namely Katarina Orbhan, is really the only way this plan can work in its entirety. Katarina's papers have been seen by the guards previously and will not be questioned. It is too dangerous to add an infant's name to an official document and would definitely cause suspicion to anyone who saw the paper. Everyone knows that Jewish babies are safer outside the ghetto, and they are told to be alert to the problem at all checkpoints. One thought we had was to fit the infant in a picnic basket, but as I stated earlier, the specifics of that part are up to you."

The oldest scribe continued the briefing. "There is another name, and you will notice it is connected to the line that states the actual employee from the Office of Social Services, namely Mlle. Orbhan. It will be a gentleman, who for these purposes will be called Christian. We have been planning to send him back into the general population to see what exactly is going on at Terezin, as well as a few other issues that need surveillance. Leaving with you and Mlle. Orbhan strikes us as an even better plan than was previously devised by the two of you. Once outside the district, he will disperse, and neither of you should ever see him again. He will not be on a day pass, but will be an office employee who was on a one-day pass. This document can be trashed once you are out of the district because we know Katarina has access to other documentation for herself if she needs it."

Rudolph Bonn was not particularly happy to learn of the last-minute addition to his newly worked-out details but realized that potential opportunities were bound to arise as more people became involved. He understood that there was a price for the documents, and he was hoping that he would not have to pay too dear a cost.

The young lady, Katarina, was taking more of a risk than he'd originally planned, as was his daughter, even though she would never be aware of anything that was to occur unless her new family told her at a much later date or if he miraculously survived the war and found her. The thought of giving Naomi a chance superseded any worries about anyone or anything else immersed in this intrigue. He thought of his wife, the love of his life, and knew that no risk was too great if there was a possibility of securing their child's safety.

He reluctantly agreed and figured he would have to wait for this Christian to appear; he hoped it would not delay the four o'clock deadline.

While this white-bearded holy man had been giving the final specifics to the doctor, the red-bearded scribe had stealthily moved toward the rear of the room. He now jauntily walked toward them with red beard shaven and a fresh appearance of youth that made Rudolph emit a laugh where no laughter had been issued in a long time.

"People always see what they want to see, Dr. Bonn; and now you see Christian, from the Office of Social Services, as stated by the papers I have in my pocket."

Rudolph noticed the yellow star was no longer on his tattered jacket; nicer wool had taken its place and was draped over him. Now Rudolph was reminded of a strong individual in the prime of his life as he gazed at the figure that earlier had been a bent–over, red-bearded holy man. Without the disarray of curly, long red hairs forming a straggly beard, his smooth face had self-reliance and assuredness written over it, although he still looked at Rudolph with doubts that popped up with or without the singular red beard.

Katarina was equally amazed at the transition before her of this Christian and was still having trouble grasping that all of this quick planning was going to come to fruition shortly. She compared the attic she was sitting in to the attic at her parents' home in a very different section of town. Both spaces were dark, but this one was alive with possibilities for helping those in need.

Her parents never spoke disparagingly about Jewish men, but such men never stepped through their door. Petra occasionally voiced concern about them, and Katarina listened attentively when she would discuss the plight of the Jews. These men before her seemed amiable and quite knowledgeable about their craft, which gave her some confidence about what was unfolding but not complete ease in the situation.

Katarina was putting her safety in their hands, and she was starting to get a little scared even though they seemed holy, which should have helped her more with her confidence level than it did. She shrugged as she turned around one more time to smile at the holy men as she stepped onto the cascading ladder. She hoped she was not traversing down to hell as she tried to find her footing on the rungs beneath her feet after momentarily being aloft in heaven.

As the three connivers in this expedited adventure walked to Rudolph's lodgings, he determined he would use Christian's expertise not only for the skillful procuring of documents, but for his savvy, which was needed to accomplish this elaborate scheme that had evolved in too short a time to be perfected and which he had quickly adopted for his own selfish reasons.

As the three voyagers scurried down the crowded streets, Dr. Bonn breathily gave the redhead more background information on this extra plan that even experienced agents might have trouble effecting.

"Everyone has his or her own motive that is driving each plan it seems," laughed Christian upon hearing how Katarina initially wanted to save the world but now was forced to save some desperate Jews, while Eva Zelinsky wanted revenge, which seemed to fit into Katarina's issues with this captain also. Meanwhile, Rudolph wanted to free his innocent baby, and finally, Christian himself needed reconnaissance material for the district.

"Aren't we a group of needy people?" commented Rudolph with a halfhearted chuckle.

Christian summarized, "Let us try to clarify our issues. You are right, dear doctor, that I can assist you with this antagonizing Nazi captain. I always have time, albeit not a lot, to help in eliminating a Nazi officer, but I am also not convinced from our short friendship that both of you are the right people for the difficult job ahead of you. What if

I go with you to the Office of Social Services? I think this will ensure that your Nazi at least has a struggle instead of a mere scuffle. I think otherwise I am leading you to slaughter, and I cannot do this. I can render this man helpless because I have at least been trained for combat. I am shocked but impressed that you felt up to the job.

"I realize that your projected mission for your daughter could also give you the strength of a golem, but it is not a guarantee. I could strong-arm him while you go the medical route. Remember, this man is a battle-trained military officer and is not a stranger to adversity.

"If we are each assigned a task, it will at least help to ensure our success. I liked your idea about having the women inform headquarters of Captain August's sudden health issues, but Katarina, you and Mlle. Zelinsky should realize that risk is always involved."

Katarina and Rudolph quickened their pace to squeeze in next to Christian so his words could all be processed and none be missed in the wind whistling around them. They noted each other's dubious expressions and assumed that they individually had come to the same realization: that they were acting like kindergarteners attempting trickery on middle-school wise guys, convinced of success but clueless about their lack of size and experience.

"In regard to your child, Doctor, I think it is a fair assumption that the infant can have placement through Social Services, though as I just stated, everything comes with a risk. Our conglomerate of players will be running somewhat solo as Captain August's death scene is enacted. Immediately after the Nazi is situated at the bottom of a stairway with no sign of breathing, I will slither to Terezin like a mink in the night, because I am bound and determined to find my dearest brother, David," he added as an afterthought.

His final words brought silence to the rapt twosome that leaned in to his every word. Katarina stopped in her tracks when he mentioned that David was his brother. She was so focused on all of the various fingers of the plan that David had delicately slipped from her mind. She now knew that David never slipped from the redhead's mind. Christian was obviously an underground fighter whose brother was in danger.

"It is important that you get to Terezin. I hope you will have luck and be able to help your brother. It is terrible of me that I did not voice more concern over his safety initially, so please forgive my error. David is an amazing guy, and you are amazing too. I feel grateful that you will be helping us."

Christian just looked askew at the young girl and nodded his head. It was not even worth discussing the way he felt about his brother. They were each other's pillars in this spinning world, and hope of his safety was what carried him away from the work in the attic and to these stumblebums who had too many agendas to be filled properly.

Rudolph's gratitude overcame his fear when he heard that he did not have to confront the captain alone with his tentative might. When he thought of extinguishing the captain's life, he quivered in shame. He never had been totally convinced that he could consciously kill a healthy individual. The pieces of puzzle were starting to fit together with less buckling and smoother borders. It began to make more sense to him why this man, whether concealed with a beard or exhibiting the affectations of freedom without a star emblazoned upon his breast, was previously so leery of him. Christian was originally helping his own brother escape a destiny now feared in all Jewish minds; he was not planning on using his skills just for a Bonn family member in distress. Rudolph decided not to ask too many specifics as to what drove him to join their escapade.

The trio proceeded into Bonn's irregular configuration of rooms by climbing yet another set of rickety stairs that led to his dismal quarters. They heard the keening of sorrow on the left side of the upper landing, and the lullaby for a baby on the right side. They chose to enter the right side, and upon opening the unlocked door, they came across a vision of an elder Madonna and child in rapture. Rudolph's mother-in-law had wrapped her tasseled and flowered babushka around her head and under the body of the tiny baby she held. It then swept around in folds of black, blue, brown, and gold, enveloping the sleeping infant. It was then carefully tucked in behind her back, with just a slight hint of cloth sticking out behind her. She was singing "Az Budes Velky," an old Czech lullaby that rises and falls in steady beats of sadness, which put Naomi in a veil of sleep and them in captivity. Rudolph's moist eyes stopped misting when he heard the wails of sorrow coming from the opposite side of the hall. They snapped him into clearing his throat as he introduced Naomi's mother to yet another person. There were so many intricacies that kept evolving on this momentous day.

"This gentleman, named Christian, is leaving quietly with us today. He will be listed as a fellow employee of Katarina's. They are not as careful about the traffic patterns of non-Jews, and it will only be my papers that they will truly scrutinize. We have to conceal Naomi from sight and recognition. A picnic basket was suggested, and I have a little numbing solution that still remains and can be used to make her a little sleepy and, hopefully, a lot more quiet. The rocking motion of the basket will put her in slumber, and the crisp fresh air should extend that sleep. Once we are out of the district, I see no reason why she cannot be held by any of us if need be."

Naomi's grandmother, Etta, continued to rhythmically rock the infant in her arms while humming the lullaby and nodding in assent. Etta looked at the trio in front of her and silently prayed that this beautiful girl, the strong-appearing youthful man cowering behind them, and her skinny, cerebral son-in-law who never even squashed a fly would be able to pull all this off.

The next hour was busily spent with preparations necessary for their upcoming mission. Etta procured a rectangular, woven, wooden box with a curved handle that looked like rotten tomatoes had been stored in it a long time ago. Red dirt splotched the sides with oddly shaped markings, and the dismal smell of something possibly sour permeated her nose when she picked it up. It would be safer to have the box appear as unusable. The smell would have to be abated somewhat if a tiny baby was to spend any time in there and not gag or cough. Various methods were tried for the removal of the smell. Etta's sadness was as pungent as the stench from the box, but she never ceased trying to make this tiny space more viable for her disappearing granddaughter.

Naomi's chance of survival hinged on factors that she had no control over, but this particular dilemma was one where Etta could assist in finding a solution. She carefully scrubbed only the inside with a water solution, in which she had added various concoctions to ease the offensive odor. She had saved an eighth of a stick of partially used cinnamon for cooking from the time she originally packed her things, reluctantly ready to squeeze into these ghetto quarters. She had tried to squash whatever she could into barely a quarter section of the small, square suitcase that she had premarked for things from her lost spacious kitchen.

Packing only one suitcase with all of her possessions in such a short time had put her in a quandary. She squandered long stretches of time trying to solve the dilemma of what to carry with her for the indeterminate time that she would be gone. She was worried that without her sepia photographs of her own mother and father, as well as her younger sister in Latvia, images would fade more in her memory than on the paper. At the end of her hour designated for packing, she discarded the ornate frames that held images frozen in time and simply threw the pictures in the stuffed suitcase.

She chose her wedding picture, taken over forty years previously, as well as a fairly recent picture that she had positioned on her stately mantel of her precious Naomi and dashing Rudolph looking so happy that any onlooker shared in their joy.

She had also remembered to put in a little sweet basil in an ornate metal thimble that her mother had given her as a child and pop it in the corner of the case. It was such a small thimble that every time she tried to use it, it just stuck straight up on her digit and did not protect her skin from the sharp points of the attacking needle. She knew she did not want to part with it even though it was a silly item. She needed the herb contained in the thimble to combine with agar-agar when she processed jelly from her harvest of wild strawberries that tangled around the back door of her elegant home.

Etta carefully powdered a little of the cinnamon stick with some old bathwater they had in the apartment and added a little agar to thicken it. Then she took this paste and rubbed it on the inside of the box, and a magical transformation happened right before her nose. The smell changed its chemistry and was no longer offensive to the olfactory nerve endings; it did not smell like vomit anymore.

The outside of the box kept its moldy impressions, looking blotched, with darkened splashes that did not welcome touch. The inside wafted a slight aroma that could even be considered soothing.

She bent over and grabbed the bottom edge of one of her two worn, old skirts that attired her aging body and ripped enough fabric from the loose hem to make a soft cushion for the box. She panicked that not enough air would flow through the enclosure, but Rudolph explained to her that Naomi would have plenty of oxygen with the open weave of the basket. To err on the side of caution, she kind of cracked the top somewhat accidentally when she stepped on it, offering apologies for her clumsiness.

A nagging thought remained that she was preparing a coffin, but she tried to keep her mind more positive while she sang "Az Budes Velky" to Naomi, who always seemed so hungry for milk that might not always be available on demand.

Naomi seemed to be stocking up on her reserves of milk, so Etta kept handing her to the neighbor, who kept latching her to her own full breast, which flowed with a creamy substance. She fed Naomi until she gently burped up little curds as milk dribbled down her tiny face. Etta was amazed at how much she was filling her little tummy. It was as if nothing quite satisfied her because none of the substance was from her mother and she was searching in vain for such nectar from the original breast that had briefly nurtured her.

Katarina's features softened whenever she glimpsed the infant Naomi. Each time Rudolph caught Katarina scanning the room for his child, it gave him more confidence that this girl would be able to procure safety for his most prized possession. He wanted to believe that everything would come together, but he was still not totally convinced. He felt the same trepidation before a swollen appendix removal performed early in his career. The appendix could be removed quite easily, but he knew there was a chance of rupture or infection in the process. Unforeseen complications from anesthesia, which were impossible to foresee, could have arisen, which concerned him, but he quickly dismissed them. He intended a full and beautiful life for his patient when he made the first cut, but this young man died under his care, with his very essence extinguished. It was that apprehension that filled him now.

Christian became more determined to pontificate once his leadership was secure; he instructed his new students on the benefits of deception and the value of presentation. The guard who blocked entrance to the city center would be the first barrier that they must hurdle.

Self-assuredness and a sense of obligation were key for Katarina, but a groveling posture was essential for the doctor. Since Katarina never had to live in a ghetto or face discrimination as a Jew, she would have no problem assuming an air of superiority, even though her sweet nature oozed a certain level of compliance that had to be overridden.

Rudolph did have experience groveling, not only because he was a resident in this hellhole, but also because he had to survive in Prague even before the Nazis took power. As a doctor, he also had an informed air buzzing around him. He still possessed a take-charge attitude for possible chaotic situations that could potentially surface. This had to be sublimated.

The lessons were over, and the tardy bell was soon at hand. It was now time for the test. Rudolph put the numbing solution on his long index finger, which Naomi sucked up greedily. With the extra milk stored in Katarina's briefcase, the group of misfits was ready to go.

Little Naomi's grandmother, Etta, lovingly tucked her in the tight enclosure that must have felt womb-like to the child, because her fussing ceased when she rested in her enclosed space. She was a tiny baby and fit amazingly well in the manipulated box.

Naomi's dejected grandmother quickly turned from the singular child of her recently deceased daughter and moved heavy-footed toward the adjacent apartment of mourning without looking back. Shedding tears of sorrow for her daughter Naomi was expected, and she anticipated comfort from her neighbors once she walked across the threshold to the other room.

Rudolph Bonn, Christian, Katarina, and a hidden Naomi tiptoed down the creaky steps and into the gray, windswept street toward the bundled sentry on duty. No words were spoken as they inched closer to the looming guard. It was a raw day, and everyone passing preferred to try to block the wind by tucking their chins as close to their chests as possible rather than getting whipped by the bitter-cold elements.

Rudolph also kept his head down and barely noticed the passing people who had their heads bowed as well as him. Christian was surprised at how Katarina did not seem to be affected by the tension, but moved her arms back and forth while holding the basket, which resembled a rocking cradle. Her sudden fearlessness gave Christian hope as they approached the disheveled guard with his bulky winter uniform and cap that was too large and fancy for his tiny, simple head.

"Halt," barked the sentry as they moved into his perimeter of control. His pistol, which they all saw bulging from his side by his thick, strapping belt, drew the group's attention.

"Papers," he demanded with brevity of words.

Christian gave their individual documents, and Katarina added the essential paper that had been painstakingly prepared.

As Naomi gurgled in conjunction with the slight wind that swept by, Christian cleared his throat concurrently.

The guard then looked Katarina up and down in what could have been construed as a leer while he said, "Bert told me you would be by today, but he did not mention anything about the group who is obviously with you. You two move to the side, please, while I double-check my books."

The error of not mentioning her relationship with the previous guard on duty to Dr. Bonn or Christian appeared sooner than Katarina had feared. She knew she had to quickly inject, "Of course he would not mention it, because these people are not going out for coffee with Bert or me. They are not staying with us while we walk the streets of Prague at twilight and glance at the castle in the distance for a connection with local history. These gentlemen are with me on business. Dr. Bonn is needed for a consultation at the Office of Social Services, and Christian accompanies me once every couple of times to keep an eye on me, I presume this time because this Jew-man is with us and therefore I cannot be alone with him. Actually, I had not mentioned meeting Bert to my superiors, so I hope we can pass today and not have you tell my little secret about being linked to your friend.

"I was intending to mention to Bert that I have an attractive neighbor Lulu, who has recently confessed to me that she has been longing to meet someone with whom she could have fun in these sour times. She is not as lucky as me about meeting a fabulous gentleman who is charming and a pleasure to be with like Bert. Why don't you talk to Bert, and I will talk to Lulu to see if we could all four go on a promenade one night? Most people who meet Lulu really like her."

This enticement was just what the married, but lonely, guard needed to quickly write the day pass and get them on their way.

He called out to Dr. Bonn, "I will be looking for you tonight, Jew," and added to Katarina, "I plan on joining you and Bert in the very near future with that silly-named girlfriend Lulu that you mentioned. Do not forget about this, young fräulein. I have done you an obvious favor and expect a payment in regard to a night on the town with your girlfriend. I will be talking to Bert later. One never should even attempt to tempt a soldier of the motherland without the might to back it up by actions. We are the iron fist here, and do not forget it."

The three figures strode toward the wider street ahead as Katarina waved in assent to the guard who was left leering at her from the distance.

Once they turned the corner, Christian added, "I sure hope there is a Lulu, and could there be anything else you forgot to mention, young lady?"

Katarina's confidence melted away as they walked farther from the guard. "I did not think it was anybody's business that I was seeing Bert. I only agreed to have coffee with him because he was a guard and I thought it might come in handy. It turns out he is a gentleman, and I do not think he would do any of us harm. Of course there is a Lulu, who really is my neighbor. I do not think it will be a stretch to get her to go out with some friends of mine. Captain August is a dangerous man who scares me for good reason and probably scares Mlle. Zelinsky for similar reasons. I have a feeling that I might have saved our precarious plan from disaster, not caused it."

Christian quickly added, "I am not interested in fault. You were cool under pressure, and I admire that. If you want to continue working with my underground group, we would appreciate it. I am not condemning you by any means. I just am not fond of surprises." Christian imparted these words while walking toward the next surprise in a long day of surprises.

Naomi slept peacefully as they moved along the streets, unaware of the perils around her. It was 3:15 p.m. when they scurried into the Office of Social Services. Eva Zelinsky had been looking out the barren window to the street below for almost an hour. It was as if she were hovering over a pot, waiting anxiously for the water to boil even though it was not nearly hot enough.

Eva's limited concentration was only for this man whom she perceived as her savior, even though he probably was a false messiah. She saw him quickly walk around the corner and enter her street. She noticed his familiar gait, his unfamiliar tattered coat, and his entourage as he moved toward her. She walked to the bleak outer office and just stood in front of the desk, staring at the closed door in front of her. She knew salvation was close, and her breathing quickened when she heard a hand on the doorknob and saw it turn in a clockwise motion, setting time on pause. She clasped her hands together in front of her favorite dress to try to control her unabashed desire to wrap those hands around her Doctor Bonn, who had silently disappeared from her universe, slinking away with the other Jews in the dead of night.

Her eyes widened in surprise when a threesome appeared before her. Shocked, she settled her glance on what must have been Rudolph, even though the man barely resembled the one whom she saw blurred in the distance. Her cherished man looked fifteen years older than at their last meeting; with tattered old gray clothes, worn shoes that did not even look like they were of leather, and a dark green jacket that had more discolored stains on it than not. She burst into tears.

"Mlle. Zelinsky," said Katarina, thinking the woman's tears were for the extra person plus the infant in her arms, "this is a strong man who will force Captain August to succumb. I am overjoyed he is here to help us. And this baby just needs to be placed in a home, which is something this office is known to do."

"What are you saying?" cried Eva, who began frantically searching for the crumpled tissue that she had carelessly left in her pocket earlier. She had not really focused on what Katarina was talking about, and tried to do it now, although she seemingly was incapable of it because she kept bouncing back to look at Dr. Bonn.

"Please, Mademoiselle, we must quickly come to a consensus of what is to be accomplished before Captain August arrives," said Dr. Bonn.

Katarina could not figure out why her superior had such a shaky, emotional outburst. Dr. Bonn, sensing Eva's confusion, continued with his more detailed explanation of why this odd assortment of souls had arrived in her office practically unannounced. He was unaware as well that it was only his shocking presence that had unnerved this normally sedate woman.

"The woven basket that Katarina holds has cargo that breathes and has a heartbeat. It is my newborn daughter who is in there, waiting to be placed with a loving non-Jewish family until I can be reunited with her. This gentleman, surprisingly named Christian, is here to help in your plan to eliminate Captain August, who seems to be plaguing this office to such an extent that serious measures were considered by you and you asked for Katarina's assistance, as she has asked for ours. We are all here to help you."

The doctor then explained to Eva that the proposed air injection would render the officer helpless and possibly kill him, although almost death was not good enough when dealing with a Nazi regime that would strike back at them with more force than a little injection. Because of August's officer status, this plan had to be done with agility and sureness, which was why the able-bodied Christian was with them. He offered his help because he was convinced that two strong men were needed to pull off this caper. With only two women and a Jewish doctor, it would be a suicide mission, and he could not condone that.

Eva Zelinsky groped for her rickety chair to listen to the scheme that had only been a storybook in her mind when she assumed fruition was not possible. Her dream of her messiah saving her was not drenched in realism. Now she saw that this weak man could not be anyone's hero, and she felt like she was listing on a sinking ship. Her momentary razor focus wavered as she glanced at the ragtag group that was standing before her.

Christian took over. "As soon as Captain August enters the office, everything must move with the utmost speed. As an experienced officer, he will immediately sense that something is out of the ordinary. Do you normally sit in the front area?" he inquired of Katarina.

After her nod of assent, he matter-of-factly added the rest of the scenario. "Dr. Bonn will be my backup, but the basic plan is that I will disarm and render Captain August defenseless, as I have previously done to other large, strong Nazis. You must trust me on this. Rudolph will give him the injection of air, and we will wait to see the outcome from this. He could die within seconds or, at the least, be paralyzed for a few minutes. It is when he is in this incapacitated state that Rudolph and I will move him to the platform by the metal and wood steps and kick him down to the bottom area with the force of two grown men. I do not expect him to survive his journey, but we will run down those steps and confirm his demise or cause it. He will end up dead as a doornail, even if by chance, he happened to be breathing after the fall.

"Mlle. Zelinsky, this is important: you must call headquarters and inform them of his heart attack, which is the story you must tell. Falling down steps while having a heart attack will seem very plausible, even for the Germans. I will be here with all of you for assistance until that call is made, and then this team is on its own to scatter, as it will. Dr. Bonn will unfortunately return to the ghetto alone. You women will deal with placement for the infant in a home, and I will move on to my next assignment. If you should ever happen to see me again, I assume you know how to feign ignorance of knowing me. I will not recognize you at all, I promise you that."

Eva's head was spinning with the intrigue that had been quickly presented to her. Processing this information was impossible for her, although her colleagues were not privy to this fact.

Christian knew as soon as the door opened that she was not functioning as well as most people who were in her position of management. He assumed that the repeated rapes had taken their toll on her psyche.

Dr. Bonn always knew that Eva was on the nervous side, but he was surprised that she was in such bad shape. Her eyes had an intense, crazy look, and she kept jutting out her neck as if constantly bobbing for apples that never materialized.

Katarina had been dealing with her oddness most recently and knew each time she saw her that she was seriously sliding down the slippery slope of sanity. Standing alongside the strong Christian and kindly Dr. Bonn gave Katarina some relief from the flood of fear that gripped her whenever she glanced at her boss. She was lucky to have them to strong-arm this Nazi criminal.

Becoming embroiled in a murder scheme put her in an out-of-body state. She was watching everything from outside the office, getting ready to participate and join herself as a mannequin inside the office crime scene. She was far over her capabilities in this matter and was slowly realizing the truly desperate situation that had evolved while she was busy bustling around the ghetto, oblivious to these many dangers.

Eva was anxiously formulating possible questions in her mind about the baby, as well as trying to decide when she should reveal that Dr. Bonn had to stay with her, when heavy footfalls were faintly heard through the old wooden door, with its frosted glass top section.

The two women looked like they had just been struck by one of those trucks that had been grabbing young men around town and never slowed down for anything else.

Christian fiercely planted his feet on the floor and crouched behind the door, which would block him when it opened.

Dr. Bonn simply raised his eyes and blankly looked at the ceiling as his jaw slackened and his mouth opened slightly while hiding by Christian and holding the syringe he had quickly procured from his pocket.

Captain August whistled through his pursed lips as he bounded up the wide stairway that graced the old building. Did he want youthful naiveté today or the uptight Eva, who housed soft, abundant breasts under a crisply ironed shirt? He slowed his gait as he pondered his sexual preferences. The young Katarina would be a firecracker in the future; he was sure of that. She was where his ultimate desires would find a home while he was stranded in this city of stupid people. It was essential to keep Eva in her place, though, while he groomed the young one, and he knew just how to do that.

He was picturing the somewhat plump Eva with the big elephant tears rolling down her swollen face and her solid legs spread open wide as he convinced himself of where he would begin his escapades this day. With these sensual taunts that livened his step, he grabbed the rock-hard, smoothly polished marble handle and turned it with a fast screwlike motion, then walked into the front area of the Prague Office of Social Services.

Katarina stood two feet in front of him with a wide-eyed expression. Maybe he was wrong about her sexual reluctance; she sensed his supreme virility, a strength that surpassed that of any silly youth that this inferior country housed.

His mind did not initially register the arms that appeared from his flank and grabbed him while rendering those arms of his as useless as if he had lost the limbs in an explosion on the battlefield. He quickly became horrified that other hands were in the room to entrap and not entice. His muscle memory overtook his inert appendages with a powerful explosion of energy that inched his attacker to his peripheral vision.

With Katarina still in his path, he turned slightly to kick her with the full force of his ironlike foot. She was thrown backward and into the office of Mlle. Zelinsky, who had simultaneously opened her door when she heard the rumble from the outer office.

Eva's hatred for August filled her with a courage that had slowly built up while hearing the footfalls that heralded his presence. She wanted to see him helpless, just as she'd appeared every time he touched her.

Meanwhile, the captain registered that this second man who lurked in the corner was gripping a small needlelike object. He bent at the waist and boomeranged his taut body around while using his head to knock down Bonn.

The doctor, whose strength was more like that of a frail woman, not a mature man, doubled over in pain; he dropped the syringe, which slowly rolled in front of Christian, who was still trying to hold desperately on to the arms entangled with his.

When Christian loosened one arm to grab the syringe, the captain advanced like a lightning strike. Using a hand that barely managed to free itself, he grabbed his pistol, which was never far from him. He then latched on to the weapon now in his arsenal and shot Dr. Bonn right through his open mouth, which was just beginning to form a scream.

The doctor's blood splattered the room and all of its occupants in a sudden gust of red spray. The always obliging Dr. Bonn did not last but a few minutes in the melee that had ensued once the captain entered the fray.

The surrounding space took on a rosy tinge, with dabs of dripping blood decorating the walls as well as its freaked occupants. Thick membranes dangled from the ceiling above like spiderwebs that entrapped weighty bug parts. The globs defied the laws of gravity as they patiently waited to send their drooping parts languidly to the ground below.

When August turned his twisted body toward Christian and aimed his pistol in his final strike on the other attacker, Eva galloped toward him with an old metal rectangular paper punch, which was the only heavy possession that she could muster so quickly. The sight of her beloved Rudolph frozen in an awkward death pose gave her some needed strength, which she had been lacking as of late. She had finally laid eyes on her beloved doctor, and even though she fretted about his sorry state, he had the potential of being nourished by her love and revived through her interest.

Eva growled with a vengeance as she barreled toward August. She felt empowered as she ran to him like a banshee into battle. She did not want him on the same earth she occupied. Her prop, that is, the paper punch, had been put neatly on her desk in the same place every day at work, so she knew right where it would be when she needed to grab this newfound weapon of destruction.

She ran toward her prey with both hands holding the metal above her head, ready to strike. She swung it into Captain August's greasy round orb, which was directly below her arms. The bang on August's head stunned him and made a dent that would pop out as an egg within a short amount of time, but it did not curtail his drive to kill the enemies who surrounded him.

With Herculean strength, he pivoted around with the same gun that had just been fired at Rudolph, and he shot Eva in a clear trajectory right through the heart. The maneuver reminded him of his early training with wine bottles and fry pans in his sacred Germany. He was aiming for her forehead, but his vision was somewhat compromised due to his recent head injury that had been delivered to him by the bitch before her demise.

Within a split second of that shot, the room started spinning, and nausea followed fast for August. His dizziness gave just enough time for Christian to grab the captain's gun-holding arm and break that limb with a crack that filled the office. His deep scream entered the street below as the captain collapsed to the floor in his own fluids.

The street below was where Bert had decided to position himself as a new sentry. His plan was to surprise Katarina when she left work that day. He was well aware of her office's location and had casually exercised by it numerous times, even though she was unaware of this strategic maneuver.

Once, on a whim, he had even gone upstairs, curious to see what Katarina's employer was like. What confronted him was a severe-looking woman wearing layers of clothes that were much too warm for the temperature of the tepid office. She severely marched into the front area, where Katarina must have sat, and with icy tones curtly asked what he wanted, obviously aware of his enlisted status. She reminded him of the old schoolmarms that had previously tried to impart some unwanted learning to him. He had no desire to entertain any type of conversation with her.

He looked around at the dingy office with gray paint on every wall and was happy to think that Katarina would not have to stay in that place for much longer.

He had been having difficulty concentrating at work and could not erase her image during the day or at night while he rested on his cot awaiting his elusive sleep. He was coming to the realization that he was smitten by her wiles.

He loved the way she slowly smiled, which immediately lit her beaming face, and he loved her raven curls and dancing green eyes. He was determined to take her home with him as if a lost puppy. These strong feelings surpassed any earlier wish that he had about simply having a fling with this local girl.

She attained superior status from the other city girls that his fellow soldiers slandered in the barracks. He even yearned to have the small-minded people in his town look at the great Prague beauty whom he had won in the spoils of war after fighting for his motherland.

All aspects of his love and chance meeting of Katarina were layering quickly in his mind. He felt he had been bestowed a love token in this war-torn nation where he was stuck as a sentry to hell. He had no experience with a cosmopolitan girl who had been raised with a servant, as well as able-bodied parents who chose to let another do their cooking and cleaning. She spoke like a trained thespian, she moved like a dancer, and she charged into her job with no cares of its dangers, which were obvious to everyone but her. No one like Katarina had ever given him the time of day or even a wink of acknowledgment. He wanted to put her in his pocket for keeps, just like a precious watch.

He did not want the war to stop his newfound love affair. Whether victorious or defeated in battle, he wanted amnesty with Katarina. And if the war were to extinguish his life or his spirit, he needed to have as much time as he could with his Prague beauty. So, it was not surprising that he appeared outside her office building that random day.

"I am just curious about the government offices here," Bert mentioned to Mlle. Zelinsky on the day he toured the Office of Social Services. "I have no plans to disturb you. Have a nice day," Bert curtly said as he left the office before noticing the sweat that was beginning to form around the hairline of Mlle. Zelinsky, who did not trust for one second anything that boy had uttered.

Bert was jolted into the present with a scream from the office above him. He carefully cocked his Ceska Zbrojovka vz 27 pistol, which was manufactured in the area and issued to the German Army. He was not that familiar with the weapon, but he drew it from his holster and ran up the stairs to the unknown.

Bert was almost halfway up the stairs when he slowed his gait and became more alert to the quieter sounds of danger. He had to use his soldier skills, which were not completely mastered as of yet. Thoughts of Katarina made him more cautious. He feared his errors might endanger her, and he was sure she was there. He did not want to take any chance of making any mistake as long as Katarina was involved.

The large office door was shut to the Office of Social Services, and he tried peering into the frosted top area. It gave him only a blurred palate of colors in odd patterns. He remembered his youthful escapades of cowboys and bad guys, so he calculatingly tromped down the steps to try to fool the person behind the door, who he knew was up to no good. He then tiptoed back to the landing and arrived at the door when Katarina suddenly peered through a crack that appeared as she eased the door open a minute amount.

"Why, Bert, what a surprise," she said in a higher than normal register. "What are you doing here?" she added with a futile attempt to normalize an obviously wrong scenario.

Before Bert had initially run up the steps, Christian had somehow managed to get the captain in an incapacitating hold through the vomit that encased both of them. After dragging the captain into Mlle. Zelinsky's office, he nudged Katarina gently awake with his foot, as he kept August quiet with a gun in his mouth that was shared with regurgitated food. Katarina screamed when she was jolted into the present as she turned her glance to the dead bodies. When she saw Captain August attempt to move his mouth muscles from under the form of the gun, she silenced herself immediately.

"Someone is coming," hissed Christian as he inched the captain over to the sidewall. "You will have to answer the door," he whispered to the frantic-looking Katarina. "It will be OK, Katarina; I know you can do this," he said while trying to sound encouraging.

The three resembled Rodin's sculpture of three bodies called *The Gates of Hell*. Why Katarina remembered that image from her one art history class, she had no idea, but thankfully it filled her head so other things could not enter. The three bodies were connected yet disparate in awaiting their entrance to hell, where they would reside forever to be tortured.

All of the living listened to the oncoming steps and then heard them slowly backing away. Katarina faintly recognized the imminent creaking step, which announced immediate arrivals. She knew the phantom had moved back up the stairway. She decided to confront her fate and sheepishly opened the devil's door as if soon to go to slaughter.

She never expected to see the soldier who stared at her in disbelief.

"Why, Bert, what a surprise," choked Katarina in a false semblance of normalcy. "What are you doing here? And put that gun away!" she said with as much authority as she could muster.

"Katarina! I heard the screams," he whispered to her as he bent toward her left ear, which appeared behind her disheveled dark curls and blood-splattered face.

"I am coming into the office," he added while pushing the door open with a force that Katarina was unable to block.

"Bert, I told you I would see you la..." she tried to get out of her fumbling mouth as he continued to push the door open to a carnage that even he did not expect. He was dumbfounded seeing a Nazi captain incapacitated with a gun protruding from his mouth.

It was right after those brief moments when Bert was pushing the door open and quietly conversing with Katarina that Christian had thrown out his leg and actually tripped young Bert, whose espionage training had only been the boyhood variety. Bert was totally thrown off-balance by the foot that came from an unforeseen spot that even his high alert status could not sense. His vz 27 slipped out of his hand.

Christian was prepared for the weight that had fallen in front of him and instantly stomped on Bert's heaving chest with his available foot and kept him captive with his powerful leg strength.

"Grab his gun," shouted Christian to Katarina; Christian was tangled with August and Bert on both ends and could not garner another move unless he loosened his hold on his two captives.

Simultaneously, Bert and Katarina lunged for the solitary gun that was placed within an inch of Bert's outstretched fingers. August then valiantly tried to free himself from the grip of Christian. He knew his only chance was during the ongoing distraction.

Christian's leg hold on Bert unfortunately became loose, which was inevitable once August began stirring. Katarina froze when she saw Bert's fingers stretch like a rubber band toward the pistol, which had previously been in no-man's-land. No one could stop him from worming over to the gun. Eventually, Bert's outstretched hand connected with the weapon.

"I will shoot her," spurted the splayed words from Bert's youthful mouth, "if you do not let the captain go."

Bert surprised himself even more than Katarina when the words slimed out of his mouth. Every cell in his body knew as soon as "I will shoot her" had been uttered, there was no way in heaven or hell that he would actually pull the trigger. It was his fatal error to say it. Katarina's sobs became uncontrollable.

No shot came from Bert's weapon. All quickly realized that he was not going to maim this beautiful young girl, even though he'd threatened it in the heat of battle. Realizing his error, Bert changed tack and whipped away from Katarina. He decidedly aimed his gun now toward the two men standing with their backs to him.

Christian's weapon remained in August's mouth as Bert switched his gun barrel toward Christian's back. Katarina was frozen, paralyzed by the horrors that had evolved in front of her previously innocent eyes.

"My hand could never pull the trigger, Katarina. I love you," said Bert in a barely audible tone, realizing that he might have just signed his own death certificate, rather than hers, but he no longer cared.

Through her sobs, Katarina looked at Bert and confessed, "This captain who you see stuffed with a gun in his disgusting mouth raped me, killed Mlle. Zelinsky, and murdered Dr. Bonn. How could you even consider helping such a man or shooting me?"

Bert then twisted his head around to look at the carnage that was before him in this normally sterile government office. He now focused on the membranes, the bloody surfaces, and the bodies around him. The corpse of the uptight Mlle. Zelinsky sloppily slumped on the ground in a state of rigor mortis, while a male body was faceless in death repose nearby. Goopy membranes were strewn across the walls and on the clothes of Katarina and this stranger, with whom she was obviously in cahoots.

Bert concluded that he was in one of those precarious situations that other soldiers mention when sipping coffee and letting down their guard. He was stuck in a vise where nothing he could do would culminate in even partial success.

Whether this way or that, the path of the next few minutes would lead to unknown territory. He had lost more than the hope of winning virginity from this dream girl. He had almost destroyed the one who he prayed would accompany him back home as his beloved wife.

Bert feared that Katarina could never erase the imprint of the gun that he'd pointed toward her in anguish earlier. He tried unsuccessfully to reverse time by speedily moving the gun away from her friend, but that did not work either. If she were to die in this tomb, he would rather be a part of the carnage with her than be alone.

The original target of Christian's back transformed with a slight movement into a bull's-eye now aimed at the captive officer. Bert's blundering moves, his instant rage over Katarina's rape, and the chaos occurring around him caused his hand to power as if under a Ouija board's spell. He altered his aim, zeroing in on Captain August during a brief second of mindlessness.

Christian's gun fired into the captain's mouth a split second after the shot rang out from Bert's weapon, which pierced August's upper shoulder. Captain August was no longer a threat to anyone.

The gun tumbled from Bert's hand as he waited for the crack of a new bullet that he assumed would be aimed toward him, but nothing filled the air. A perfect silence ensued while those barely breathing tried to soak in the violence that had disrupted the tentative calm that had started their morning so very long ago. Soon Katarina's heavy intake of loud breath shook them from their reverie and caused the three survivors to survey the bloody mess.

It had become obvious to Christian that this sentry was blindly in love with the young Katarina and that to somehow use him was the only exit plan that made sense in their dire situation.

Christian spoke first as he looked directly at Bert and asked, "How far into this muck are you willing to sink, soldier? Katarina's life is by no means secure right now. It is in serious jeopardy, with only you between her and the entire Nazi army's revenge. If you intend to ever assist her, now is the time of reckoning."

Katarina irrationally got anxious about being beholden to anyone, especially a Nazi. She futilely tried to assert her independence from all present by proclaiming through her tears, "I do not need anyone's help. I am just going to walk out of here and go home."

That statement made the two survivors flanking her realize how scared and naïve she truly was about the consequences of their actions. She would not survive long in this intrinsically messed-up scenario even though she'd created most of it. She needed more than the help of the two profoundly different men before her. She needed a miracle.

"Home," they both chimed in, "is not an option," added Bert. He sadly understood that home, whether in Germany or in Prague, would not occur for him either as he looked around the soiled room.

"I will do whatever it takes to extricate Katarina from this death sentence," said Bert as the muffled cries of a baby startled him.

Nobody had paid attention to the infant's cries previously. They had been buried beneath the awkward sounds of the death gurgles emitted from Mlle. Zelinsky, Dr. Bonn, and the Nazi conqueror, August, as well as the tense air that thickened the atmosphere and deadened the child's delicate utterances.

Now all eyes tried to locate the spot that was teeming with high-pitched crackles. Katarina slowly heaved herself up to her knees and reached past the inert body of Eva Zelinsky. Mlle. Zelinsky's arm had unnaturally draped itself over an enclosure that originally held tomatoes and now held an even more precious cargo. The arm had been successful in keeping the lid down while giving some warmth and padding to the noisy contents inside.

Katarina's hand was now frantically scratching the covered lid as Christian respectfully stepped over the sprawled corpses. He moved Katarina's arm aside as he scooped up the contents and managed a smile for the crying baby now residing in his worn and tired arms.

The sight of the infant girl vanquished the carnage around them. Here was a new life, and everyone in the room hoped that if life were an option for this babe, no matter what the consequences were for them, they would opt it for her. It might help justify the deaths if this innocent child could live free.

Neither Christian nor Katarina wanted those who had perished to do so in vain, especially Naomi's father, who had risked everything he had, including his own life, for her safety.

"Let me introduce you to Naomi Bonn," Christian said to Bert while he rocked the infant, who suddenly stopped her fussing. "Her father's remains lie before you, and her mother died a natural death, something that almost seems unnatural in these fragile times. Should we put our heads together as a team and figure out how to get out of the tightening hold that is strangling all of us now? Can we come out of this with one another's help? Are you capable of collaborating with us, Bert?"

Once the lovesick Bert had made his leap over the great divide to his maiden's side, it was not that hard a step for him to make this decision.

"You are right, sir. We might have a slim chance of success if we can work quickly to find a way out of this mess. Even though my uniform says otherwise, my loyalty toward Katarina was pronounced when I aimed my pistol at a commanding officer. I will not waver in these final steps to somehow manage to get at least Katarina and the baby out alive. I promise I will see this through for her and am going to work with you, not against you. I am giving you permission to use my status as a soldier in the Third Reich to your advantage in order to ease out of this disaster," he said with an amazing amount of sudden self-assuredness.

"I have no moral dilemma over this decision. I would gladly murder Captain August again if I had the opportunity," he added while looking off in Katarina's direction. "I have seen horrific things I never thought possible. I admit that a disillusioned soldier stands before you. I am not saying I have had a complete change of heart because, as you see, I wear the German Nazi uniform, and I do not plan to take it off until this conflict is done. I realize that I am a pawn in many games here, but I am also a proud German. I will not kill more of my own countrymen, but I will make a stand with you now for the woman I love and will work to do anything that can get that love returned.

"The war has me jaded, and I want my humanity back, even if it is in only a small parcel. The day I met Katarina was the day I became fortified with a stronger purpose for my life, even if it took me a bit to realize it. Give me a chance to prove my loyalty to you, even though I make no future promises to help others against the regime."

Katarina and Christian listened intently to Bert pouring out his heart toward Katarina, who sat soaked before him in bloodstained clothing, not uttering a word. The only thing that really came close to keeping her focus was the baby.

Katarina was conflicted in her thoughts, but focused in her gaze toward the resting infant, who looked almost angelic. She sensed the stare of Christian's bright blue eyes in her peripheral vision hovering above the child.

She looked at Naomi's small face and remembered her doll at home, which was now stuffed in a box in the back of her wardrobe. The doll was supposed to be a newborn baby, which was quite a different presentation than the other ones that she played with using her china tea set adorned with gold shamrocks. She would sit on her miniature chair, at her miniature table, and have hours of enjoyment. She adored that doll, and she never really outgrew it, which was why it still occupied coveted space in her limited wardrobe. She just wanted to be sitting by that little table cuddling her newborn doll, not sitting here facing a bleak future while staring at the real thing.

Meanwhile, Christian only planned to trust this soldier as long as he had his gun handy and his iron will intact. He understood the German status this boy had. Bert was still a young boy, although he pretended otherwise with the silly, elaborate uniform that adorned him. Christian needed to keep Bert thinking like a boy and not acting like a soldier whatever ensued.

Parts of the original plan had already vaporized before solidifying a new one, but the one thing that did not change was that German Headquarters still had to be alerted of the murder of one of their own. This tricky dance of getting everyone who was presently still breathing out of this office alive was going to have to be carefully choreographed, especially in regard to Katarina and Naomi. He assumed in regard to himself that it would be fairly easy to just slip away, as he had done many times before on previous missions. He had a plan.

Katarina's shaking began with her teeth chattering as soon as she heard the strained sound of the Gestapo's siren inching toward her. Her teeth clanged so much that her body started to pick up the rhythm of the syncopated beat. She had practiced her part a half dozen times with Christian and Bert in the previous sixty minutes when they had hashed out the details. It did not instill security though.

It was agreed that Naomi's safety had to be the goal of this new team, which was trying so hard to trust one another.

Christian had a sister who had taken the identity of a Ukrainian named Inna Nobis Gerse, who had secretly left for England before her own country was invaded. Inna had no intention of living through any type of conflict with a husband who repulsed her with his coarse manners and greasy hair.

It was with this unkempt man that Christian's beautiful, Jewish sister was forced to live in a state of matrimony when his family paid for papers that gave her a way out of a desperate situation. His sister's life was successfully spared by this deception, because she had never even stepped foot in the stuffed ghetto when the rest of the Jewish population had been corralled there. An elaborate plan was hatched that actually had his sister supposedly buried in a coffin, which thankfully was empty. The family had registered her death certificate in the city records.

Christian and his parents had mixed emotions as they reluctantly sent the statuesque beauty to live with Johann, the real Inna's husband. At the time, there were many vocal Jewish community members who felt that times might get rough, but never so critical that lives would be extinguished. Christian felt otherwise and convinced his parents to send their Deborah to live as Inna. Deborah had little say in this decision but abided with her parents' wishes and moved out of the family home.

Life was not easy for this well-bred Jewess, but being aware of how degrading it was for her family in the ghetto, she tried never to complain and to be a civil companion to Johann. Johann's manners were more than coarse; they were barely civilized. His clothes were always filled with a little potato smear or some juice that had dripped from his drooling mouth while he ate his sauerkraut and talked at the same time. She constantly washed his attire, but he was so quick to dirty it that it appeared she never could even get it into the soapy washbasin. His hair was always too long and in need of a washing, but he would not compromise on this issue.

After four months of crying off and on during her occasional moments of solitude, she was finally able to discern a little good in his heart. His heart was what she assumed initially made him risk his life for her and be involved in duplicity of sorts. It never occurred to her that it was because she appeared so delicate and beautiful with her long, wavy, light brown hair, her striking brown eyes, or her Caucasian features that did not look at all Semitic like the posters all around Prague informing the populace how to spot Jews. Johann Gerse was immensely happy in his present marital state because the obvious repulsion from his first wife grated on him as well.

Christian's plan for little Naomi was to give the infant to his sister and Johann for safekeeping. She was a newborn, and it would be easy for Inna to register the child with the Nazi bureaucracy as her own. He knew Inna was always scared and rarely ventured out except under deep cover. Her neighbors were completely unknown to her, so they would not have noticed any type of growing bump that could have been forming under Inna's bulky attire. Nobody would be surprised if the young wife had conceived a child.

His worries centered on Johann, the slob. He suspected that Johann would agree to accept the infant, because he knew that his sister was his spoil of war and there would be more of a chance of her sticking around when life returned to normal if there were a child to glue her to him. Inna had insinuated that Johann was pressuring her to have a baby, but she was so thankful that she was unable to conceive. Her body must have been in tune to how unhappy her soul was during this time of conflict.

Naomi had the potential of a safe haven with them. Christian would deposit the baby himself after talking to Inna that night at her apartment.

Bert's friends knew that he was to meet Katarina later that afternoon, so that piece of information would be corroborated if a task force decided to pursue the story that they would soon receive from Katarina and Bert. Nobody would think it odd for Bert to arrive at the office a tad early for his date with Katarina, which was what Bert planned to tell the officer in charge who arrived at the scene.

The three planners were like huddled children thinking up lies to tell their all-knowing parents. The hope was that the Nazis were not as clever as any of their knowledgeable parents had been.

Christian decided that Bert would call headquarters to tell them that the Prague Social Services Director had shot Captain August before Bert had even arrived there for his intended rendezvous with an office employee. When the arriving soldiers saw another man dead, the plan was that it would be inconsequential to the Gestapo because the dead man was a Jew. Civilians, and especially military personnel, felt that it was no big deal if one popped up slaughtered on the street or otherwise decimated. Shooting a Jew did not seem too much of a problem for anyone within the Reich's reach. If it made the military happier, they could even blame the entire fiasco on Dr. Bonn. From their viewpoint, it should be just one less Jew who needed to be eliminated, so either way the good doctor was not really at issue in this case.

Once headquarters was notified, Bert was ordered not to touch a thing, but simply keep the young lady on the scene and relax until personnel arrived. The "relax" part had elicited the only bit of levity that the three on the other end of the phone line had experienced in hours.

The Gestapo arrived with horns blazing and doors flipping open, then cracking shut. Whether Jewish, Gypsy, homosexual, learning disabled, or simply at home in one's kitchen, the wail of the sirens brought fear to those who heard it.

Even though Katarina's ears were in tune to their footfalls ascending the steps, she still registered shock when the door opened, and six looming men in dark black uniforms with high shiny boots marched into the dimly lit office with their loaded guns all aiming at her.

All of the blood drained out of her face, and she stopped shaking because she was now frozen in fear. She had never been aware such an anxiety existed before the door smashed open.

Bert instantly clicked his heals and saluted the officers. They responded with a resounding, "Heil Hitler!" and clicked their boots simultaneously, but kept their weapons still aimed toward a combination of mainly Katarina but also a wary Bert, who was within their gunsights.

Christian had snuck out moments earlier, with Naomi safely tucked in her somewhat rotten tomato enclosure doused with those odd, delicate flavors that were lovingly rubbed in by her grandmother. The vision of her father, dead in a pool of blood, would only appear to her in a dreamlike trance many decades later that was brought on by the scent of cinnamon for some reason.

"Explain," the Gestapo officer in charge curtly demanded, and Bert hurriedly obliged.

He told them how the bodies actually told the story themselves, with Dr. Bonn's gun lying near his corpse and Mlle. Zelinsky looking like she was tossing something before her death pose sculpted her.

"My friend Katarina is really the hero in this room, sir," sputtered Bert. "She brought the doctor to the office at the request of Mlle. Zelinsky, her superior, having no idea what her plan w—"

The Gestapo officer cut Bert off in midsentence, turned to Katarina, and pointedly said, "She will give me her account in a moment. Soldier, the two of us will chat later. At this time, I want you to go to headquarters accompanied by two of my men and wait for me there. Since this is an investigation of a murder, please hand over your gun," he added as he waved off Bert with a flick of his hand.

Bert was shocked that they sent him to headquarters under guard, even though Christian had been convinced of the inevitability of this happening and had warned Bert and Katarina to be prepared. Bert paid no attention to the warning though and assured Katarina that she would not be left alone, while dismissing Christian's words as "improbable."

As to what Christian thought would happen next, there were lots of possibilities, depending on the answers from

Katarina and Bert and the kind of man that the Gestapo put in charge of the case. Christian refused to be specific, since Bert had no intention of paying much stock to what he said anyway.

The SS officer dipped his head toward Katarina to continue the dialogue begun by Bert.

Katarina's eyes exhibited her complete panic as the scary soldiers led off Bert to headquarters. Her nose began to drip as she tried to hold her tears back. She kept pinching her nose, hoping to stop the flow that started falling into her open mouth and trickling down her raised arm.

The Gestapo officer surveyed the scene and was well aware that no matter what either of the witnesses proclaimed as true, he knew that they were lying the minute they opened their mouths. His desires fell in places other than hearing anyone's false statements as he looked at the carnage before him.

The open mouth of Captain August showed a different story, with damage done by more of a professional than an out-of-shape doctor, a stocky female director, and a pretty young girl. The naive soldier played more of a part than he was saying, or another skilled person was at the scene.

The Gestapo officer knew Germany needed its entire cache of soldiers for battle, especially in losing fronts, so he wanted to be clever about dishing out justice for this fighter.

The young girl was more at fault than she admitted. With only a few remaining men left in the office, he quickly dismissed them to act as sentries outside the door. He took off his hat, which always felt a tad loose, and moved toward Katarina. His coat slipped off his shoulders while he encased his arms tightly around the shaking girl and murmured, "Don't worry, my little flowering bud. This will not take long and will be the most pleasure you will have for a while."

His hold became a stronger vise, his eyes became steely, and he added, "One sound from you, dear girl, and your corpse will be added to the cart that will shortly arrive to collect these quite dead bodies."

Katarina closed her eyes and kept repeating the mantra "War is hell" over and over and over. She knew that he was right and it would be over fast if she just kept her mind occupied with the mantra.

Within moments, the Gestapo leader was outside the Social Services office telling his few remaining men that when they finished with the girl, they were to take her to the new camp Terezin, now ready for occupation.

He had no regrets about sending this girl away...after all, she had killed a Nazi officer whether she was Jewish or not. He considered himself soft in his mature years since he did not exterminate her on the spot and was hopeful that Terezin would do the job for him after using her up for some hard labor. He heard there were many Jews being stuffed into that camp, which was also used as a distribution center to other crematoriums and work camps.

Because Katarina was not Jewish, she could be used for a lot of services by the attending guards, who refused to touch Jews but needed to have some relief from their difficult service. He hoped his decision would bring a smile to many of those faces. The faster the Jews and enemies of the state perished, the better off Germany and the world would be. After all, was not the Jewish doctor found dead at this

Social Services crime scene a good thing? He probably was the one who devised the deaths for those around him by using his Jew intelligence against them. That girl, as well as the German soldier, must have somehow been in cahoots with him. They were obviously incompetent.

It would be easier to send the soldier to the Russian front than shoot him as a traitor. The end result would be the same, and he might just help Germany a tad more before his time was up on this planet, which obviously was shortly.

The three remaining soldiers, one skinny with a belt holding up his baggy pants, one with fat cheeks red from the brisk air, and one with a uniform that looked like it had been in battle for years, glanced hungrily toward the closed door and instantly formed a line as if in a cafeteria.

By the time the fat cheeks entered the office, the bodies, the blood, the tears, and the disarray of the girl before him took away all desire. He had lost the lottery by being last in line. It was simply time to clean up the profound mess in front of him. Next time he was going to be more aggressive and make sure he was first for such an important queue.

After a quick perusal, he simply did an about-face and left to get his buddies and order the cart. Once alone, Katarina only halfheartedly tried to cover her bruises that were beginning to form and the blood that started dribbling down her leg. There was no more mantra repeating in her head. There was nothing but the silence of being too numb, too weak, and too pained to do anything but lie there in shock.

Katarina's despondent mother, Margharite, cried constantly for three days straight, then simply went to bed and refused to leave her cocoon-like bed amassed with blankets.

"George," she cried to her husband, "Katarina could never be involved in these murders that the Gestapo claims happened. You must keep going to their headquarters until you find out how we can get her removed from that Jewish fortress that they have sent her to. She is not even Jewish, and this is an outrage! Where is the trial?"

George, who felt pain from his sad eyes down his painful back to his flat feet, was also beside himself with worry but still functioned better than his hysterical wife. Daily, he took the long, arduous walk to the Nazi headquarters, with its ornate rooms and foreign workers. He dutifully entered each room to talk about the plight of his beautiful young daughter, always showing them a picture of a smiling youth, sitting on her father's knee. Each room that he dragged himself into contained a sergeant, a private, or some sort of lieutenant who barely listened to his woes before sending him out of their sight and definitely out of their minds.

Each day his head hung lower when he entered through the stately door of his home with the brass knocker that Katarina had been particularly fond of using.

One gray day, months after his daughter's disappearance, George did not fiddle with the knocker before entering his home after his daily visit to Gestapo Headquarters. He just never came home from his visit and never made contact with his worried family, which everyone knew meant only bad news.

It was the day that George failed to return that Margharite became mute to the world around her. She stayed in her darkly carved wooden bed with her fluffy, down, cream comforter that felt like puffy clouds, easing her aching frame. She refused to go downstairs, and she refused to have anything to do with the running of the household.

She never saw Petra adjust the curtains but assumed they simply opened and magically shut according to the amount of light seeping in to her chamber. Her eyes sprung open and clamped shut with complete disregard to the clicks of her grandfather's grandfather clock in the darkened downstairs hall.

Each morning previously, George had awakened, dressed in his dark suit, donned a yellowed shirt, kissed his crying wife whose eyes seemed permanently swollen, patted his son on the top of his curly blond hair, and waved goodbye to Petra, the ever-present housekeeper.

Before the door would slam shut each morning, Petra would call to her employer, "Please, Monsieur Orbhan, do not leave the house today. This is the Gestapo, not like any police force that Prague has ever seen. Who knows why they do what they do? Let me try to find some answers. It is safer."

Then George would call out before the door totally muffled his saddened voice, "Katarina is my only daughter. I will never stop going to headquarters until she is released."

So, after two days of watching Margharite incapacitated in bed because her husband was now missing, Petra sat down with their son, young George, and valiantly appealed to him.

"Georgie," she said in a tone she used when he was a mere child on her knee, "you must trust me now and not follow in your father's footsteps. I was able to procure the news about your father and am still trying to get the release of Katarina. I have already found out that your father was struck by a policeman and never moved a muscle after that. He died then and there, and they are not going to release the body because they have no intention of answering questions regarding the death."

Young George stifled his cry, blocking it with his sweater. He knew his mother would construe the anguished sound as more bad news if he did not muffle it.

"What are you saying, Petra? Is there no hope?" he finally whispered through his heaves of quiet sobs.

Petra grabbed his shoulder and blew hot bursts of air in his outstretched ear with the words, "He is dead." She then enfolded the young man, who had been teetering around boyhood for many months. Her body blocked his cascading tears, which flowed uncontrollably.

Petra had been born in Odessa, Russia, and immigrated to Prague with her parents and her teenage daughter. They had wanted a life without starvation around every corner and felt that Prague held that opportunity, even for peasants who spent what little they had fleeing.

Petra's initial job with the Orbhans had turned into her life's work, and she never regretted it. She knew the travesties of the poor and was happy to live in such a beautiful city, far from her roots.

The Orbhans proved to be decent people, who were exceptionally kind to her through the years. They even increased her pay when they found out that she was supporting her parents, who raised her daughter. Petra's stipend enabled her parents to stay in their sunny flat with a big window that showed a glimpse of the castle that majestically towered over the old city. Her daughter married and moved to Serbia, which meant that Petra very rarely saw her.

Petra was wholeheartedly accepted by the Orbhans, which brought her peace as the years progressed. She was forever grateful to them for giving her this security, especially after her parents passed on from what the doctor termed "old age." In these shaky times, she realized that such death proclamations were a luxury that most people were not afforded. Very few people died from old age. The accidents occurring seemed to be more planned than by chance. The young seemed to be dying even faster than the elderly, and there was nothing natural about those youthful deaths.

Petra was savvy enough to know that a Russian-born immigrant was in a very precarious position inhabiting this German-occupied city, and she was happy she'd previously had contact with a group that came to be known as the underground. She was not an active participant in the underground, but she knew of them, and they knew of her. All potentially trustworthy volunteers were worth the effort. The more people with the same beliefs as they, the stronger the organization could become.

The main thread that wove through all of the different sections of the underground was the need for secrecy. It was taking a while to build up a network in Prague that would not be extinguished by the Germans, but the effort was paying off.

Petra began giving bits of information to her friend Ted, the local butcher, who gleaned what was important and then passed it on to his contact higher up in the organization.

Petra knew that something was afoot recently and was not surprised when Reinhard Heydrich was found critically wounded and later succumbed to his injuries. What dumbfounded her was the attack on Lidice and Lezalcy, the two villages that were razed because the Gestapo for some reason assumed that the attackers hailed from that area. She read that all of the males in the villages were murdered, with the remaining women and children put in camps or executed.

Petra became certain that the Gestapo was much more deadly than any group in Russia, even though she had known some terrible mobs doing terrible things there to innocent people. The Gestapo's willingness to sacrifice two local towns scared her, and she pulled back in her dealings with the group. She saw Ted all of the time, but rarely had information that he could use.

It was only because her dearest family had tragedy on their doorstep that she reconnected with the underground more seriously, to get answers about Monsieur Orbhan and his daughter, Katarina. She felt ready to take on more chances with this secret society because the lives of the Orbhans were spinning out of control. They were her only family now, and she would willingly risk her life, where previously she was not willing.

She offered her services to Ted if he should need them at any time. She had no doubt that she would be called on to do something somewhere down the line.

Ted easily found out about George Orbhan, because German Headquarters had many a vocal laugh that the crazy man was no longer going to bother them on a daily basis. They were all amazed that he had lasted so long anyway before someone just shut him up permanently. The news about Katarina only came out when pressed.

"Katarina Orbhan has been assigned to the Terezin Fortress for political prisoners and bears a new tattoo of numbers on her forearm. Because she is young and strong, she was instantly put to work, rather than the alternative, which at that camp comes swiftly."

Ted continued, "We are getting a clearer picture of why the groups of camps exist there, and it is safe to say that the devil inhabits them and stokes the fires that burn the soles of those who step over the threshold. I would not count on seeing her again, and if you do, let us assume that a miracle has occurred."

He said all of this in a deadpan manner, which resonated as a truth that was nonnegotiable to the saddened Petra, mutely listening to Katarina's death knells.

Ted decided not to tell her of the underground person who occasionally switched places with a camp inmate and brought back intelligence. The information received was passed on to other pockets of the underground and eventually into the Allies' hands.

Powerful allies had chosen to ignore this accurate intelligence given and close their eyes to what was going on in the death camps of Terezin. This mortified the local fighters.

It was not worth the effort to tell Petra all of the horrors that existed in those camps. She also would probably not believe it since even great, powerful countries chose to ignore the facts being presented. No one seemed to think the atrocities mentioned could possibly be true.

⊨◁ ▷⊨

Within a relatively short amount of time, Katarina knew that she was carrying a child from one of her many rapes. Her inability to understand how it could survive in such dire circumstances took a while to overcome. She finally realized that her fetus was tenuously holding on to the delicate balance of life that both of them occupied precariously.

Thankfully, the rapes had ceased once she was tattooed and ingrained in the desolate camp life that now encompassed her. The small amount of food ingested made it a nonissue for anyone to notice her pregnancy. Her layers of rags that became her clothes masked what little growth was even discernible.

Her initial vomiting was par for the course with the inmates, and it did not lead anyone to question her health or even her state of mind. Nobody around her resembled a robust or healthy female anyway. Conversation was minimal since a combination of exhaustion, fear, hunger, and guards kept it at bay.

She woke up, she slept, she toiled, and she also had something that most people suffered: depression. Because of her status as a non-Jew, she was given the job of gathering up hard objects, such as any kind of metal, from the female prisoners' clothing that lay strewn in an ad hoc manner throughout the initial undressing chamber.

She went through the clothes while imagining vignettes of the women's lives; the women were as crumpled as the clothes strewn around her. All the fabrics were somewhat tattered, but many held the telltale semblances of their former glory.

There were taffetas that had at one time been rich in color although presently were so stained and dusty that it was hard to decipher what had once been the beautiful material of wealth. There were undergarments that must have cost plenty earlier, although the dirt and tears overshadowed their glory.

Jewelry must have been sold or stolen long before the inmates had arrived, but occasionally there appeared a hidden treasure, sewn in the folds of an undershirt or among the stitching of a girdle. These women were forced to strip naked and walk to the next building in the intake process; they were unable to keep anything. Any hidden fold of skin or opening was thoroughly examined, so it was of no use to try to hold on to any ring, gold coin, or locket whatsoever.

She would hear periodic claps of gunfire and know that someone had risked keeping a memento or maybe holding on to a little treasure with the hope of using it for bartering purposes.

She knew of no reason to risk holding on to anything that passed through her hands. She threw everything in the provided dirty burlap sack until it was filled, then tied it with the one bit of small twine that was included in the sack, just long enough to secure the tie. She then walked to the exit, where a gruff guard collected the sack and gave her another one if necessary. She would watch him weigh the sack and then write something down in the journal that was located in the guard's grimy pocket. Before giving her another sack, the guard would rub his roughened hands all over her to make sure there was nothing hidden on or in her thin frame.

At the end of the day, he would make her open her mouth and would also stick his fat little index finger up her vagina. He would wrinkle his nose and let out a grunt, with his tongue sticking out. She knew that the baby within her must be very strong to fight off the intrusion of such an unwelcome assault.

Katarina always felt she was carrying a strong-willed girl, and she was certain that she would find a way to save her. It was that bit of certainty about her own child that kept her from the worst levels of depression, which often descended upon her young spirit at awkward times. Her strength was from knowing that she was put on this earth to save baby Naomi Bonn, and now she felt the same resolve about the fetus burrowed deep within her. She had to stay alive to complete her mission.

Terezin was a town that Hitler designed to hold Jews. Over one hundred fifty thousand of them eventually lived there. Conditions were not like a town, but were more like a death camp or a portal to even more lethal environments. Hitler himself had decided to house Jewish musicians and artists to play chamber music as Jews arrived from all areas of the Czech nation. From there, they were dispersed to other camps, with larger gas chambers that could accommodate more than the one that was being built at Terezin.

The Red Cross even came to the camp occasionally. When it did, a fake atmosphere descended temporarily, and illusions of tolerable conditions were instantly deployed. Musicians played, and artists were visible painting, while young, serious children drew pictures before being carted off to certain death. The most amazing part of it all was that the illusion worked and the Red Cross returned to its various countries and reported to the various offices that this camp was in accord with the Geneva Convention.

One time a Red Cross worker, devoid of the usual accompanying guard, walked up to Katarina and said, "These conditions look good!"

Katarina responded demurely, "Yes, and make sure you truly look at how good they are."

This comment, even though it had layers of possibilities, many of which could have been misconstrued, brought Katarina no food for the day. It endangered her unborn child and taught her that Red Cross workers might not be worth it.

This particular worker did not even wink or say anything other than, "You must enjoy the beautiful music that you hear every day to inspire you."

One typical cloudy, damp day in spring, a woman in her shared dank, sparse bunkroom, started staring at her with more than the usual gawks that various inmates delivered.

Katarina had never made friends that easily, and she was especially wary in these new surroundings. This woman's harsh eyes bored right through her when she woke up, they stared mindlessly at her when she collapsed in bed at night, and they darted back and forth when Katarina gobbled up the insignificant rations that were issued. When the sun finally peeked out from the gloom that had immersed them for weeks, Katarina edged over to her and asked her name.

"They call me Anya, and you may do the same. I know who you are and what ails you. You seem to have some important friends who are concerned about you."

Both women then heard the siren that alerted them to the ever-present roll call, which happened right before the sun rose and again when the sun sank behind the sticklike structures. They both scrambled to the front of their bunkhouse and silently waited for the roll call to finish.

After attendance at the roll call, a liquid with unrecognizable organic forms floating in it would get distributed. When that was choked down, the women were dispersed to their various workstations.

There had been no time to pursue what Anya had said. It did give Katarina a glimmer of hope, though, when she probed the various possible meanings of the woman's words. She wondered if her family was finally going to get her out of this muck that she had fallen into all of her own accord.

She truly wished she had listened to her wise father when he was simply trying to keep her safe. She thought of her parents when she woke, before she fell into her needed sleep, and while she worked.

The image of her brother chasing her between the leafed trees on the promenade often seeped into her mind.

She was always worried about her family's safety and knew they must be fearful of hers.

In the early evening, there was another roll call, and then came the final gruel, which barely seemed worth the effort to stand in line to receive. A hard bunk without even a blanket to cover themselves awaited those who survived the day.

Time passed in ways that befuddled Katarina. It was hard to tell exactly how much time had elapsed before she could actually finish the conversation that Anya had started days earlier. Katarina knew that Anya was still closely watching her though, and that oddly gave her a jolt of peace, which had not existed before their exchange of words. She liked the thought of there being someone out there concerned about her, and she liked the idea better that there were people outside the camp who were pressing for information regarding her travails.

She pictured her father demanding in a stern voice to someone in power that they absolutely return his dutiful daughter to her loving parents. She could almost smell the yeast from the biscuits and the crispness of the bitter chocolate brownies that filled the lively house in anticipation of her return.

Her silly brother would probably not even give a hint of a tease for at least twenty-four hours after her precious homecoming.

It was these images that occasionally gave moments of relief that were associated with Anya's stares, which Katarina sought out whenever possible.

Eventually Anya slinked over and whispered frantically in Katarina's ear, "As soon as the baby is born, there is a chance that it can be removed from the camp. This would be a miraculous feat if it succeeded. If the wrong guards find out you are with child, you will be immediately killed as a whore, and your story will end there. Try to fold into yourself and disappear to all of the Germans who watch us like lab rats." Then she slinked away in silence.

Anya and Katarina did not speak again until the pangs of labor racked her weakened body. Meanwhile, Katarina kept her head down and did her job with nary a complaint. Her depression lessened as her spirits soared in anticipation.

At times, Petra the housekeeper had given the underground leader Ted more solid intelligence than Christian had; Christian carried out his own war in fighting what appeared to be a losing battle against the aggressive German force that occupied the region.

Christian became devoted to helping Katarina once he found out her fate. His guilt was immense for leading her down such a bleak path. He was determined to now help Katarina as well as his own brother, David, who was rotting in the inferno labeled Terezin.

Christian never returned to the oppressive ghetto after the gut-wrenching events at the Office of Social Services. He skirted through the surrounding forests and did various reconnaissance missions from there.

He watched Katarina's darkened house for many nights before coming to the conclusion that the housekeeper was the calmest spirit who traversed amid the shadows. He felt that he could make his initial contact with her. He knew from various rendezvous with disjointed underground soldiers that it was ultimately safer to seek a non-Jewish covert fighter rather than a passive couple, such as the two Orbhans residing in the home.

He had come across Ted in an earlier mission and had indirectly heard about Petra from him. The common ground that the two secretive men shared was the thread of Petra and Katarina, not David, who was an unknown to Petra.

The strongest link to his brother and Katarina was through one greedy Terezin guard named Gunther, who was soaking Christian for as much jewelry, money, and stocks as possible from what he had secretly accrued before the ghetto was disbanded and moved completely to Terezin. His previous work with the other forgers in the ghetto provided interactions among needy people who were not apt to accept no for an answer in these times of imminent danger. His work was gratis often, but there were certain clients who were so appreciative of alleviating the pangs of their sorrow that he was given what little remnants remained of their former hidden treasures. These had been kept for emergencies that could never have been as serious as those they were presently experiencing.

Desperate and unusual bargains were constantly being made. Sometimes it was for news, sometimes food, and sometimes for a chance of anonymity. When that finite supply of his wampum ran out, he knew that his tunnel into camp life would come to a halt.

Gunther had a singular purpose in giving his assistance, which was to garner as much as he could in the short time before all of the Jews were exterminated and the well of his resources ran completely dry. This capitalistic Nazi, who only cared for what he could get his hands on, was never willing to truly take gigantic risks with his own life but did give bits of information that Christian managed to use and pass on to the more organized forces around him.

"I knew Katarina was involved with Jews from the minute she took that job at Social Services," Petra told Ted one afternoon when he came to the house to deliver the few pieces of beef liver that he had saved for the Orbhans and a few other families in the area, who gave more coins than many for the product.

Ted had explained to Petra that he needed more cash to uncover information about Katarina as he looked around the quite comfortable home in this well-to-do area of Prague. He knew that their Chinese vases and the Viennese teacups strewn on the shelves were worth more than Petra realized.

"You must talk to Madame Orbhan about the objects that grace these shelves. If these teacups are on display, there must be more valuable objects hidden in drawers and under lock and key. If they part with these things, which are just things, they might get something more tangible in return. This possibly will be the only chance they will ever get to really help Katarina."

This culminated in the tenuous connection that Petra forged with Christian, whom she would rarely see in person, although he frequently kept his eye on her. The birth of Katarina's child would soon be added to their worries about their loved one. This information was unknown to

Petra or the Orbhans at that time, but Christian kept apprised of her situation.

"Madame Orbhan," said Petra to the almost mute Margharite, who still could not face getting out of her immense bed, which practically smothered her with warm feathers. "Please, madame, we have a chance to help Katarina, but it calls for large amounts of money and expensive objects that I alone cannot supply. Your daughter's needs are extremely serious now, and there is a slight possibility that we may be able to help her by immense bribes."

Margharite Orbhan did not respond to much conversation these days, and this one only brought the faint response of, "Ask George." Petra knew she was referring to her husband and not the son who went by the same name.

Despondent herself, Petra went to the youthful Georgie, who frequently acted like the immature young man that he perpetually was. She cradled his head in her loving hands again, and just looked at him to let him know that this request was a heartfelt one and he had to trust the nanny of his previously stress-free childhood.

"I can assist you, Georgie, in finding your sister by moving cash along to a reliable person, not just someone who will rob you of your money and livelihood. Your bedridden mother is in no condition to make either monumental decisions or even slight ones that are inconsequential. I can relieve this family of the day-to-day issues that come up in running a household, but this matter is different. You need to give me your approval, and not just orally, but written and signed. Your sister is fighting for her life in that awful political death fortress, and we need to take ownership here. Your mother and sister both need our help. Those monsters need to be fed with cash at Terezin. This requires more money than I have to give, but I want you to know that I am willing to give everything I have to add to yours. This family has become my family too. I hope as the man of the house now, you will provide the necessary approval of funds for your poor, desperate sister."

Georgie looked into Petra's eyes and realized he had to step up and be the adult that she had raised him to be.

"My father's top drawer in his dressing room has everything catalogued and how much things are worth. Whether it is a bank account or a vase, he would constantly tell me that the top drawer was where I should remember to look if we ever needed money and he was not available. I guess I should have been more thankful that he harped on this," he quietly told Petra, while still being cradled as if a small child.

"Thank goodness George Orbhan was obsessive," Petra thought.

Katarina continued to gather up the hardened remains of people's lives in the boring everyday drudgery of the dismal camp life. Death was everywhere, and friendships were hard to come by.

David, located in the same camp but in the Jewish men's section, never once saw Katarina. He knew it was his brother who was piecing plans together. David tried to make very few waves in his sea of sadness. He worked here or worked there and slept each night. Every now and then he ate something stale and soupy, which tended to disagree with him. He was young and at one time very strong, so he was used repeatedly for the harder labor in the camp.

Watching the older men toil as they dragged their heavy shovels doing backbreaking work, enabling them to live another day, was painful to see. David preferred to work the harder details if it meant saving another from such hardship. He hoped someone perhaps more frail than he was doing something else that would not break the body quite as much as the excruciating slave labor he was forced to do.

He found it hard to believe that he and his brother Yitzhak, or Christian as many called him, would change places for a short time. Their similarity to each other had always been striking and was even more pronounced as they aged.

In primary grade school, they had secretly switched classrooms, which was not noticed for two hours by the busy teachers. By the third hour that had passed, though, both of them were in the director's office, and a note was sent to their embarrassed mother. Even being punished was worth it for the young, carefree brothers. They laughed over this for many years, and it even brought a smile to their faces when times got tough, which happened around a corner that neither of them had ever predicted.

Yitzhak convincingly messaged David that he could get his needed strength back easier outside of the harsh camp, which made sense if the scheme worked and the guards never figured out that there were two brothers who looked so much alike that they could switch identities and locales.

David was worried about his brother in this hostile camp, but Yitzhak brushed that off, pointing out that it was only for a short time, and then David could finish his own allotted time, even though no one was really sure what that allotment was.

What David was not aware of, though, was that Katarina was also an inmate in the same camp area and his brother was in the midst of a precarious negotiation for not only David's life, but also the life of Katarina's unborn child, who was the only part of that duo under negotiation.

The guard Gunther's appetite for riches constantly consumed more and more of their resources. Gunther began to accumulate more than he'd ever thought he would see in his lifetime as a dirt farmer with no formal education. He became almost giddy with his continual acquisition of treasures, and he now understood the joy that Midas had in hoarding his cache. Gunther only had to give the guard in the women's jewelry depository room a mere fraction of the amount that he would have demanded had he been in his position. Finding people to accept even a little extra cash and jewelry was never a difficult task in the depressing camp.

The pieces of the plan were coming together for the two guards, the male inmate, the female inmate, her unborn child, and the civilian Christian who had set this in motion. Gunther did not think about anything other than getting his piece of this flowing pie. Why anyone would want to come into the camp even for a second confused him, but he did not spend too long worrying about it. Everything was now in place, and they only had to patiently wait for the whore to drop her bastard child and the final payment of cash to be paid.

﹦﹢ ﹢﹦

Katarina had been feeling cramps for hours before the piercing alarm sounded for roll call. The sensation was tolerable, but she also knew this feeling would not last. Anya could tell as soon as she lifted her swollen lids in the crowded bunkroom and stared at the far-off bunk, which she always had within her sights, that Katarina was at last in labor.

Anya slinked toward Katarina without disturbing the others and whispered to her, "You must go to roll call and ask for a pass to stay in your bunker for just one day. They should give it to you, but be careful not to let anyone figure out what is going on—or inevitably coming out."

The siren then loudly wailed, and the forlorn women dragged themselves to the ragtag line that always formed in front of the wooden bunker in rain, wind, snow, or sleet.

When Katarina's name was yelled, she bravely eked out, "Pass, please, for today due to stomach problem," and then looked down as a trickle of warm liquid moved across her calf and stained the dirt below her, as well as staining her shoes, which barely covered her feet.

"You are disgusting, and I do not want you near any loyal guards who could glance at your grossness. Go back to the bunker, you pig," said the guard in a most disgusted tone.

Katarina crept back to her bed and silently moaned through the long day of her own intense labor. At times, she breathed deeply and knew that she could accomplish this natural feat, but there were other times when her whole body shook and she had to bend her head to the side of the bunk and vomit into the available bucket placed conveniently next to all of the bed frames.

She was anxious, but she was also quite hopeful. Bringing a new life into the world, even though it was to a dysfunctional environment, gave her the stamina to continue her monumental task. Her mind leaped among thoughts of family, Mlle. Zelinsky, David, Christian, Dr. Bonn, and the beautiful tiny Naomi. Images popped in and out of her head with the rising intensity of contractions that proved beyond a doubt that the baby really was coming and she could not stop it. She focused on the flickering panels of obscured light peeking through the tiny bunker window; as many distraught women were housed there as could be squeezed into the bacteria-ridden space. She felt relief that her bunkroom only had one person per bunk, which happened because the women in there were political criminals, not Jews by birth.

The hours inched slowly by as her pains steadily increased. The new sharp intensity brought even more nausea to the mix as she realized that the baby must be even closer. She feared she would have a deathly labor, like Dr. Bonn's Naomi. She felt like she was miraculously having a virgin birth because she did not know the identity of the father, and that, of all things, made her feel content.

It was in the middle of one of Katarina's extreme nausea attacks with accompanying vomit that the women skulked in the door from their exhausting day of work, weak from their lack of food. Anya rushed over to her and wiped her sweaty brow with her own hand, blackened with imbedded dirt. She wadded some ripped cloths that had a moldy and tattered look to them and gently put them slowly in Katarina's mouth. Eyes started darting in all directions from the surrounding women, who were taken aback by this surprising imminent birth.

All eyes settled on Katarina's bloody bunk, with shocked looks of horror mixed with surprise as well as a glimmer of hope. Women started slithering over to delicately offer a variety of opinions, and then slither back as the crescendo of pain descended on Katarina, and she lost her sense of awareness. A young, stronger woman than most, called Zita, who was new to the camp, began to take charge of this most unusual situation and quietly barked orders for everyone to return to their bunks except for Anya. Zita hovered above Katarina and began pressing on the top of Katarina's belly, right under her swollen breast. This caused Anya to see the head burst through the birth canal from her vantage point as she ran to the foot of the bunk. A tiny, piercing cry was emitted from the lower regions of Katarina's bunk.

This infant surprised all of the women with its ferocity for life and caused all of those eyes to light up with the momentary joy of witnessing a new, innocent life begin in the world.

Zita placed the infant, a tiny little girl with just a small amount of hair on her tiny little head, onto Katarina's belly, and they waited for the afterbirth to be expelled. Zita then bent her head down and moved toward the infant. She opened her mouth and bit through the umbilical cord with her jagged teeth. Zita then turned to Anya as Katarina engulfed the now-resting child in her arms.

"This baby cannot survive here, and both of you must realize this," said Zita, who continued to bare those jagged teeth as she tried to keep her voice down from the panic that was now replacing her previous calm.

"There is a plan, and it will not jeopardize any of the women here. The infant will be out of this hellhole soon. It is important that nobody here extinguishes this little being, who was born today in the worst of circumstances," said Anya. "Just let the plan work. Please, no one mention anything about the baby. If Katarina can get to work tomorrow with the baby, the infant will be transported out of the camp. That is all we need to know. Let destiny take it from there, and let none of us interfere with that."

Zita knew better than to ask any more questions, and the word dripped around the bunks, down the rough wood, and across the room to inform all of the inhabitants who were trying to stay alive in any way they could that they just had to let destiny play its part and not change what was meant to be by talking about it to anyone.

Anya then put the baby to Katarina's swollen breast and waited for her to suck, which she did with a ferocity that astonished both Katarina and Anya. It surprised the mothers of old to hear slurping sounds from the decrepit bunk that housed the new mother and child. There was hardly enough nourishment for one person on the sparse prison diet, and it was truly miraculous that two could manage to share even a drizzle of food.

Anya, who was by now wrapped around Katarina, whispered into her ear, "Tomorrow you must go to roll call and then report to your workstation as usual. Muster all of your strength to do this. Women through the centuries have survived labor and gone to toil in the fields within the day. No crying and no complaining from you at all. When you are at work, the first sack that you fill will be with your own precious jewel, your most precious infant daughter. Do not shed any tears over this. Your daughter will be safe, and that is what you must think about as you hand her over in the porous sack. The guard will take the sack with him, and your infant will leave the camp in safety and breathe the fresh air of freedom, which is more than any of us here have a chance of doing. This is your only option if you want her to live, so you must keep this in mind with every movement you make. You cannot change your mind at the last minute or waver in any way. Do not trust anyone except the guard who takes the sack. I truly am sorry, Katarina, but this is really a miracle that is happening, and you must approach it as such."

Through her tears that had begun to drip sporadically down her pale cheek, Katarina choked out the words, "Thank you." Then she dropped her gaze to the beautiful little baby girl that had emerged with a hoot and a howl from her broken body. She did not stop looking at her until the early siren rang through the camp to let everyone know that they had survived another night.

Katarina wrapped the soiled rag around her and the tiny infant close to her breast. The child would be able to get air from the opening by her neck. Her clothes would block any awareness that there was something suspicious. Nobody in the camp ever assumed a child could be born in any of the bunkers. Katarina did not have the same fear that she'd had when she carried little Naomi into the fray of that chaotic day that ended in a hidden life, shut off from the world.

The shift that she was wearing was sewn with ample space for various body types. She could be tall, short, big, or skinny, and the shift would not be any different in size. All female inmates received a similar article when they entered the camp, and this oddity ensured that the baby would have plenty of room while absorbing the warmth of her mother's body.

As the women lined up in front of the bunkroom, they each periodically cleared a throat, gave a little cough, or emitted a sigh. This directed attention away from Katarina, who sensed their thoughts of hope for a new generation that would not know such inhumane hardships.

The faint gurgles coming from Katarina's bent body went unnoticed as she trekked to her repetitive job of collecting discards from the doomed women who were arriving in droves each day. Once alone in the tomblike enclosure of the undressing room with the usual disarray of discards, she placed herself on the filthy floor and rocked her sleeping infant in her arms.

After forty short minutes, she gently encased her in the burlap sack, kissed her on both cheeks and the top of her head, then tried to keep a pleasant face so her daughter would not sense her growing fear. This was the second time in her life that she would be carrying a baby through hell to the light on the other side.

She experienced calm in her normally jumpy mind, and this made her task easier. She no longer cared about her hunger that kept her up at night, her pain that racked her frail frame, or the immense sorrows that she sometimes dwelled on for hours and hours. She was now experiencing something that made her other thoughts pale in their quake. She was enabling her daughter to have life.

Katarina soon became anxious and rapped on the door. It was time to let the German guard abscond with her own precious Jewel. The three light taps were barely perceived by the guard, but they were heard, and he did respond. The squeaks and clanks of the locked door slowly opening filled her now-attentive ears. As usual, silence then ensued as the guard went to grab the sack that Katarina was gingerly cradling.

"Jewel," she said audibly, and then added, "is her name," in an even quieter voice.

As soon as the guard had agreed to take money from his friend Gunther, he knew that this woman had to die no matter what Gunther had planned. There was no way that he ever wanted it to slip out that he had helped a prisoner relieve herself of a bastard child. That was not worth the extra flow of money if it became known.

Because Gunther was immersed in this crime as well as being German, he was confident that nothing incriminatory would come from him.

He also knew that the woman, who was Czech, was not reliable, no matter what anyone had said about her. As for the infant, he knew that she was part of the insurance for the expected fortune to come his way and had to be kept alive, at least for now.

So he whispered to the sorry-looking Katarina, "I will take your bastard child to safety."

She looked up at his pock-ridden face with a tear forming in her right eye.

The soldier kept her gaze but quickly and without any remorse aimed his handy pistol at her shocked face and pierced a bullet cleanly through her temple, which made her collapse in a sudden heap on the ground.

He felt no guilt, because the death came so quickly she barely knew it happened, and the direct shot could not have caused much pain. She would have experienced more pain had she continued to live in the squalor that had become her life. He also knew that killing one of these whores was not a problem in Terezin, and called immediately to the nearby guard, who came running,

"The whore was trying to steal from the discards and even tried to lay hands on me, a soldier of the Third Reich. You would think she'd be smart enough not to touch a soldier after trying to steal. She was probably a Gypsy," he added in order to make sure this guard would not be concerned about her death.

"This is one less problem to worry about, friend. Dispose of her," he said, as she was kicked over to the wooden wheelbarrow, with old wooden wheels that were well worn from its heavy usage. There was always one available to cart off the bodies, which were constantly stacked up all day and all night, every day and every night.

The busy guard never even noticed the sack with the real Jewel inside as he went about his business of clearing the corpse from the room that would soon be occupied with another inmate who could continue with the endless task of collecting more discards from the Jews, who never seemed to stop coming.

Gunther, holding the breathing sack that had been passed over to him twenty minutes previously, waited for Christian at the fence behind his outpost with David in tow. Gunther knew that Christian was due to come at any moment because he always arrived at exactly 10:02 a.m.

Christian's meeting had always been timed by the train that left Prague at 8:30 a.m. It was a three-mile walk from the train station to the ghetto, but Christian's path had to be a little more circuitous than that of the other train occupants, who were wearing the mark of a Jew with the visible Jewish star emblazoned on their outerwear. They were slowly herded to the massive old entrance to the fortress after the long trek that they endured with their few possessions. None of them really knew what was in store for them upon their arrival.

Musicians, who were inmates as well as accomplished in their craft, played lively tunes to keep the spirits up and the crowds moving.

New train tracks were being laid in another section of the camp and would facilitate extradition to Germany for the thousands who would come and go through the fortress. Most of the inhabitants would be exiting into those crowded, airless cars to other concentration camps in Germany. It was all part of Hitler's Final Solution, which was clearly in play.

Gunther knew that by 10:03 a.m., the plan that he had hashed and rehashed over and over until the inevitable outcome was to his liking would begin. On this ominous day, he would be able to execute his solution, which had already brought him many riches. There were shiny trinkets that he could give to his wife, and there was cash that he could use for his livelihood when the war finally ended. He felt like quite the entrepreneur and knew that all would be jealous of him when he returned to his town a wealthy hero.

Gunther had previously grabbed David at gunpoint and yelled to the other guards that he planned on roughing him up because he did not like the way he glared at him during the prisoners' daily forced walk to the hard labor area. Jews knew not to look their conquerors in the eye. Gunther's fellow guards were more than happy to give the boy David up for a punching practice, whether it was a valid reason or not.

The other prisoners, with their guards, trudged on through the dirt to begin their day's toil. Few of the men even cocked their heads to watch David trail off with the menacing guard. The two odd, mismatched fellows—one an overweight, burly guard with a belly big from drinking, and the other an emaciated inmate whose sustenance could barely keep him alive—walked in the opposite direction of the other prisoners and moved behind the wooden guard station, where Christian would appear from the other side of the double-stranded barbed wire as was previously planned.

It was not as difficult to enter the camp as it was to leave it. The old forest had been there much longer than anything humans had made. The forest was dark and foreboding to some, but to Christian it was a blessing. The heavy trunks of the old trees were custom-made for blocking and camouflaging, with their shades of browns and beautiful canopies that spread over the carpet below.

As predicted, Christian was right on schedule. Yitzhak instantly threw his arms around his wispy brother and lifted him off the ground with as delicate a bear hug as he could muster. There was so little meat on David that it was not difficult to whip him in the air, which was not lost on either man. Christian knew that the brother exchange had to be completed in as few minutes as possible. He desperately needed David to slip under the sharp fence before he had a chance to change his mind.

Gunther shoved the bulging burlap sack he had been carrying unobtrusively into David's now available arms once freed from the hug. David had not focused on anything other than his brother's arrival and now glanced at the sack that was being transferred to him. Nobody expected a baby to be anywhere in the camp, so it had not been very difficult to carry her around when procuring David from the work detail or traveling to the meeting spot. Local birds, squirrels, or snakes, which abounded in the woods bordering the enclosed area, could have made those occasional noises that were emitted from the sack.

Gunther quietly said to the brothers, "Her name is Jewel, and her mother is now dead, and never ask for anything like this again," which caused David to look quizzically at his brother.

Christian said with very little emotion, "Katarina is the dead mother, and in this sack is her infant, still alive."

David's jaw dropped and his head slumped in complete surprise onto the sack he held, having not heard Katarina's name mentioned for any of the months of his incarceration.

Yitzhak added, "Now you must go to our sister to deposit the baby as quickly as you can. Do not worry; we will pull our famous switch again in two months, when you have your strength back and I need mine. Now let's switch clothes and make this more believable."

Gunther then focused his weapon at David's heart, which was dripping with emotion, in an attempt to force the boy to mindlessly scurry away with the beating burlap sack before more tragedy could happen to him, his brother, or this baby, who surprised everyone the most.

David finally took heed and slithered away in his new clothes into the forest with the precious Jewel in tow. Before leaving, he clasped his brother's arm and whispered, "This is only temporary," and then left without another word.

Christian gave Gunther the last of what was left from the Orbhans' stash and waited for the beating that he expected once his brother had departed. His face needed to be unrecognizable to the guards on the off chance that they had noticed what David's face looked like.

"Get on with it," demanded Yitzhak to this gigantic man, who oddly was his brother's savior.

Gunther obliged and beat him almost senseless, centering on his face, which swelled to a big round melon, with tiny cuts for the eyeholes. He grabbed his dirty shirt by the collar and bounced him on the stone-filled dirt to the workstation that had all but forgotten him. This proceeded just as previously planned by the two men, right up until they arrived at the work detail.

Gunther approached a young, pimply guard who must not have been any older than seventeen. He had the reputation of a bully in his ancient village outside of Munich and not much of any reputation in the camp. When the young punk realized how useless the worthless Jew had become from his obvious beating, he froze.

It reminded him of when he berated the baker's son, Alfred, who then told his father, who quickly marched to his house with Alfred in tow. His papa made him do all of the chores for the rest of the week himself, without any help from his younger brothers, which gave him terrible blisters on four of his toes and exhausted him each night for the remaining five days.

Because of this hateful memory, he fumbled for his gun and, without much ado, shot the swollen-faced man who looked strikingly like Alfred did when his father presented him as evidence. The gun fired twice—once in Yitzhak's chest and once in his head—before Gunther could interject anything to prevent it.

Even though this was not what Gunther had planned for Yitzhak, it realistically saved him the messy job that he was certain to have in the future, especially when the money stopped flowing, which it always does and probably had already.

Because Yitzhak was no longer alive, the wooden wheelbarrow appeared and carted off its new passenger. The same wheelbarrow then wound around toward the back of the camp, where a mountain of bodies reeking from death was angling toward the cloudless sky. The rotting corpses, mangled, with a hand stuck here and bits of hair flying there, were waiting patiently for an even larger pit to be dug by bone-thin prisoners.

Yitzhak's body was thrown on the leeward side of the fly-ridden pile and flopped right on top of his friend and coconspirator Katarina. The two bodies looked like Siamese twins, with their two mangled heads awkwardly angled at 180 degrees from each other.

There were so many piles that had been made and so many holes that had been dug in the vicinity of Terezin that when the young soldier threw down the discarded body of another worthless Jew, he laughed to himself, "The land has become Swiss cheese here, with dips and spaces and holes all around, but I imagine it will be very fertile in the future for growing wheat. The people who live around here are so lucky."

Johann Gerse rolled over and told his sleeping wife, Inna, to remain in bed as he threw on his plaid flannel robe and lumbered down to the heavy door that was trembling from the knocks that had been hammering it for the past three minutes.

Johann used to spend many hours worried about the Gestapo arriving in the middle of the night to cart off Inna and end his marital bliss, but now his worries concerned her worthless brothers asking for more favors.

He remembered another dark night when knocks had assaulted the door to his home in the middle of his sleep. Nothing good ever came from nighttime knocks. Inna's crazy, Jewish brother had endangered them by demanding a favor that never should have been asked. There was no way that he was going to keep that Jew baby whom the brother dropped off well past midnight, with no consideration to any of their safety, especially his sister's.

The nuns of Assisi had a convent in Prague, where Johann dropped the baby off the following morning amid Inna's protestations. Johann was an avid churchgoer who attended Mass daily and always gave generously when the offering plate was passed through the congregation. He always had a soft spot for the local sisters.

He went to Mass as usual the next day, but this time with an infant whose screams echoed throughout the cavernous church. When a hefty nun with a foot dragging, which always drew his attention, came up to him, he furtively spoke to her about the child. He figured this plump nun had the physique to ward off evildoers should they try to enter the nunnery and ask too many questions. He needed the sisters to take in the child immediately. After looking into Johann's shallow eyes, this Sister of Mercy gently held her arms out and scooped up the poor child.

Inna had been in no position to barter for an extra mouth to be fed because her own precarious life was entangled in the iron control of Johann. He made it crystal clear that he did not want a squeaking girl baby disrupting the already tenuous situation in his home, especially if she was of Jewish extraction. Inna's choice was to agree to send the baby to the nuns, or he would block the baby's mouth and nose with a pillow and extinguish her young life. Inna wisely chose the former.

Johann felt quite magnanimous when he brought the baby to Mass with the little picture of her parents tucked in her soft blanket, as well as a thimble hidden in the cushy blankets that Inna had not shown to Johann. He was confident this donation of a soul would send him directly to heaven; in addition, he felt it was an added insurance policy just in case his previous act of mercy was not enough to open the pearly gates. Oddly, the nun did not seem to focus on the Jewishness of the baby and did not even thank Johann profusely, like he thought she should have done for donating a heathen child to the church for redemption. It was the last he saw of this nun or the baby, but it did not faze him in the least. This child held no importance to him, nor did the hefty nun who received her. His life was in more danger than either of theirs could be if anyone realized the ruse that was occurring under everyone's nose.

This Inna imposter that shared his home had turned out to be the best thing that had ever happened in his sad life so far. He definitely appreciated a nice-looking woman in his bed, because ever since his own childhood, his parents had made it very clear to him that no one of any standing would ever enjoy his caresses. For this attractive Jewess, he was willing to take some risks. He was aware that it was not as dangerous as it could have been, though, because she had so completely taken over the identity of his long-gone, good-for-nothing wife. No one had ever seriously questioned him about this new Inna with any severity as of yet, and he did not want to alert neighbors or police that his household had changed in number or dynamics.

He finally made it to the locked door, where he instinctively knew it was not the dreaded Gestapo. Those who had either had a door knocked upon by Gestapo or knew someone who had Gestapo enter their home were well aware that they rapped with heavy weapons and broke through a door with very little encouragement. He assumed correctly that it was one of Inna's brothers but was shocked when he saw it was the incarcerated David. It really did not matter, though, whether it was David or Yitzhak, because whichever one, they were always the bearer of bad news and were truly not welcome anytime in his home as far as he was concerned.

"Get in here quickly, you fool," Johann commanded to the partially covered man plastered against the door frame.

Without even a cordial greeting, David instantly revealed his mission. "Johann, I am told by Yitzhak to bring one of God's gifts to you and Inna," he blurted to the awe-struck man.

"This is insane! How can you be out of the camp, David? And what are you doing with yet another child connected to your family? I am not an orphanage!" yelled Johann with as much restraint as he could muster. "Is that camp a revolving door with an infant for every contestant?"

David saw Inna as she came running into his somewhat occupied arms while crying hysterically. She never thought she would see her brother again and clung to him with tenacity.

"Let us sit together calmly, and I will explain how this infant came to be in my arms," said David, trying to keep his shaky voice from revealing his worry and desperation. He glanced at his sister while she frantically pawed him and thought how well fed she looked. She brought shock to his darkly etched face and made him realize the limits of his own frail body and his inability to emote the correct signals from his shriveled frame to his dearest sister. It was as if he were still residing at Terezin. He feared retribution for displaying any emotion that ran through him. He would never really lose that feeling completely and would always feel that the best part of him was left at that horrible death camp as a payment for being on the outside.

As soon as Inna moved slightly, Johann came barreling into David and Jewel and pinned him against the wall with a sideways block, while throwing Inna forcibly on the floor. There was not much girth to David anymore, and he flew like a feather, which blows in the wind and dissipates into the atmosphere.

"Remove your stinking body from my house, you dirty Jew, and take the devil's child with you, or I will call the police on both of you," growled Johann.

David managed to get the words out that inevitably saved the two of them. "What would you tell the police, Johann? Your Jewish wife, who is not really your wife, let her Jewish brother, who just unexpectedly arrived from Terezin, visit her in the middle of the night and give you another child to rear? This one is not Jewish though, so the thought was that you could have one of each."

"You think I would ever help you by raising one of your discards? That other little pile of shit is long gone. I pawned her off on the church. Those eunuchs are always happy to save another heathen soul from the devil. Take this miniature skeleton out of here before I smother her with simply my hand, which is stronger than any part of you. We both know you are in no condition to fight anyone or anything. Now, get out of my house, and be thankful I am not throwing your whoring sister out with you," spit Johann, with eyes popping and girth bulging out of his open terry cloth robe.

David peered at his lovely, poor sister crying in a lump on the cold floor in the home of this disgusting man and knew that Johann was right about many of the things he put so ineptly. He gave a quick glance to his sobbing sister with the hope that she could remain safe in this house of torture by living with this horrid man and staying away from any Nazi camp, which was inevitably worse than any man could possibly be, no matter how unscrupulous. Terezin, he knew, was a death sentence, and he refused to add his sister to the family lot there. Pleading his helpless case would only prolong the inevitable. He knew this avenue for the child was closed permanently.

He dragged himself out of the home without even closing the door. He could hear his sister sobbing into the night as he walked away from her sorrow.

The cool fresh air filled David's lungs and gave him the strength to continue. He cradled the little baby, who needed nourishment if she were to continue on her perilous journey. He was almost resigned to his fate of wandering without purpose when he realized other options had to be considered for the child in his arms.

He knew she would already be dead if she had remained in the camp. There were children there, but they always seemed to vanish into thin air, and then new innocent children would arrive who suffered the same fate.

Empty transports continually clanked on the new tracks that now went right into the fortress. They always left laden with cargo stuffed into the squalid spaces that smelled of excrement. There were rumors that the shipments went to Germany and were just transports of living dead until their dismal destiny was fulfilled at the new facility. There were always those who voiced their hopeful rumors that the new camp would be better than their present conditions, but eventually even they realized the folly of their thinking. The longer the war went on, the more

Jews seemed to move through Terezin, and the worse the conditions got for everyone.

He had only hoped to save the infant from the imminent death of camp life while he puttered around in the vicinity of Prague. He knew that this precious Jewel was the vivacious Katarina's miraculous child.

Yitzhak had sent an obscure message months ago regarding his sister and Johann caring for another Jew's child. He figured out that Katarina had found her Dr. Bonn, and this was where another child's destiny must have come into play. He was at first shocked that Johann had agreed to this humanitarian gesture, so hearing that he immediately passed this baby on to the church did not surprise him at all.

His face burned with failure for Jewel, knowing that even though she was presently safe, she was anything but secure. The plan for this baby that his brother had devised had failed. Plans were constantly failing around him, and he hoped that he would live to see something succeed other than having his brother take his place at Terezin.

He had been so entwined in Katarina's life and death from the moment he saw her disheveled and confused in the Jewish quarter.

He was never convinced that he would be able to survive the trials that had befallen him since the Nazis took power. His survival had never been solidified in the fabric of his consciousness, and he realized this as he inhaled the crisp air. To breathe fresh air again gave him a moment of serenity.

Living was the ultimate decision he made for the two of them. He lifted his weary spirits up from the heap that they had been thrown into, and he comforted the crying miracle of life that clung to him for survival.

The pangs from David's own hunger, the fear that jangled his nerves, and the cold that permeated his body made it harder to carry his burden. His thinking was distorted as he tried to imagine a solution for the hungry infant, who needed a warm breast that he did not have. He stuck his free hand in the small opening that was located on the inner side of the waistband of his pants. He could feel a crinkle of paper as he pinched it with two of his fingers and slowly took it out to read.

Yitzhak had written Katarina Orbhan's name and address on the slip, as well as the words "Contact Petra."

David actually had few recollections about Katarina's family. She had nervously talked of a pleasant home with a brother who drove her crazy, a father who was somewhat overbearing, and a sweet mother. This long-gone conversation seemed more like a dream than a reality because he could barely picture how Katarina even looked. He first met her so long ago on the sad streets of a ghetto with the hope that somehow she could save him from the horrors that he could barely imagine happening back then. He remembered wanting to kiss her, and he could not believe that he was now saving her offspring and she was dead.

From the bulging population at Terezin, he figured the entire Prague ghetto was now at the Terezin compound. He initially wanted to check the streets where he used to reside, but he realized that even though there might be people living there, none of the current residents could possibly have Jewish roots or a hidden grandparent with Jewish blood or even a yellow star sewn on their shoddy garments.

Yitzhak had come to his rescue by having that scrap of paper hidden in the clothes he gave him to wear. The answer to his dilemma resided with Katarina, just as it had so long ago. At least her family might offer some solutions, especially once they were aware of what he brought with him.

David's new quest was to get the baby to safety through the dark of night. The avoidance of the occasional street-light was fairly easy, but it was harder to avoid the military soldiers who milled around the city in packs like they owned the walk, the river, or whatever came in contact with them. Not wearing a star made quite a difference to maneuvering around the city, as did having the correct papers that his brother had put in his jacket pocket just in case he was stopped. He even had papers for the newborn, which should have surprised him but did not, because he knew his brother was always so thorough and always so thoughtful.

The attitude on the street was very different than the attitude that he had gotten used to in the camp. The total despair that he had smelled for so long had not wafted through the streets of Prague.

He darted, he dashed, and he maneuvered until he arrived at the treed avenue where the Orbhans lived. In Katarina's initial ramblings about her family, she mentioned her home had a crazy brass knocker consisting of a capped young man bent over as if old. He pictured in his mind a youngster who was crippled like Atlas because of all the woes of the world, and he knew just how he felt.

No household flickers of light could be distinguished through the darkened windows that were laden with sloping drapes in the early morning hours, but he sensed a family must be there. There was no sign of a military presence on the street as he walked openly toward the brass knocker on the door.

There was a square glass milk container that had been left by the front door just waiting for replenishing. Fresh milk was something he had not seen in a long time. This would brood well for the baby he was holding. He moved his face around the baby's mouth to make sure that she was still breathing. He had occasionally strained his ears and heard a shallow whimper, so he knew she had not given up previously. Jewel needed any mammal's milk for survival. Whether it was the perfect nectar or not was not an issue in her delicate state. David thrust one foot in front of the other faster and faster. He then grabbed the capped boy atop the knocker, tightened his grip, and let it drop.

Margharite Orbhan could not understand why the faint knock went unanswered. She was not aware that this rapping happened in the pitch black, right before a hint of the morning appeared. She did not realize her son and Petra were in a deep sleep. For her, sleep was something that she could not do very easily, which was odd because she rarely left the safety of her massive bed. She tossed, she turned, she counted, she thought of her husband as a young man, she thought of him as a middle-aged man, and she thought of him never coming back. Images of Katarina always made the tears flow. She felt responsible for her taking that ridiculous job and should have stood by her stalwart husband and not interfered. It was the weight of that decision that rendered her useless in the world outside her bedroom walls.

She so rarely left her bed that she did not even think to throw on a robe and gingerly walked downstairs only in her old voluminous nightgown. Then she cracked open the heavy door, which traditionally made a slight creak whenever it moved. There stood a gaunt young man who wore only slightly more than she did to block the chill of night. He awkwardly carried a burlap-covered bundle that she knew had to contain a baby from the squeaky sounds coming from the interior. To see a boy in such a defenseless way cut past her recent lethargy, and she quickly gathered him into the warmth of her home and the bosom of her heart.

He was startled but succumbed with no difficulty. Tears welled in her eyes and dripped down her cheek while hugging him tightly. He let down his defenses for the first time in a long time and reveled in her warmth and the ring of security that she temporarily wound around him.

Jewel stopped her whimpering, and he began his. The tears continued to fall as he sobbed into this strange woman's motherly embrace. He cried for his horrible existence, he cried for his brother and his sister, his parents, and he cried for the infant in his arms who did not deserve the calamity that had befallen her.

The commotion finally awoke the sorrowful inhabitants who had long ago lost their joy in little things. Georgie cautiously moved down the steps as Petra peeked around the corner, where she had her own small quarters. Both froze upon seeing Margharite Orbhan out of bed and embracing a street urchin who had appeared from nowhere.

"What are you doing, Mother, and who is this stranger?" yelled Georgie to the duo who were now cautiously moving apart from each other.

"I was a friend of Katarina's," started David, who within seconds realized that this was too shocking to just throw out to these people who still had sleep in their eyes.

"Why did you use the past tense in regard to my sister?" yelled Georgie as he abruptly pushed David.

Because of David's weakened condition, he instantly fell to the floor, but he did not give up his hold on the burlap sack that held Jewel, who was making barely audible tones.

Before anyone said anything else, Margharite quickly grabbed the baby and began rocking it, which quieted both down while she carefully removed the infant's soiled sack.

Nobody dared talk as they watched Margharite complete the task. Shock and confusion ensued when a beautifully formed infant appeared from the confining quarters that had enclosed its delicate form.

Petra knew that it was time to step in when it dawned on her that this boy must be the one that Ted had said was scheduled to help Katarina at Terezin. She figured something must have gone awry if this young man had taken a chance and traveled to Katarina's house, especially with this child. Ted never mentioned a baby or to expect a disheveled boy who could only be a runaway Jew from glancing at his decrepit condition, but he did say he would soon have news about Katarina.

"Please, if you have news for us, we are hungry for it," begged Petra while she helped the young man up from the floor and ushered him into the kitchen, which kept its warmth better than the rest of the chilled house. "Georgie, tell him you will not hurt him. He must be the link to Katarina that we have been seeking."

"Yeah," muttered Georgie, resigned to wait before again pouncing on this stranger.

David began unraveling his fragmented story of how he happened to come to their home in the wee hours before morn. David carefully omitted any mention of Johann, his sister, or his incarcerated brother, but included everything he had gleaned about Katarina.

He ended with, "I need your help, as does Jewel, to survive the hell that is around the corner but cannot be seen so clearly in these warm, beautiful homes."

Margharite could not stop clutching and rocking the baby in her arms. She whispered, "My Jewel, my precious Jewel," softly into the baby's little belly. Jewel had to be starving for nourishment and love, especially from a despondent grandmother.

BACK TO TUSCANY AND 1975

Delilah, Carmine, and Dr. Rescondito were like silent slabs of marble in their respective positions around the cell. They never questioned or commented on the mesmerizing tale that Sister Katarina had woven through long hours of waiting for their ride to appear. Not a peep was heard from anyone except for the small nun, who captivated her audience with an amazing tale from the annals of her personal history.

A crisp rap on the door preceded the grand entrance of Philip, escorted by the Mother Superior.

The silence was shattered with a panicked voice emitting, "Oh, my God! Oh shit, forgive me, sisters, for my blasphemy. Dee, I cannot believe you had an accident and are not in a hospital. You have got to get out of here quickly."

He rushed to the simple wooden bed frame where Delilah peacefully lay with her head on the gentle sister's lap, with no obvious need for hospitalization.

"We need to get her out of here and back into the real world right now! Nobody touch her," Philip went on.

"Young man," Dr. Rescondito sternly responded, "Delilah is in good hands here and does not seem to be complaining. I am a doctor, and we would have found a way to get her to a hospital if she actually needed to go to one. It appears only that her arm was bruised and she experienced a little disorientation. I have a feeling she is doing much better because, as you can see, she is resting quietly but alertly, with no complaints. Would you like to speak for yourself, young lady, to assuage this man's fears?"

Delilah began with a flurry of words that Philip immediately construed as nonsensical.

"The most critical thing here is that the Nazis never got Jewel. Can you please continue your saga, sister? I am not starving or weak or cold. I have not been without companionship. I am perfectly OK, and I will not tolerate you barging in like this.

"Are you Naomi, Sister? Is that why you carry the picture of the Bonns? What happened to David? Where is the precious Jewel? Do you own an intricate thimble?

"I refuse to leave now, Philip. This place has healed me, and I do not even have a headache or any symptoms that require a hospital!

"May I stay with you for a few days, Sister Katarina? I could rest here, and I would not have any distractions from this crazy wedding. I could just take a little time off and let my friends see the local sites without me to bother them."

Philip gawked at the strange sight in front of him: this tiny nun; Carmine, the driver who caused the problem, yes, problem, in the first place; and this way too handsome doctor, who was probably just a proctologist and knew nothing about anything except assholes, because he sure could act like one. The bizarre request of his fiancée, who was talking in tongues or at least it sounded that way to him, was upsetting and put him on edge.

"Maybe a few days in time-out might be a good idea for both of us," stammered Philip, who at this point was turning beet red. "Aren't you even concerned about Anna?" Philip whined.

The thought of her friend did snap Delilah out of her reverie. Anna, moaning in the backseat of the car, had not been a concern of hers as she listened to Sister Katarina pouring out her heart. She brushed the hair from her eyes and tried to appear compassionate, even though she was not sure she was feeling the emotion.

"This does shame me, Philip. Is she OK?" she quivered.

"She has a broken leg and is quite shaken. She was extremely worried about you, which is more than I can say about you in regard to her." Philip was disgusted with Delilah and let it show in his snarly words and sarcastic tone.

Philip's accusations caused the tears to tumble from the emotions pent up in Delilah. She was embarrassed about Anna, but the emotive outpouring was for the young Katarina, Mlle. Zelinsky, Naomi, Rudolph Bonn, Yitzhak or Christian, and the millions more who all had a story of untold heartbreak. The survivors of Prague concerned her now, not the man standing in front of her or friends who traveled here for a party. She yearned for information about the survivors. Were any of them still alive? Did the sister know where these brave souls resided?

Sister Katarina gave her voice to only a few of the many statistics. Millions had perished, disappeared, or were shot, burned, buried alive, gassed, starved, or maimed. Billions had intimate stories she would never hear. It had been so hard for Delilah to comprehend the magnitude of the Holocaust, but she felt she had gained a miniscule amount of insight that night.

A thought flickered about the intolerance that had been earlier mentioned by Dr. Rescondito in regard to the mosque. She remembered Dr. Rescondito exclaiming that the local inhabitants were refusing to tolerate a renewed Muslim presence because of imminent projections to erect a gigantic temple. She was worried about the enormity of the crimes people were capable of doing in the name of ethnicity, religion, and righteousness.

She noticed the tremor of her hand as it rested on the muslin blanket covering her and realized that she definitely was not ready to move from this tranquil convent environment that she came upon through happenstance.

She no longer was shocked to see a nice Jewish girl in a convent, whether it was she or a transplant from a foreign place, as was Sister Katarina. She was aware of the unsteadiness in her emotions, which seemed to be bubbling out of control.

Delilah reined in those bursting emotions, gathered her thoughts a little more concisely than she had earlier, and asserted to her fiancé, "Philip, I intend on remaining here for a few more days. I cannot walk down an aisle right now, and literally, neither can Anna, so it is obvious that more time is needed before either of us attempts it. I know I disappoint you, but I beseech you to uncover the understanding in your heart that I know is residing there."

Philip's awareness of the situation was different than what Dee was intending, because he stormed out of the room with large, heavy steps, ran squarely into a wall, started swearing profusely again, then finally found a circuitous path to his waiting car.

Carmine was confused about the particulars of the crazy Americans' conversations, which sped along at warp speed, but managed to add, "I will find my way home, no problemo."

Philip was nowhere near them to even giggle about that problem, which was no problem for Carmine or Delilah.

Mother Superior added in Italian and then English, "Carmine, you and Dr. Rescondito may stay in the guest cottage tonight if you want. There has been enough excitement here."

The doctor bowed out, citing his car nearby, but Carmine opted to spend the few hours before daybreak in the confines of the nunnery's guesthouse. He had never slept around so many women in his life, especially the pretty American nearby, so he succumbed to the offer and both men headed toward the cool air outside.

The remaining hours of Sister Katarina's night consisted of watching Delilah toss in the simple cot that usually held only her own frame securely through the night. It was an odd juxtaposition to see such beautiful, full hair falling delicately on a perfect oval face in the sparse surroundings, which usually did not house such representations of beauty.

At one point, Dee's arm abruptly escaped from the coarse cotton blanket and dangled toward the cold tile below. Katarina relished the task of painstakingly raising it, then placing it against the bed and tucking the covers neatly around the appendage. Later, when the young girl shuddered from some unwanted thoughts, the sister delicately rested her own hand on Delilah's back and imperceptibly patted the space that encompassed the shudder.

Meanwhile, Delilah's thoughts rambled from the convent to her childhood bed, where frequent nightmares made her father come running, tripping over the dolls, key chains, and clutter that surrounded her bed, to wind up near her side, always out of breath.

As the sister kept up her vigil, she knew a story had been buried between the folds of her habit and the recesses of her mind. Telling it to strangers was not how she thought it would emerge, but she guessed it did not matter.

Her mind wandered back to her early years in Prague after the war. The sisters in the Czech convent knew that she could not stay with them for the duration of the war, so they made plans to send her to a distant order in a safer area. They had a facility in Assisi, Italy, which was known to have fewer hardships than Prague. The Germans used the city as their hospital headquarters, which protected it from bombings by either side. The Catholic Church, particularly in that city, tried a little harder to protect the Jews. Before the war, the holy city officially had no Jews living there, so it really was a peculiar situation. Papers were procured for the arriving Jews by using identities from incommunicado-occupied territories, where confirmation would have been impossible to obtain.

By the time she, little Naomi, blinked, she was in Italy, where her living really began. As she grew and prospered, her dedication to those who risked everything in order for her to survive became more acute. She never looked back in regret at her decision to stay with the good sisters, who gave her security and helped her become an asset to them also. They enabled her to achieve contentment and keep most of the scary skeletons at bay, buried in the closet where they belonged. Using the name Katarina seemed like a sensible choice once she read about Sister Caterina Cittadini, an orphan who dedicated her life to children. She would be forever grateful to the nuns, who dedicated themselves to saving her. It became clear to her when was called upon to say her vows that Katarina was the right name. The slight difference in spelling seemed more Slavic, which made it a good choice for her.

Dee cracked open her swollen eyes, basking in the light of early morning with a renewed vitality. She rotated her vision around the room and eventually rested her eyes on the tiny Sister Katarina, slumped in a small wooden chair, whose rigid back rose straight up from the soft orb of her body. Katarina's eyes fluttered briefly, then flipped open quickly as she woke from her gentle snooze. The sparkle of recognition from seeing Delilah lit up the entire tiny cell around them. She knew joy had begun her day with this curious girl near her.

After a smile that lasted longer than it needed to, she spoke. "I will show you the bathing room, Delilah, and will put some clean clothes outside on the chair by the door for you to wear. Do not worry, my dear. It will not be a religious habit but clean clothes from the large collection that is stored. They are always available to the occasional young women who frequent our convent with a variety of reasons trailing behind them."

"I would love to chat with you, Sister," interjected Delilah, ready to continue the story from the previous night.

"Get clean and then get you some nourishment, my angel. There will be time tonight after my day's work and our vespers, when we can continue our conversation. I will be occupied with tasks today, but you may roam wherever your spirit takes you," Katarina said, which surprised Dee because it was not in her plan to wait a full day to get the final details about Katarina's intriguing life.

"I am looking forward to tonight then," said Delilah quietly as she was being ushered into the large bathing room, which contained a deep white tub and a large showerhead in the middle of the space, with no containment around either to block the splashing water until it hit the walls at the room's exterior.

Carmine had been assigned an uninhabited cell in a visitors' section specifically cordoned off from where the sisters slept. Upon waking, he went to look for a toilet at the spot he remembered from the previous night. He came across a sign between two closed doors on a three-by-five card taped to the wall directly between the two. There was a roughly drawn picture of a toilet, indicating one could be found behind those doors. He barely moved his fingers across the door because he had no intention of disturbing the nuns, who seemed to keep noise at a minimum. He knew that they were busy in the other parts of the nunnery, consumed with their various jobs. He could distinguish faint sounds in the distance that corroborated his theory.

Carmine waltzed into the large, open bathroom only to find Delilah naked in the middle of the room under the shower, with her head lifted toward the heavens and her eyes closed. As he stood there with his mouth agape, he began to understand what déjà vu was, because he was almost familiar with Delilah's naked body now. He could picture himself back in the villa staring at Delilah in awe. Then within a fraction of a second, he tiptoed backward and gently closed the door, hoping that the noise of the water would block out his some-what innocent invasion that continually seemed to occur.

"Ah, marone! No peace will be mine if I do not stop see-ing this Madonna in her Garden of Eden just waiting for me to bite her apple," he thought as he went outside to find a deserted tree and finally relieve himself.

Meanwhile, Dee finished her shower without any hint of the momentary desire that had welled up in the voyeur who was following her footsteps, whether intentionally or by chance. The warm liquid gushed around her taut body and sprayed the walls with a fine mist that slowly dripped down to the white tile floor. She lifted her face to greet the water and sensed that she was a very lucky person to be here and not there, where Jews had perished every day in such multi-tudes that it was impossible to even fathom the devastation so many years later. With six million Jews murdered in the war, it was difficult to get a spiritual connection to any of those who were lost, which was why she just felt that she was given a jewel.

She always liked the theory of six degrees of separation between unknown persons connecting for the first time. Connections to connections to connections were possible in six or fewer steps. She was determined to find her degree of separation from Naomi, Rudolph, or David's family.

It fascinated her that the name "George" popped up in both Sister Katarina's story and hers. George was a common name, but it still seemed "cool" to her that the name occurred in both their families' stories.

Jews name after the dead, which made her curious why the name popped up on her brother's birth certificate. Why would her parents pick the name George? She did not remember them mentioning a dead uncle, grandfather, or cousin with the same moniker. Getting this answer meant calling her mother from Italy. Conversation did not always flow smoothly with her mom, and adding distance on top of age made it even tougher. Her mother was always argumentative when the conversation steered toward her dead father.

She needed an answer though so she retrieved her handy cell phone, which luckily had been recharged and was ready for action.

It was possible this simple question had surfaced before and she'd forgotten the answer. She dreaded discussing her nonexistent wedding, but her mother was never that anxious for Philip to be her son-in-law. She could now pursue a minimission that would keep her busy until she could sit down with Sister Katarina and hear the rest of the tale.

After discussing her mother's sleep patterns and various ailments that were quite real and not imagined, but hard to listen to because it required her to use lengthy descriptions of her bodily functions, her question finally arose about why Delilah had called her in the first place. It became clear that her mother did not remember that she was in Italy to get married, and Dee was not interested in going into details about that, so the conversation trotted at their usual slow gait. She found herself thumbing her fingers on the table, which signified the nervousness that her mother always brought to the surface. She needed the pace to quicken so they could delve into why her brother happened to be named George. She still was baffled why she had never broached the subject previously. Her mother's memory was much better for past events rather than present ones.

She finally blurted out, "How did Georgie get his name?" even though it interrupted one of her mother's descriptions about an encounter with her eccentric hairdresser with the orange hair.

"That is an odd question, Delilah." Her mother paused before continuing, "because I asked your father the same thing when my little man was born. He would not entertain any other names besides George, and you know as well as I do that your father never budged when his mind was stuck on something, so I decided to just go with the name George. It did not bother me to have birthed a George, but I would have been quite happy with a Harvey or a Bernie, both names from my family's group of names."

"But, Mom, why did Dad insist on that particular name? Where in the world did that name come from?"

Dee held her breath, waiting for her mother to actually ponder what was broached.

"Your father said that 'George' was not actually in his own family or even from a Jewish man. He did not want this suffering young man, who died with only your father's hand clutched to his shoulder, to have such a lonely death and no namesakes. This poor boy experienced horrors that your dad never could really articulate other than saying there were conditions in his life that no person should be forced to exist in, and he did, only to die when finally liberated. No one was there other than your father when his spirit passed away from this earth. I had to agree with your dad, who felt very strongly that 'Georgie' had to be named in his honor. The dying man's name should not cease to exist without a namesake."

"Mom, what were you and Dad thinking? There are a lot of Georges in this world, and that name is as popular now as it was thirty years ago."

"Yes, dear. But none were named after this particular George except for your brother."

"How did Dad come to hold this stranger's hand? Dad never seemed that sentimental."

"He said that George was the first man that he literally picked up when he entered the Terezin internment camp as part of the victorious team of Allies. Your dad had been temporarily assigned to the Russians and would join his own group of men shortly. He refused to speak of the horrors he encountered when they walked into the fortress, except when he wanted to convince me to name our newborn son a stranger's name. He told me that he would never forget carrying George's bag o' bones to the waiting ambulances that were lined up with more than enough people to fill them. He knew that this very sick, emaciated man would

242

probably not have the strength to survive the night and decided to stay with him during his last hours. The only thing he ever really said about him was, 'George was a jewel.' I guess this dying boy kept muttering, 'Jewel, jewel, jewel," in the moments before he expired."

And with those words, Delilah dropped the phone and firmly closed her eyes, squeezing out the drops of tears that had already formed.

After a moment, she picked up the phone and rounded out the conversation, hearing more details of her mother's life. The numbness throughout her stiffened body made her immune to the conversation as she blankly listened to noise droning in her ear. She concluded with a "talk to you soon" and disconnected her bridge to her parent.

Could it possibly be that her own father had played a role in the story that Sister Katarina had told her? She knew very little about her father's years during the war, because he never brought it up and changed the subject if anyone else did. She did realize early in her childhood though that it was impossible to sneak up on her father when he was sleeping. Once she did attempt this feat, when not yet eight years old. Her father was snoozing on the floor, which he liked to do, lying atop the lush Moroccan rug, which graced their somewhat modern living room and always felt comfy to him. An Andrews Sisters' record was playing softly in reminiscent tones on the state-of-the-art stereo machine while she pirouetted and sashayed all around her snoring father, as she often did.   While standing over him, she bent down to whisper, "Hey, daddy-y-o" because she wanted him to wake up and see her graceful moves. As she bent forward, he suddenly popped open his eyes, lifted his arm up, grabbed her, and flipped her over him, which made her crash flat against the cushioned rug. She burst out crying, which woke him from his stupor, and he instantly started hugging and rocking her. She remembered being scared more than injured.

"The war never takes a nap when I do, darling. Waking me is a dangerous job. Always do it from a distance."

And after that, she always woke him from afar, whether dancing, singing, or reciting a poem. That phrase was the sum total of what she knew of her father in the war. It was time to fill in some of the blanks, even though he was not around to help her complete this task.

Delilah enjoyed her lengthy walk around the trees, which reminded her of the stark birches of New England. She meandered through the property filled with little huts and winding paths. What felt like minutes lasted for hours. The world was filled with so many things to discover when time permitted. There were explosive flower gardens in reds, yellows, and pinks beside lush vegetable plots. The plants oftentimes had the illusion of wax, because no dirt dusted their intensity.

Occasionally nuns could be seen in a variety of habits, smocks, or work clothes passing by in blurs of blacks, grays, or brown tones. Most took the effort of peering from their dark head coverings and smiling in her direction. None of the women were at all interested in stopping for a little chat. She was definitely a voyeur in this idyllic scene, not an active participant who had a hoe in toe.

She anxiously waited for the moment when Katarina would continue to whisper shreds from a distant tale that had not materialized with a final chapter yet.

At last she heard a faint, tinkling bell that signaled imminent prayer or a possible dinner. Either way, the alert spread out to the flock, and they returned to the convent. It turned out to be prayers and then supper. All of these trappings reminded her of the vow that she was soon to take. Granted, it was not to be a nun married to the church, but it was to be a marriage nonetheless.

The continuing percussion of bells, which gently floated through the air, also floated up thoughts of Philip. Their last explosive argument drove him away in anger but surprisingly resolved in a peace within her. She was relishing these short alone moments, which surprised her. She knew all of Philip's imperfections, those little idiosyncrasies that chinked at his armor.

She had previously acquiesced to his flirtatiousness, his somewhat know-it-all attitude, and his continual need to direct the show. She used to bask in his positive points, which drew her to him initially, but something was amiss now. She tried to concentrate on his intelligence, kindness, and capacity to love her. A future without him never seemed possible until recently.

She appreciated his tall, handsome physique and knew they made a lovely couple. She realized she had a yearning for something more, but she was not sure what it was.

The yesteryears of Prague's lost families were her focus now, not whether Philip was the one for her, which seemed trite in comparison. She just wanted to put him on a bookshelf to be grabbed later on if she needed a book to read or a Philip to love. She needed to concentrate on another tale from the archives, just for a wee bit of time, before she moved on to her destiny on that shelf.

She was convinced that she somehow was entwined with this nun, who was more than happy to comfort her when the long, scary night of darkness crept in, and her father was nowhere in sight.

⤝⤞

Delilah eventually met Sister Katarina in her cell and anxiously waited for her to continue the saga that had been interrupted by the light of day and all of its encumbrances.

"Tell me about Georgie," blurted Dee as soon as the nun finished her group prayers.

Katarina knew that the positioning that occurred the previous night had something to do with making her spurt stories that had been long buried in an ancient well of emotions. She was not sure if she could commence where she left off just by opening her mouth.

After preparing for the night's sleep, Sister Katarina, who had once carried the name Naomi bestowed by Jewish parents by the name of Bonn, began to move her mouth with words that had been begging to exit.

Petra, the Orbhans' housekeeper, was conscious of the dangers that would exist with housing the runaway David and the infant Jewel in the main body of the home and immediately sent them to hide in a dank root cellar that was inaccessible from the interior space. She garnered minimal supplies in a worn shopping bag for David.

"I am going to get some goat's milk from the old goat Karel, who has miraculously hidden an even older goat. I think I can coax him to quench Jewel's thirst from his friendly animal. The milk of a goat is better for an infant," she told the stunned occupants of the house before leaving on her errand.

"Please, I know I am able to help. Do not decide anything until I return. I know this sounds obtuse, but I really can get our two visitors to safety with extra nourishment for the baby. Just let them stay in the cellar for now. They cannot be seen in the main home."

She had a double purpose in leaving that day. She not only needed the milk, but she had to locate her contact Ted and plead with him to get these two delicate survivors out of the nest of danger.

Petra had no idea that the Gestapo had let Karel keep the goat as long as he informed the office of everyone who begged him for milk. So, as soon as Petra left her seemingly magnanimous neighbor Karel, he bicycled to headquarters and blurted out his news that the Orbhans' servant, Petra, had asked for milk. He knew full well that there were no babies in the home. He also knew something was cooking.

Upon looking up the name Orbhan in their files, the Gestapo came to the conclusion that this was the same family that had a daughter in Terezin who recently died and that the head of that household had previously died in custody under classified circumstances.

The sun was setting by the time the contingency of soldiers arrived at the Orbhans' beautiful home and rapped the brass lad dressed in brass knickers and donning a brass cap.

Petra had returned from Karel's and also had stopped by her meeting place with Ted.

She crept down the old wooden steps leading to the basement and tried to focus her eyes in the claustrophobic dark space that held the two captives of large and small frames. She discerned the outline of David holding the tiny baby and groped to where they were leaning against the far wall, amid some precious potatoes that she had saved in case even more starvation than they had already experienced was in their future. She gave David a large container of milk and a baby's bottle that she had bought at the local market on the way home. She told him not to feed Jewel at her first whimpering, but to wait unless he knew he had an ample supply of milk stored for the next few feedings in a safe place. She then left them and walked through the back kitchen door of the home just as the Gestapo contingency was entering the front.

After aggressive searching of the home for a baby who could not be found, the officer put a gun to the stalwart Petra's head and told Mme. Orbhan that she would be shot unless one of the occupants told where the baby was now hiding. A short silence ensued, which was shattered by a loud gun emission. After Petra crumpled to the ground dead from a single shot to the brain, young Georgie blurted where the baby was hiding over his mother's desperate screams of useless protest. As Margharite filled the night's air with her protestations, the soldiers entered the dark root cellar from the outside of the house, only to find it empty.

After the soldiers returned to the cloaked interior of the home and informed the officer of the barren room below, the officer walked over to the screaming Margharite and pulled the trigger of his gun at her temple, which quieted the space filled previously with screams. The officer then told a shell-shocked Georgie that he had had enough and therefore it was this lad's lucky day. Georgie would enter Terezin instead of heaven on that fateful day.

Sister Katarina said these last words very quietly after Dee asked if she knew what happened to Georgie after he was taken prisoner. Slowly the nun whispered, "I know only that he died right after the camp was liberated."

Delilah breathlessly told what she knew of poor Georgie's death. It was a synchronistic moment.

"I knew when my mother repeated, 'Jewel, jewel, jewel,' as Georgie's last whispered words that our stories interlaid and one Georgie transcended into both of the tales. You are a cloistered nun. How did you put all the pieces of this together and end up where you are now? What happened to Jewel and David?" said Dee.

"My dear child," said Katarina as she wiped the tear that was dripping down Dee's cheek, "it is because of David and Jewel that I am in Siena."

Ted followed Petra with a slight distance between them when she returned to the Orbhans' home. Ted had already entered the root cellar when the Gestapo arrived with their loud pomp and circumstance that always accompanied their pursuits. He realized right away what was occurring. He silently ushered the two quickly from the home without detection by the soldiers, who were already inside the premises and ripping everything apart as they made their search.

Ted procured a hiding place for David and Jewel on a friend's farm in the Czech countryside, where Jewel thrived, David survived, and Ted did not. Ted was captured a week after they were placed in their Valhalla but thankfully never breathed a word about their whereabouts to the German inquisition that arrested him and questioned him for days before finally ending his life.

After the war, David, with Jewel in tow, sought out information on his sister, Inna. He uncovered that the Germans found out that Inna was Jewish and sent her to Terezin, where she was quickly put on a transport to Auschwitz and gassed upon arrival. Johann was sequestered at Terezin and became a stoolie for the camp's commandant. After the Allies entered the camp, Johann was taken by the Russians and tried as a German informant, found guilty, and died in a prison hospital in Siberia from cancer.

David and Jewel were soon housed in a displaced persons' camp after leaving the farm. Realizing there was nothing to keep them around Prague, with no one who would even miss them, they luckily got to Israel before that route was extinguished to Jews. David had no desire to raise Jewel in the chaos that ensued after the war was declared over and was always thankful that he took the road to Palestine.

Jewel thrived in Israel. David found meaning to his broken life through his only child. She matured, she laughed, she loved David with all of her heart, and she called him Abba, for he was the only father she ever knew. David had many girlfriends, but he never could settle down with anyone other than Jewel to share his life. He truly dedicated himself to his charge.

David eventually enrolled in the university and earned a doctorate of history. Jewel found her passion in art masterpieces and traveled to Siena's unique program of art restoration at the university there. There was never a question that David would ever be far from his Jewel. Because David was so adept in research, he eventually uncovered my whereabouts. After a short phone conversation, accompanied with a subsequent meeting, it became obvious that we were destined to make our unusual mix a family unit. David had procured a position at Siena University, and I requested a transfer to this convent to be near him and Jewel. I was meant to serve God, and I have never regretted my decision or even choosing Italy as my home territory. My God and my family of David and Jewel have been my sanctuary."

Delilah interjected, "I would be so excited to meet David and Jewel!"

A gentle smile came to the nun's face as she explained that David had recently passed away. For her, it was not a sad thing to move from the land of earthly beings to the kingdom of heaven and be reunited with his loved ones that he had not seen in a long time.

"It is his precious Jewel, though, that cannot be consoled and has been in a tailspin of despair. He decided to raise her as Jewish, since Judaism molded the era in which she was born and comforted her during her years in Israel. There had always been a part of David that had a darker side and periodically disabled him. He had tricked death and felt that Yitzhak was the one who belonged with the living, not him. He could never truly comprehend why he was saved and his brother and the others were not.

"David and Jewel lived a devout existence here in Siena while they both pursued their blossoming careers. David became a learned professor, with the little quirks that men of academia sometimes acquire. He never lost his accent, and students sought him out in his lectures as well as his times of leisure at the espresso bars. He taught at the University of Siena, as Jewel continued on her path to become somewhat of a local celebrity in the field of art restoration. Her precision for detail and her ultimate patience in slowly peeling off layers from the beautiful church paintings to show the glory of God became well-known.

"David's burial was at the local Jewish cemetery just last week, and the rabbi, who was a great friend of his, followed all of the traditional customs, which I know would have pleased him. Jewel has been inconsolable in her grief. She has spent many hours at the synagogue praying and chatting with the rabbi who was so fond of David."

Delilah knew immediately that she had met Jewel on the day that she and Philip had tried to enter the synagogue when touring the city. She remembered the coarse German tour guide who brought Jewel to tears that day and realized that part of her upset must have been because that aggressive woman also had a sharp accent that obviously struck a chord with Jewel's muscle memory of German people.

Delilah could not wait to say how her brother happened to be named Georgie. It was miraculous that her own father had been with Katarina's brother at the time of his horrible death.

Upon hearing Dee's tale, Sister Katarina suddenly dropped to her knees and started uttering Italian words,

Czech words, and English words that bubbled out in an outpouring of prayers.

"We hold a connection in this modern world as well as the past, because of our entwined histories," said the nun after quietly praying with her head raised and her spirits soaring.

Dee peered in awe at this tiny speck of a woman, draped in the dark voluminous cloth of someone dedicated to her faith. Here was a soul who shared a minute part of a jangled moment with her.

It was no accident that her brother had been named Georgie and her father just happened to be at the Terezin camp outside Prague to ensure that Georgie Orbhan would not be alone in his final moments, which cemented the crossing of those divergent paths. Two souls traveled a circuitous path that entwined future generations to cross paths in their own time and space.

Dee knew that her quest would now take her back to Siena and was hoping that her friends and Philip would share in her joy by meeting the most precious Jewel of all— a survivor.

In the early morning hours, when the sun peeked into the convent, Delilah bowed her head in reverence to this woman perched in front of her. She knew their tenuous connection would continue to grow and gather strength. The time was right to move on and leave the convent to its rightful inhabitants, the sisters.

She delicately tiptoed to the only phone in the darkened space and dialed Carmine's number.

His deep "Buongiorno" made her smile, and hearing her American-sounding voice made his heart beat faster. It was not easy to convey her thoughts to him when he was not before her, watching her arms flailing in the wind and her actions triggering the meaning of her babbling of words. He did not care what her words meant; he just knew he liked hearing them. Their conversation ended with Carmine abruptly asserting, "I come," and he did.

On a very different path back to the city of Siena, they sedately rode in an older-model car that was not luxurious at all and happened to be procured from his childhood friend Nico. As they each glanced out of their respective windows, their visions both passed over the plot of land that was under contract for a Muslim mosque. It was this particular tract of land that brought the marchers out on that eventful night and ended with her spellbound in a convent.

Religion was capable of rearranging the mood of the world. The machinations in Prague, as well as other parts of Europe at that time, affected the population in adverse ways. The Muslim dilemma, rearing its head on this innocent tract of dirt, rocks, and weeds, could change the face again in positive or negative ways, depending on bigotries or tolerances. Dee realized that religion not only separated people into their own congregations, but also had the power to extinguish the bright lights of future generations when annihilation from ethnic cleansing happened.

Seeing the land triggered a switch in Carmine. His face began to blotch, with red circles forming around his cheeks and reaching down his neck. His voice got a tinge higher as he began a diatribe that made her muscles atrophy as she collapsed into the cushion of the worn automobile seat around her. As if ice water had been instantly thrown over her, she was shocked out of her stinging attraction to the handsome driver that had been accelerating since the day she met him.

"No Muslims, not here," he practically yelled in the small confines of the car. "No building near Siena for a mosque, not now, not never." He then broke into a fast Italian that he muttered under his breath, with Delilah gleaning the meaning by his dramatic positioning of his one free arm that moved through the vicinity of his bucket front seat.

His multilanguages left her speechless as she just looked out the dingy passenger window and felt a tiny tear moving down her pale face.

Carmine soon realized that her reaction was not what he had expected and became silent as they drove toward Siena and her American fiancé, who had been anxiously awaiting her return.

Delilah first spotted her sleeping friend Jamie slouched on the couch, with her legs spread-eagle and her mouth exhaling a noise that some might interpret as a snore. She pounced on her friend, who woke with a start and a snort.

Carmine carefully watched the two beautiful Americans hugging each other with pats and squeezes. This new American looked like a piece of sweet taffy, and Carmine started licking his lips as if he could almost taste the sweetness coming from the pull of the candy.

Delilah's friend opened her eyes, which had been squeezed shut during the heartfelt hugs, then pushed her friend aside and came leaping into Carmine's arms, which shocked all of them.

"Thank you for taking care of my dearest friend," she gushed at the surprised driver. She then planted a kiss on each cheek, and finally landed one right on his lips.

"Jamie! He is not French!" giggled Dee as she watched the shameful display of a now-effervescent Jamie.

"I know, Dee. That is why I did not just kiss him on both cheeks!" laughed Jamie with such an infectious joy that Carmine joined in the gaiety, happy to finally be around a happier American.

After the displeasure that Dee had shown him during the car ride back, he was ecstatic to be near this long-haired blonde who enjoyed kissing him in any kind of fashion. He carefully placed himself on the couch and quietly observed the two animated women. There was no need to converse because he really could not participate in any of the ongoing conversation, which proceeded way too fast for him to comprehend anything at all.

Jamie listened intently to all of the stories that Delilah had heard during the last few days. Anna entered the room limping, accompanied by Kerrie, who was holding Mike's hand. Philip also arrived and reminded Delilah of a tornado ready to touch down on the closest projection, which conveniently was the upright Delilah, whose smile was transforming to apprehension very quickly as her body inadvertently started to crouch in anticipation of the on-coming onslaught.

Carmine, who was reading the body language better than the spoken language, leaped from the couch and placed himself before Delilah, facing Philip and speaking such a mishmash of Italian words peppered with so little English that nobody had any clue what he was saying. It was clear that he was somehow defending Delilah, though. This infuri-ated Philip so much that he placed his arm, which had ex-ercised at many gyms and carried many weights, heavily on Carmine's sloping shoulder. Then he took his free arm, which had played a variety of racket sports growing up through his adult life, and placed it in a punch to Carmine's jabbering jaw so hard that he fell backward into Delilah, who was stand-ing with her right foot slightly in front of her left foot. This made her topple to the right, which was the exact spot where the infirm Anna had come to greet Dee, who then fell on top of her with a piercing scream that brought Sylvie running from the kitchen with flour flying through the air, giving a light dusting to the immediate area.

Sylvie thundered Italian words so hard at Carmine that she did not notice that Mike, a policeman by trade, had taken out his small revolver that he always had somewhere on him to use, just in case people took his small stature as a lack of strength. Mike was not quite sure whom to point the gun at, but he decided that Carmine was the logical choice because he was not speaking English. Jamie saw this, shuddered in horror, and knocked into Mike, whose hand was delicately on the trigger, even though he had not intended to put much force on the mechanism. The gun went off, causing Mike's whole body to shake just enough to make the gun aim in a projection that was a little off from Carmine and toward Philip, where the projectile pierced his armpit in that fleshy area that did not contain any vital vein or organ. Blood started flowing, and all peered in shock at Mike, who looked in disbelief at the gun that was now limp in his hand.

As soon as Philip comprehended that he was shot, he quickly fainted, which elicited a collective "Oh no" from the entire entourage. Carmine then expedited a call to Dr. Rescondito from his pocketed cell phone. He rightly assumed that since the doctor had previously helped these crazy Americans, he would be able to assist again at this even crazier time.

Dr. Rescondito was immensely pleased to respond to the SOS when made aware that Delilah was involved in this new catastrophe. He enjoyed just being near this stunning and alluring woman. Americans seemed so different than the familiar Italian women he knew.

The tales spun that eventful night in the convent had added to his intrigue. The nun's story seemed to bring Delilah to life after her auto accident, when she'd looked so deflated from all of the commotion and bruising.

The matronly Sylvie greeted the young handsome doctor as he entered the crowded foyer of her palazzo, which was quickly becoming a crime scene. She rattled off a quick synopsis of events but made sure she ended her story with a long description of the shot flying through the air and piercing the fiancé of this odd couple who had alit in her home with all of their problems.

It was just supposed to be a simple wedding that had the potential of bringing some much-sought-after money to her abode, which was starting to droop a little from age.

First, Dr. Rescondito sought out Delilah from the crowd that was hovering around Philip and gave her a warm smile, which brought an equally warm response from the previously downcast girl. Then he assessed the wound on Philip, which was minor because of its clean exit, and asked for assistance in placing him in his own bed in his own room.

"Doesn't he need to go to a hospital?" asked Jamie incredulously. She had recently arrived in this picture-perfect country and really was not aware of their unique customs.

"No need," said Sylvie with race-car speed. She did not want hospitals or police involved or coming to her bed-and-breakfast, which had a variety of violations from various pedantic codes.

Dr. Rescondito on cue added, "I can easily dress the wound and give an antibiotic to him, which is possibly more than the hospital would do. It is only a little flesh wound, and there is no need to make a master deal about it."

Mike piped up from his slump against the heavy old door, "I am at fault here and should be prosecuted."

"What is 'prosecuted,'?" whined Sylvie, assuming it was something that was not good.

Anna chimed in, "Police, courts, juries, jail…"

And at that, Carmine and Sylvie gave such a look of disdain to Anna that everyone knew those words were poison to the two of them when they comprehended what would happen if the crazy Americans had a say in the outcome of what had unfolded that day.

ONE YEAR LATER

The rabbi, dressed in a flowing white robe, looked at the chatty audience seated before him. His wife sat in the first row, clustered with the immediate family of the beaming bride. It warmed him that Delilah's mother was able to make the long trip, as well as her now famous brother, Georgie.

This celebration felt more in line to what a celebration should feel like versus the request Delilah had initially asked of him. There had been no drama this time leading up to this service that blended familial Italian culture, Muslim roots, generations of Judaism, and even a hint of the Catholic Church as he looked at the minute nun who was seated next to Dee's serious-looking brother, Georgie.

Effervescent on this happy occasion sat beautiful Delilah's fun-loving friends, who placed themselves next to the serene Sister Katarina, with only one male rounding off that row: the driver, Carmine, who had become more than a driver to this mixed group. The perky one named Jamie sat next to the handsome Carmine, holding his hand comfortably, which made the rabbi's smile grow a little more in proportion to his teeth, which were gleaming out from his slightly parted lips. Dee had told him that Jamie's previous boyfriend was not a good fit for her, so it was nice to see this American happy. The virile Italian man grasping her hand obviously produced smiles because she was glowing almost as much as the resplendent bride.

There had been a few twists and turns since his initial meeting with the bride, who was poised in front of him ready to take her solemn vows with a learned man whom she barely knew at the beginning of the previous year. Her ex-fiancé had scurried back to the States immediately after the fiasco of the gun-toting US policeman, who probably would have been better off if he had not ventured out of his own realm of security in his home turf. But then again, he was the catalyst for the final breakup of the doomed Philip and Delilah.

She shed very few tears when he left, which told him that it was a good thing she did not marry him. The year gave her time to contact Jewel, a close friend of his wife.

Roberto Rescondito, intrigued by the sad story that Sister Katarina told, repeatedly accompanied Dee to the temple where she would meet Jewel. He often ushered her back to the medieval convent where she would quietly chat with Sister Katarina. Their interactions gave each of them an internal peacefulness.

He watched, he listened, and he benignly added his own words, which were sought out more and more by Delilah.

Eventually, the coffees, lunches, and dinners with Jewel not only led to Dee's friendship with her, but an even deeper connection to Roberto, who hung on her every word and was always gazing at her from a distance, or closer if he could manage it.

The two began to enjoy long conversations that were always lively and stimulating. Delilah grew to relish their time together and realized he was what she needed in a partner.

Her brother, Georgie, who arrived to save the day after hearing of the calamities with Philip, realized quite quickly that she was not the one who needed saving; rather, the one in need of saving was the image that appeared when he gazed in the mirror. Georgie had come out of a marriage that was rife with unhappiness His joy in life had diminished as his union ended. His life was crumbling, and he jumped at the chance to travel and assist his sister. He needed a change of pace as well as a change of scenery, and coming to Italy provided the needed cure. He definitely stepped livelier around Siena.

Their mother, who always seemed to rally from her maladies, arrived soon thereafter to make sure that her children were not falling into the evils of a foreign land. Not only did she find them safe, but she also saw a joie de vivre that had been absent from the two of them for a while.

Seeing her children in such a good way brought renewed strength to her. She enjoyed the weather, the scenery, and the new people to talk to. It did not matter that most of them did not speak English; as long as they were good listeners, she was happy. Her health continued to strengthen in this country that enticed her daughter and gulped her son. Delilah was very comfortable in Roberto's arms, and

Georgie found himself spending more time alone with the artistic Jewel. She felt content.

When the time finally arrived to smash the wineglass and seal a marriage, the crowd whooped and cheered so loudly that the cows in the distance joined in with the merriment. The dancing of the Jewish hora and Italian tarantella, the eating of the pasta accompanied by appetizers of lox and capers, and the imbibing of regional wine as well as trusty Manischewitz lasted well into the clear, starry night.

"The part of the service where our rabbi talked of war-torn Prague and the terrible losses that occurred there during the war brought a tear to my eye," said Dee to her new husband, knowing that he felt similarly about the need to remember.

"I also liked that he brought up how we met, with demonstrations against a proposed mosque, an issue that still has not been resolved," added Roberto, who was seated next to her holding both of her hands.

They smiled intimately at each other. Their thoughts were in sync.

In three days they were going to fly to historic Prague for their honeymoon, but they would not be traveling alone, as most new couples did. The little Sister Katarina, whose presence was amazingly large, finally agreed to join them on the trip. Jewel and Georgie begged to come with them, but they did not have to beg very hard.

Delilah felt drawn to the cobbled streets of a city that had been preserved beneath the Iron Curtain and now found a new capitalism in today's world. She wanted to walk down the old avenues that David and Yitzhak had known and see if the other Katarina and Georgie's house lasted longer than their lives did.

She knew the Jewish ghetto was as it had been for decades. The many temples survived, even though the throngs of people worshipping and doing their daily rituals there did not. The Jews were mainly deceased, but a smaller, newer crowd of religious dwellers occupied a section of the Jewish quarter. She wanted to be in that space with her brother, Georgie, the survivor Sister Katarina, and the amazing Jewel, who was birthed under impossible circumstances and led to safety. The young social worker who had been named Katarina was no longer alive, nor was Katarina's lively brother, Georgie, who could no longer run and play with his friends and family, but there were remembrances and survivors.

At least there was a Georgie in the here and now and a Katarina who still walked in their shadows. She could not see the handsome Doctor Bonn or his attractive wife, Naomi, trying to heal the sick and comfort the wounded, but their daughter, Naomi, could walk those same streets habited as a nun whose aim in life was the spiritual and the healing.

The long-gone Katarina's very precious Jewel survived to sparkle for those around her. Delilah's own brother, Georgie, was particularly dazzled by her brilliance.

The names were similar, but the lives were different. What did make it through the camps and murders was at least their tales, to bear witness to a time that many refused to acknowledge. For that Delilah was thankful.

Delilah needed to walk where they walked and see what they did not live to see. It was time to rehash those hidden memories that slip so fast and are easily forgotten as the years pass and the new generations evolve.

She suddenly lunged for Roberto's strong hand, looked into his dark Mediterranean eyes, and exhibited a smile that lit up the dark skies from Prague to Siena. She was ready for her new journey. An Italian wedding was even more delightful than she had ever dreamed was possible. There were so many jewels in the night sky to discover. She felt their presence all around her and bowed her head in awe.

Made in the USA
Middletown, DE
23 July 2018